KILLER MATH
A Dave Levitan Mystery

Stanley Cutler

Published by the Author
Philadelphia, Pennsylvania

r

Book Layout ©2013 BookDesignTemplates.com

Ordering Information: www.stanleycutler-dot-com

Killer Math / Stanley Cutler – 2nd ed.
ISBN-13: 978-0985734336 (Stanley Cutler)
ISBN-10: 0985734337

ENIAC; (*Electronic Numerical Integrator And Computer*) was the first electronic general-purpose computer. It was Turing-Complete, digital, and could solve "a large class of numerical problems" through reprogramming.

MONDAY

1

Dave Levitan had been ordered to meet an FBI agent on the Boardwalk in front of the *Traymore Hotel* in Atlantic City. Running red lights and overtaking cars on the way from Philly, he passed places that triggered memories of Helen: a road shoulder where she'd leaned against the guard rail as he'd fixed a flat tire; the produce stand where they'd bought a basket of peaches that she had approved with a trickle of juice on her chin; the diner where she'd first refused his marriage proposal.

They'd finally had the big wedding that made everyone happy except Helen. She'd left for New York three days before. As the road took him through the scrub pine forest, it crossed his mind to miss a curve and hit a tree. Then there were no curves or trees, just straight four-lane road through the salt marsh with the high-rise hotels of Atlantic City on the horizon.

The *Traymore* was the biggest hotel in the busiest resort city in America - a sixteen story edifice topped by three tile domes like a cathedral or a capitol building, occupying an entire block of Boardwalk frontage. On the crowded beach in front of the hotel, more women were wearing two piece bathing suits than would have dared before the war. On the far side of the throng, down at the water's edge, a lifeguard stood atop a plywood platform blasting his whistle at kids playing in the surf. He'd walked this beat and knew it well. On Labor Day, 1946, there was as dense a crowd of vacationers as he'd ever seen.

Levitan stood next to FBI Special Agent John Brixton at the railing. "Why here, John?" he asked. "Why not in your office?"

Brixton said, "To save time. I was here anyway. I need you to work a murder, Dave. The victim was an atomic scientist, a top guy. He worked at the same place as Einstein."

"Einstein! At Princeton?" said Levitan.

"Not exactly. The Institute For Advanced Study is near the campus, but not part of the university. It's a place where the professors teach each other. There are no regular students. The IAS pays geniuses like Einstein to hang out with each other. The victim was one of those."

"Was he famous?"

"Only to other scientists," said Brixton. "His name was Robert Weber, age thirty-five. He'd been at the IAS since '38 – a boy genius apparently. After Pearl Harbor, he enlisted and served in the Artillery, as a Lieutenant, and then as a Captain at the proving grounds in Aberdeen. He was mustered out last December and went back to the IAS. That tells you a lot right there - that they kept a place for him. His murder could be extremely significant, depending on who killed him and why. This can't get into the press."

"I understand," said Levitan.

"I need your help with the local cops. The murder might have nothing to do with atomic secrets, it might just be your garden variety street crime gone bad, so the ACPD has to do its job. But they're dragging their feet and we need them looking at a robbery angle. They'd been on the scene for over an hour when my men arrived."

Levitan said, "So, by now everyone on the ACPD knows about the murder, and probably everybody in the D.A.'s office, and the medical examiner, and the hospital people, and the neighbors, and the cousins. The horses have left the barn, John."

"Well, let's keep it contained. The cops don't know who he really was. Tell them as little as possible. Understood?"

"I've got it. Did he have a wife?"

"Yeah, and two daughters, eight and eleven. She was at home with their daughters on Saturday night, the night of the murder. She'd been expecting him to come back to their house from Atlantic City yesterday, Sunday morning, and she was worried about why he was so late when she got the news."

"I don't get why the ACPD informed the FBI. Knowing them, it would have been the last thing they'd do."

"They didn't. The head man at the Institute called us. The ACPD had the Jersey State Troopers bring the bad news to the wife. The wife called a friend, who told her husband, who also works at the IAS, and he immediately informed their boss. The Director of the IAS is the one who called us."

"So this victim is a big deal."

"A very big deal. There's cabinet-level weight hanging over us on this one, Dave, and a lot of military brass too. I have to report directly to Hoover. But I need someone – I need you – to work with the Atlantic City Police Department. They're not real fond of us around here."

Levitan said, "Just avoid dark alleys."

There were some on the ACPD who would have enjoyed beating up a G-Man. The three trials of Enoch "Nucky" Johnson, the final one in 1941, had been the culmination of an FBI investigation into the famously corrupt South Jersey political machine. Most everyone connected to the machine believed that the trial had been a vendetta, that the relentless prosecution had been J. Edgar Hoover's way of getting even for something that Nucky had done to incur the FBI Director's wrath, although no one knew exactly what that sin might have been. Everyone connected to the municipal government, including the cops, was beholden to the revered Nucky and therefore despised the FBI.

"Nobody blames you for Nucky's conviction," said Brixton. "I need you to get them working on it as a street crime."

"What makes you think they're not?"

"I'm having a hard time getting information from Chief Rafferty," said Brixton. "I'm counting on you,

Dave. We've got to hurry this thing along. If push comes to shove, if you can't persuade the ACPD to do their old pal a favor, claim the Admiral's jurisdiction over the coast and ports. Just do whatever it takes to get them to cooperate."

"The Admiral ordered me onto the case, so here I am," he says. "I'll do what I can, but I work for him – not for you, not for Hoover. Just the Admiral."

"I understand," said Brixton, and related the facts he knew.

Robert Weber had been strangled in his *Traymore Hotel* room, his body discovered by a maid on her rounds at 11 AM the previous day, Sunday, September 1st. Overturned furniture and a broken lamp indicated that there had been a struggle. The fully-clothed body had been taken to the local morgue where a post mortem examination confirmed a compressed hyoid bone, most likely caused by a pair of strong thumbs. The extent of rigor mortis suggested that he had been killed late Saturday afternoon or early in the evening. Weber had been registered alone, and there had been no signs of another occupant in the room.

The victim had lived in Pennington, New Jersey. He had a top-secret clearance and had been on The Manhattan Project, an expert on wave theory and on electronic computing machines.

Brixton finished, "The possibility of espionage has got to be my main focus."

"As it should be," said Levitan. "I have no idea what an electronic computing machine is."

"Neither do I," said Brixton. "Apparently, they can use radio tubes to somehow do equations. That's all I know."

"And this has to do with the A-Bomb?"

"Yeah. Apparently, solving the formulae involve so many thousands of separate computations that they need machines to speed up the process. That's all they've told me."

"Radio tubes?"

"That's what they tell me."

Levitan couldn't get his mind around the A-Bomb; a weapon that turns a city into radioactive cinders in the blink of an eye was too big and horrible for him to comprehend. The only comfort he found was that his government alone in the world could make the terrible things. Germany and Japan were in ruins. England, Spain, France, Holland – all the old European Powers - were withered empires clutching their colonies, probably too weakened to hold them. The Soviet Union was a threat, bellicose and ruthless, menacing the Allies from Stalin's conquered lands in Central Europe. But Americans had been assured that Communist Russia was many years, even decades, away from the ability to produce an atomic bomb.

"What was Weber doing in Atlantic City?"

"Gambling. That's why it could well have been a robbery gone wrong. Can you believe it? A guy like that? He checked in Friday evening and booked his room for two nights. He won a couple of hundred dollars playing poker on that night, August 30th, the night before he was killed. He was supposed to go home yesterday and was due back at work tomorrow, the day after Labor Day. Happy Labor Day, by the way."

"Same to you, John. I have tickets behind third base for the Phillies-Pirates double header."

"Sorry about that."

"I'll send you the bill. His boss? That would be Einstein?"

"No. He's not the Director. Weber was on a team led by a guy named John Von Neumann."

"A German?"

"No, a Hungarian Jew. And Weber was Jewish too," says Brixton. "Weber's father called the morgue and told them to leave the body alone. Apparently, autopsies are forbidden in the Jewish religion. So is embalming. They like to get the bodies buried the next day."

"So he was Jewish. What else?"

"I've got people looking into his friends and relationships at the Institute. I've got scientists looking into what he was working on. But I need someone I can rely on looking at it as if it were an ordinary crime. Let's go inside and I'll get you started," said Brixton.

Levitan looked at the vacationers riding the waves and crowding the beach. He said, "Before we do that, tell me who you've been talking to. Don't make me go tripping all over things. You must have a few leads."

"Nothing. None of the hotel workers knows anything, except for the guys running the hotel card room. That's how we know that his cash is missing. But nobody else remembers anything about Weber."

"Do you have your people in there now?"

"I've got two men posted in the lobby, just keeping an eye on things. And the cops have posted a patrolman outside the room to protect the crime scene."

"Don't even bother introducing me to your Agents. The less I'm seen with you guys, the better. Just let your guys know who I am, and tell them to give me a wide berth."

"You'd rather I didn't come in and, you know, authorize you?"

"You'd be doing me more harm than good, John. Trust me. You'll be in the loop, I promise. How will we stay in touch?"

"I'll command the investigation from our Philly office. You know my number."

"Okay. When?"

"Call me tomorrow morning." said the G-Man. "Let's say nine o'clock. I have to call Hoover at ten."

2

The Traymore Hotel's lobby décor showed signs age. The columns soaring to the high ceiling could have used touchup paint and the carpets on the two staircases that swept to the mezzanine in half-spirals on either side of the lobby showed a few frayed edges. The Manager on Duty stood at the center of a walnut reception desk wide enough to handle a dozen guests at a time. His name was Gerald Percy and he still wore a three-piece suit, a pearl stickpin, and a white carnation. The only difference Levitan noticed between his current and his pre-war appearance was that he sported a pencil-line mustache.

"Well, well, well. Detective Levitan," said Gerald Percy. "Whatever can I do for you? I hope you're not here for a room. It's Labor Day, don't you know."

Levitan's relatives stayed in one of the special hotels or in boarding houses when they came to Atlantic City. *The Traymore*, like most of the hotels on The Boardwalk, did not accommodate Jewish guests. The Traymore was not quite as blatant about it as its pretentious next-door-neighbor, *The Marlborough-Blenheim*, which was proud to advertise itself as a "white family hotel". Gerald Percy would have turned Levitan away, claiming to be fully booked, whether there were rooms available or not.

"I'm told you've had yourself a murder," said Levitan.

"Yes. But who sent *you*? You left town, did you not?"

Levitan removed his wallet and placed it open on the reception desk, the better for Percy to see his Commodore's credentials.

"Isn't that interesting. My oh my."

"Tell me what you know."

"Just that they found him in 803, where he was registered."

"He'd been here before, right?"

"I'd have to check."

"Listen to me... Gerald. Do not fuck with me. I will make you pay for every smarmy remark you make from here on. I've given you the first two for free. Now you will be completely forthcoming and extremely polite, do you understand?"

Percy blinked like a chameleon and switched on his welcoming demeanor. "He has stayed here before, now that you mention it. I happened to have checked, after we found him in his room. He'd started coming back in June."

"Often?"

"Once every week or so. Friday nights."

"Why, Gerald? What was the attraction?"

"*The Palm Room.*"

"Who's running poker in *The Palm* these days?"

"I don't think you know him... he's a vet... name's Tommy Worshevsky."

"Call him. Tell him to expect a visit from me. Find someone to cover his table while we talk. Has Room 803 been disturbed since the body was discovered?"

"I wouldn't know. The cops and the G-Men have been all over it since yesterday. We'd like to put it back in service, if you don't mind - the eighth floor guests have been complaining about the cop in the hall."

"Not my call. I'll be going over to the station house later on. I will relay your concerns."

Percy reflected, his face tight.

"Good man," said Levitan. "By the way, Robert Weber was a Jew."

"Do tell!" said Percy.

"Imagine that."

§

A man with whom Levitan had walked The Boardwalk beat for a year, ACPD Sergeant Burton "Buster" Fulton, was sitting on a chair at the end of the eighth floor corridor, one door down from the entrance to Room 803. He was in full regalia, bare-headed, a wide- brimmed campaign hat covering his lap.

"Dave!" he said, rising. "Holy cow! What the hell are you doing here?"

"Good to see you, too, Buster."

Fulton was a powerfully-built six-footer who seemed made for his uniform, a getup more suitable to a parade ground than a boardwalk, kit that had seemed a little absurd when Levitan had worn it himself: twill riding breeches, riding boots, a starched khaki blouse, with a black billy club and a .45 in a large holster attached to a wide belt with loops around it for a dozen, fat bullets.

Levitan knew a lot about bullets. During the Spanish Civil War, he had carried dead and wounded comrades on stretchers. He'd fired hundreds of rounds himself, killed men in the brutal house-to-house battles in Teruel and in the forests and rocky slopes surrounding the city. On the job, he carried an S&W Thirty-Eight Special revolver with a four-inch barrel in a GI khaki holster under his custom-tailored sport jackets.

The crime scene appeared to have been put back in rough order, the furniture upright, a lamp with its shade askew on the desk. The bed was made. There were no clothes or toiletries.

"They took everything," said Buster.

"You were here yesterday?" Levitan asked.

"Yeah, I got here just after the Detectives."

"Who caught the call? Which Detectives?"

"Turner and Staup."

"Good – so they both made it back from the war."

"Yep… fit as fiddles. You're still with the Coast Guard? Is that permanent?'

"I guess so. So whose great idea was it to make the bed?"

"Nobody. That's the way it was, I think."

"It hadn't been slept in?"

"Didn't look that way. When I got here, there was glass on the floor from the light bulb that got broken.

It looks like that got cleaned up. The desk chair was knocked over, so we stood it up so's we could move around. Maybe the desk was put back straight."

"Anybody take a picture?"

"Not us. The FBI took over as soon as they got here. Maybe the FBI got some shots last night. I went off shift at four."

"What happened when the FBI got here?"

"They chased us out. They came around three-thirty in the afternoon, the arrogant bastards."

"Listen, Buster. I'm taking charge of the case. Got it?"

"Sure, Dave. Great."

"Lock the room and come with me. I need your help down on the mezzanine."

"What do you want me to do?"

"Just stay near me. You don't have to say a word. I want to find out more about the poker game that Weber played on Friday night. Let's keep everyone inside the card room for awhile. We'll pull them out one at a time, starting with the dealer and the cashier, and see what shakes out. You with me?"

"Let's go," said the Sergeant, placing the campaign hat on his head, running his fingers along the brim to make sure it was on straight.

§

Levitan asked Fulton to station himself just outside the doorway of *The Palm Room* on the mezzanine, and to allow no one out.

Card rooms like *The Palm* were legal in Atlantic City so long as chips were in-play instead of cash. The rooms met the letter of laws crafted to Nucky's specifications by his friends in Trenton. Besides serving as permanent, honest games for recreational players, the card rooms were a way for ill-gotten revenue from all over the city to be entered into hotel accounting ledgers as the proceeds from room services. The dealers and bellmen who ran the rooms were highly paid, highly trusted hotel employees.

The Palm featured a pink wall with a mural of a hula dancer and a palm tree sketched with white and gray paint. There were two card tables covered in green baize, a wood-top table for board games, a man-tall safe in a corner, and a small bar behind which a bellman in hotel livery stood.   A man wearing a Hawaiian shirt and pegged pants of white gabardine stood at the bar, facing the tables, holding a bottle of *Coke*.

"Tom Worshevsky?" Levitan asked.

"That's me. You're Levitan? This is about Bob Weber, right?"

On the mezzanine, they found a bench upholstered in leather.

Levitan said. "Would you mind going over what you told the FBI? Bring me up to speed?. How well did you know the guy?"

"Bob was a regular player, as good as they come. Fast. Always the same – two beats and he says his play; Bam! Bam! Like a machine. Always the same – Bam! Bam! – a really a good gambler. Never ate. Never drank booze, just *Pepsi*. Usually, end of the night, most times, he cashes-in as a winner."

"Tell me about the last time you saw him."

"Friday night? He did good. Won about two hundred dollars. Next thing you know, they tell me he's dead on the floor of his room."

"What was he like?"

"I can't say. He hardly ever says anything except to bet. I think maybe the war? He wasn't real cheerful. I had the feeling he's one of the guys having a hard time coming back. Know what I mean?"

"Where did you serve?" asked Levitan.

"Me, I was in Normandy - Saint Lo. Went all the way into France. You?"

"I was in the Coast Guard Auxiliary, sad to say."

"You were lucky."

"I didn't think so."

Levitan's short leg had disqualified him. The old ankle wound, incurred under sniper fire when he'd leaped into a ravine, had long since stopped causing problems, but being stuck in civilian clothes while his countrymen soldiered on far off battlefields had been frustrating. His anger cooled when the war ended, but he was sorry that so many others, men like Tom Worshevsky, had been sanctioned to do what had to be done while he had been forced to stay out of the fight.

His war in Spain had been swept under the rug, his service in the anti-Fascist cause dismissed as a bit part in a premature political sideshow, his experience denigrated as vainglorious, even treasonous. So be it; he hadn't gone to Spain to be a hero. Still, he would have liked another chance to soldier against the Third

Reich. His hatred for the Nazis had only increased after the war ended, after stories about the atrocities had appeared on the pages of the newspapers.

"Did Mister Weber ever talk about his service?"

"No, not that I remember. When he first started coming, I think he said something like being a clerk or an accountant, something like that. He never said much, like I told you."

"What was his game?"

"Any kind of poker. Wild cards, as many as anybody called. Two-card, three-card, five-card draws. He didn't care. It was all the same to him. Bam! Bam!"

"Take me through who else was playing. As of right now, you are the last person who remembers seeing Weber alive."

Tom Worshevsky nodded slowly, as if he'd just retrieved a card from the table and was inserting it into a hand. "He was the only regular, the only one I knew."

Levitan knew that there were men who habitually frequented the card rooms, men who also sat in the wire rooms in town tracking race results on chalkboards, men whose lives were in thrall to the highs and lows of winning and losing. Inveterate gamblers were attracted to places like *The Palm Room* like drunkards to saloons.

"It's been a busy weekend. They were just players, know what I mean? And the players, they don't always use their real names anyways."

"Think, Tom."

"Well, yeah. The last hour or so, there was another guy that I know. He calls himself John Smith. He's sat-in a couple of times lately, started showing up maybe a week or so ago. But I wouldn't call him a real regular. He's a pretty bad player. He went bust Friday night, like he did the other times. Lost a couple of big pots."

"Was Weber the winner?"

"Yep."

"Do you know anything about Smith?"

"Nope. He's an old guy, maybe about fifty. Kind of fat. Kind of a country bumpkin. He may be a local guy - you know, not somebody here on vacation. He has big hands, big fat fingers with dirty nails, like he works with his hands. You know, you could check the book, the player register. Even if they walk in and there's a seat open, we put their name in the book. We keep it on the bar."

"But you say they don't always use their real names. John Smith... Really? Do you put down addresses and phone numbers?"

The dealer said, "If they're staying in the hotel, we take their room numbers so they can run a tab. But we don't take nothing from anybody else. We don't take checks for chips. We got no need for nobody's address or phone number."

"So, the only person you really know from Friday night is Bob Weber and this guy John Smith."

"That's it."

"What's your bellman's name?"

In Atlantic City's card rooms, senior bellmen took care of everything but the games: tending bar, handling the cash and chips, taking sandwich orders, and emptying ashtrays. He asked the dealer to return to the card room and send the bellman out to talk to him.

Worshevsky tilted his head in Fulton's direction, "What's with the cop at my door?"

"I want to talk to the people inside. We are not messing around, Tom. Bob Weber was an important man. Send the bellman out.

He stood at the bronze railing overlooking the lobby, watching people in a hurry. The bellman joined him after a minute.

His name was Harvey Dawkins, a suntanned man in his thirties with the symmetrical features of a shirt model. His uniform was a tan sport jacket with "*Traymore*" embroidered with blue silk across the pocket. He could add nothing to the simple portrait that the dealer had drawn for him; the dead man had been an extraordinary gambler who kept to himself.

"Did he ever ask for anything special?" Levitan asked.

"Like what?"

"Girls, for instance."

"Nope."

"Boys?"

"Nope."

"Drugs?"

"Nope. He just sat down and played. He'd buy twenty dollars worth of chips, the same every time, sit down and play. That was him. Oh, and he drank a lot of *Pepsi*. I got him cigarettes when he ran out - *Tareytons*."

"Tell me about the other players on Friday night," said Levitan

Dawkins looked puzzled and claimed that he knew nothing about the players - they were just customers, patrons.

"They trade cash for chips, Harvey. You left out about the cashiering," said Levitan.

"Yeah, that too."

"Let's go back into *The Palm Room*, Harvey. I need to look at your books. I'm taking your ledger and the register."

Dawkins said, "No way! I can't just let you do that."

"Sure you can. Take a look," said Levitan, and flashed the glassine covered card showing the crossed-anchors emblem of the US Coast Guard and the bold black letters "Commodore". He placed his hand on the bellman's shoulder and turned him toward the game room. "Shall we?" he said. It wasn't a question.

They passed Patrolman Buster Fulton. "Follow me in," said Levitan.

A canasta game was underway at a table of men and women, the players leaning-in to take cards from the fat decks in the middle, careful not to disturb the arrangements displayed in front of them. Three women at the games table were clacking *mah-jongg* tiles. Worshevsky was dealing to a four-man game at the table nearest the bar. The room could hold twice as many players: the holiday rush seemed to have petered out. The hula dancer hadn't budged.

"Tom," said the bellman to Worshevsky, "He wants the books."

"I don't think anyone's allowed. I mean, are you really allowed?" said Worshevsky.

"Fetch me the books. Now, Harvey."

"Can you wait a minute?" said the bellman. "I'll call Mr. Percy. Let's let him decide."

Levitan leaned forward and said, "Harvey, you are now the person who is refusing to let me see evidence. You do not want to be that person. Fuck Gerald Percy."

Worshevsky started to rise.

"Uh uh," cautioned Levitan.

The dealer settled down.

Unhappily, Dawkins walked to the tall safe standing in the corner. He hesitated, looking at Worshevsky, who remained impassive, and reluctantly turned the chromed dial.

The safe door was hinged so that its contents were hidden from everyone but the person who opened it. Dawkins reached in and removed a clothbound ledger, swung the door closed, and handed the book to Levitan. As soon as it was out of his hand, he stepped behind the bar, picked up the phone and dialed a single number.

Levitan opened the book.

Dawkins spoke into the phone, "Mister Percy? Can you come up here? I've got a problem." He returned the handset to the cradle and said, "When can I have my ledger back?"

There were only a few entries, all on the first two pages, dated September 1st and 2nd.

The player's register lay open next to a pen stand at the far end of the bar. Levitan walked to it and thumbed it back to the first page, a date in mid-August. "Let me have both sets of books, going back to June,"

"Seriously?"

Gerald Percy must have taken the stairs two at a time. He came into the room breathless.

"As serious as blitzkrieg," said Levitan. "Now, please. Get me both sets of books for the whole summer."

"Stand where you are," Percy said to the bellman.

The canasta, poker and *mah-jongg* games had ceased, all of the players watching the unfolding drama.

"Mister Dawkins has no choice, Gerald," said Levitan, keeping his eyes on the bellman. "He gives me the books."

"You need a... a... whatchacallit, a warrant!" said the Manager On Duty.

Levitan walked to the safe. The handle was a long, brass lever. He pulled the heavy door and looked inside at stacks of currency, chips in trays, a metal lockbox, assorted envelopes, and a stack of ledgers. The top three were the ones for June, July, and August. He took them in hand.

"Where's the player register from before this one?" he said.

"Long gone. We throw them out," said Harvey Dawkins. "They're only to keep track of the games."

Levitan studied the bellman and decided he was being truthful. All the poker players at Worshevsky's table rose, as if to leave.

"Gentlemen and ladies," said Levitan, addressing the room, "I am Commodore Levitan of the United States Coast Guard. Please stay at your tables. Keep playing. Sergeant Fulton of the Atlantic City Police Department is here to take your names and ask you a few quick, questions. Then you'll be free to go or continue your games. But stay put until we say you can go."

"This is an outrage," said one of the canasta players.

Levitan went to Buster blocking the doorway to *The Palm*. He spoke very softly, "Get the names and addresses of everyone in the room. Find out whether or not they were at the table with Weber on Friday night."

"Aren't you staying with me, Dave?"

"Can't - I've got to get some more manpower. After I stop by the morgue, I'm going to the station house and talk to Rafferty. I'll make a call to you here in a little while and you'll tell me how you did. You okay with that?"

"Terrific," said the cop.

3

The big hotels, the Convention Hall, the train stations, the bus depot, the hospital, and the municipal buildings were just blocks away from each other in the densest part of the grid of streets between the beach and the bay. The Boardwalk counted as a street. The streets behind it, in parallel, were named after the oceans. First, a block west of The Boardwalk, was Pacific Avenue, along which the eight-seat taxis called jitneys traveled; then came Atlantic Avenue, with tracks and overhead wires for trolley cars; then Arctic, Baltic, Mediterranean, and lastly Adriatic nearest the bay. The cops and firefighters preferred to use the four lanes of Atlantic Avenue when traveling upbeach or downbeach.

The cross streets were named after States of The Union and grouped by region. *The Traymore* was in the "Midwest," looming over The Boardwalk between Illinois and Indiana Avenues.

The morgue was in the hospital on Ohio Avenue just a block from the hotel. Levitan took his time studying the face of Robert Weber, trying to fix the humanity of the victim in his mind. His hair had been light brown, curly, and in need of a trim. Levitan lifted an eyelid and saw that the cloudy eye had been blue. As expected, there were dark bruises over his flattened Adam's apple and around his neck. He'd been of below average height and quite thin, his ribs prominent.

The corpse of a genius is just a corpse - a dead thing. Levitan pulled a chair next to the marble table on which the body lay and stared for several minutes, trying to visualize the man animated: walking, talking, smiling, reading, making love, writing on a blackboard, sitting at a card table, driving a car, watching a movie, sipping *Pepsi*. He imagined a living man, killed in his prime, and felt a bolt of rage.

He spoke to the morgue attendant on his way out. "Who identified the body?"

The attendant checked the file. "A Missus Miriam Weber is expected any time now. The wife I guess, or maybe the mother. But she hasn't shown up yet. And the undertaker's van ought to be here soon. This one's Jewish, they bury them as soon as they can."

Atlantic City's downtown didn't look like a resort because The Boardwalk hotels pictured on the postcards were shielded behind office buildings and department stores with rooftop billboards. The police station was on Atlantic Avenue in a cluster of municipal buildings two blocks inland from The Boardwalk.

Levitan's former boss was Chief of Police Francis Rafferty, whose office on the second floor was the only room in the police station with a rug. Rafferty's walls were decorated with framed photographs of himself with Nucky Johnson and other politicians. Levitan's last case as a member of the ACPD had made headlines across the country and gotten Atlantic

City favorable notice by the high and the mighty. Rafferty was proud that one of his own Detectives had cracked the case.

"Jesus, Dave," said Rafferty. "What the hell are you doing here?"

"They've asked me to join the investigation into the murder at *The Traymore*."

"Well I'll be damned."

Levitan shrugged. "What do you think? Is it a good idea?"

"Let me think about it."

"No time, Chief," and he explained the pressures from Washington, and the fact that the victim had played in Einstein's league on a government team. He finished by reminding Rafferty that such a man had been killed in his town.

"Exactly," said the Chief. "And whatever happens, you know that bastard J. Edgar Fucking Hoover is going to find a way to smear us. You know he will."

"He didn't last time,"

"It was the last year of the war, no doubt he had other matters on his mind," Rafferty says. "But the war's over now and we all need to work out who's who, you know what I mean? It's not just me, you know. Lots of Chiefs, from all over the country, we are really worried about Hoover. He's nuts. No one elects him and everyone's afraid of him. And he's already come at us right here in Atlantic City for the sole purpose of eliminating one guy - our guy - who had the guts to stand up to him. So, Dave, why the hell should I give that bastard the least satisfaction?"

"Because he can squash you like a bug anytime he wants to and you know it. You're better off playing nice. I've got a foot planted inside the Federal Government. I can keep an eye out, make sure the FBI plays it straight. And here," he says, placing the card room ledgers and guest register on the Chief's desk, "These are the books from the *Traymore's* card room. Can you have them put in the evidence locker for me?"

"Oh shit, Dave. Please tell me that you're not getting involved with *The Traymore* people. I don't need that kind of crap."

"If that's where this goes," said Levitan, "That's where I'm going."

The Chief frowned. "Just be careful, that's all. The hotel manager over there, Gerald Percy, he's on the Chamber of Commerce. All kinds of people own shares in that place. Just be careful. Why did you take their books?"

He said, "Weber was a regular at *The Palm*, just the kind of guy they'd use to launder cash. Now, I can use a little manpower help. I'd like Buster Fulton. And I'd like Turner and Staup to stay on the investigation."

Rafferty agreed, but not until he reminded Levitan of how great his sacrifice of three men happened to be.

The Chief's office shared the second floor with a clerical office and a conference/storage room. The conference room had a big table, a few chairs, and a wall phone that Levitan used to make a series of connections to *The Palm Room* in *The Traymore*.

"Buster, it's me," he said. "Did you get all the names?"

"Got 'em."

"How about Friday night? Were any of the players you talked to there on the night Weber was playing?"

"They say 'no'. None of them was here. I got their addresses and phone numbers. Two of the canasta players were from Canada. Everyone else was from Philly, New York, or New Jersey. Nobody played on Friday night."

"Okay. Bring your notes with you to the station house tomorrow morning. We'll put them in the case file. And, guess what?"

"Uh oh."

"We'll be working together on the case. Rafferty's okay with it. And he promised overtime pay. We'll start tomorrow morning. I'll meet you at the station house at eight-thirty. Wear plain clothes."

Detectives Calvin Turner and Lou Staup were on a call, expected back soon. Levitan occupied himself during the wait by talking with people who came into the Detective's bullpen to shake his hand, surprisingly glad to see him.

Levitan had been an oddball in the Atlantic City Police Department, an organization so accustomed to collecting cash from the town's illicit operations that the payment system has become institutionalized, reaching down from Rafferty to patrolmen trainees. Levitan had never participated. He had not objected to the system, even understood it as a way for the city to exercise some control over those who satisfied the yearnings of people looking forward to a few nights away from their homes and the opinions of their prudish neighbors. Absent the whores and the gamblers, the appeal of Atlantic City - *The Queen of Resorts, America's Playground* - would surely fade. He had been okay with the system, but he had been averse to owing anyone for anything.

He had not socialized with the other cops, spending his off hours at home with his books, his fishing tackle, and his girlfriend - now his wife - to drinking with the guys.

ACPD cops were local, with long South Jersey ancestries and close ties to the church communities of Atlantic County. Levitan was a Jew from Philadelphia. Even more exotic, Levitan had come in through a seldom-used door; his patron had been a legitimate businessman who rarely exercised his influence. Levitan had been the only man on the force who'd owed his job to Al Rubin, known to everyone connected to South Jersey politics as Nucky Johnson's very good friend and closest adviser.

Rafferty, a political dancer, had initially resisted having Levitan on the force, only acquiescing after Nucky, at Al's request, had interceded. As someone who'd regarded himself as an outsider during his time on the force, Levitan was surprised by the warmth of his welcome that afternoon. Absence, he supposed, made the heart grow fonder.

As he expected, there were exceptions; the two men not pleased to see him were Detectives Calvin Turner and Lou Staup. They insisted that Levitan come with them to Rafferty's office so that they could hear about his legitimacy from the horse's mouth.

"I want you helping him," said Chief Rafferty to his Detectives. "Let him take the lead. Be nice."

"Overtime?" asked Turner.

"Yeah, yeah. Overtime," said the Chief.

"That's good," said Staup. "But why, Dave? Who was this guy? What makes him so important? Nobody has told us nothing."

"The A-Bomb may be involved. The victim was an atomic scientist."

"Holy shit."

4

Detective Cal Turner was a fair-haired man going to fat. Levitan had worked with him before he quit to join The Army. He was smart and quick to anger. Turner's partner, Lou Staup, was a dark-haired, barrel-chested man, with short powerful arms and stubby fingers. He, too, had quit during the war to go into The Service.

A box from the morgue containing the victim's effects had been delivered to the station house while the Detectives had been meeting with Rafferty. It was sitting atop Turner's desk, somehow sad, a reused carton made of cardboard.

"This couldn't be everything," Levitan said, opening the box and regarding the few contents.

Calvin Turner was indignant. "No kidding!" he said. "The FBI took everything except this."

Lou Staup's expression was of faint expectation, as if he was waiting to hear the punch line of a joke. In fact, he was too vain to admit that he needed to wear glasses and was squinting to see better. He said, "Listen, Dave, you have to picture what happened yesterday. We were doing our jobs when they showed up. They just come busting in, telling us to get out. And we're telling them to go fuck themselves. And they keep on giving orders when they got no right! And I told them so. And Calvin did, too. Right Cal?"

Cal Turner said, "We don't let people push us around, Dave. Do we? Are you kidding me? Nobody tells us what to do in our town. Nobody. And, Dave, let me tell you, they don't know what they're doing. This one guy goes right over to the desk and starts opening drawers and throwing clothes on the bed, going through the pockets, and this other guy is packing up the guy's suitcase with everything in the room. He doesn't ask any questions. He's just messing everything up as if it wasn't a crime scene... our crime scene. Unbelievable!"

"I'm surprised they let you stay and watch," Levitan said.

"Let us stay! What? They're going to pick us up and carry us out?"

"Why didn't they just take everything? Even this stuff here?"

"Because they aren't cops. They don't deal with crime scenes like we do. These guys just come walking right in after we'd sent the body to the morgue. We had no idea that the victim was some kind of secret guy. He was just another dead guy in a hotel," Turner said.

Staup, seething with righteous indignation, said, "I even said to them, 'Keep your hands off.' I told them, 'It's evidence.' When they figured out that we weren't going nowheres, they just took all the effects, his clothes, his magazines, and everything else, packed them up and walked out the door."

"They didn't even say goodbye," said Turner.

"So we'll have to find out where they took it all," said Levitan.

"Why's that, Dave? For what? It's not our case anymore."

"Sorry, but it is your case - it will be tried here. It will be up to your District Attorney, not the FBI, to prove who killed this guy. You have to look at the effects from the crime scene," Levitan said. "It is your responsibility."

"What the fuck," said Lou Staup.

"Stay out of the national security stuff – that's where the heat will be. Just do your jobs as if it's an ordinary murder. You can't dodge that part of it."

Staup and Turner, as workingmen paid for a day's labor, despite their indignation, would have been pleased to distance themselves from a case that was shaping up as a legal train wreck. The more entities and jurisdictions involved in any case, the more time a detective spends in court, the more reports he has to write, the more administrative 'T's he must cross and 'i's he must dot, and the more asses he has to kiss. Levitan had just delivered bad news - this one was theirs, whether they liked it or not.

Turner challenged him, "What about you, Dave? Do you have jurisdiction? I mean where does the Coast Guard fit in?"

"Nowhere, if I can help it," he said. "I'm doing this under orders and because the Chief of the ACPD wants me to lend a hand. But it's your case to make, no doubt about that." Then, after allowing them a moment of reflection, he said, "Shall we see what's in the box?"

Turner, head bent, showing a bald spot, removed the items from the carton. The bald spot hadn't been there when they'd worked together before Turner had gone off to the war.

There was a set of keys; a pair of glasses with tortoise shell rims, a used deck of playing cards with the Hotel Traymore's image on the backs; a ticket for the parking lot at the intersection of Indiana and Pacific Avenues, a half-full pack of *Tareyton*s, a half-full pack of matches from *The Breakers* - another Boardwalk hotel - a comb, pocket change, and a wristwatch.

Levitan said, "Where's his wallet? Where's the money? He'd been a winner the night before."

"So he could've been robbed," said Staup. "How much did he win?"

"About two-hundred dollars. Did you see whether the FBI found any money?"

"Not that I noticed," Staup replied.

"Where was his room key?"

Turner and Staup looked at each other. "It was on the floor," said Staup, looking to Turner for confirmation.

"Calvin? Do you remember where the room key was?" asked Levitan.

"If Lou says it was on the floor, then it was on the floor," said Turner, pursing his lips, causing his orange and white moustache to bristle.

"Alright," said Levitan. "Here's what I need you to do. We don't know anything about his day before he was killed. Go find this guy's car in the parking lot. Find out when he parked it - it will tell us whether Weber used it on Saturday. Go over it, see if there's anything of interest. But leave it where it is. Then go to the hotel and talk to the staff and see if anybody remembers any contact with the victim. I'm going to pick up a hoagie and I'll catch up with you at the hotel. You guys want me to bring anything back?"

"Where are you going?"

"*Palermo's* on Arctic."

Levitan's personal itch, his weakness, was a fondness for the foods of the ethnic neighborhoods on the bay side. The Sicilians, in particular, ate very well indeed, flourishing on imported Italian delicacies, the local produce, and the blessed bread of their ovens. You couldn't beat an Atlantic City hoagie when the tomatoes were ripe.

Staup said, "You think we're going to be working tonight? It's Labor Day, remember – a holiday."

"I intend to," Levitan answered.

"Well," said Turner, "We're with you. It's overtime, right? Why don't we just come along. I'm hungry."

Levitan, Turner and Staup were on their way out to *Palermo's*, standing at the tall duty desk that confronts visitors as they enter the Police Station from Atlantic Avenue, explaining the temporary reassignments to the duty officer, when two women and a man came in through the double doors.

The younger woman said, "I am Miriam Weber. I'd like to talk to whoever's in charge."

5

Leaving the parents in the bullpen with Turner and Staup, who were unhappy at the postponement of their supper, Levitan escorted the widow to the conference room. Miriam Weber was haggard and red-eyed; a small, slightly built woman whose dark hair was beginning to silver. "Could it have been some kind of accident?" she asked.

"You saw him?"

"Yes. I mean the mark on his throat? You don't think he could have taken a fall or something like that?"

"No, ma'am. I'm afraid there's no question. He was killed deliberately."

"Then catch this person. You must. And he must be punished. Anyone who would kill my Bobby is a monster. This cannot be allowed. Find out who did it."

"I am so sorry. Truly. But you can be helpful… if you're willing to answer some questions."

She sat up straighter. "I want to help. Ask me the questions."

"How much time do you have?"

"Not much. I have to get back to the girls."

"How were you notified about your husband?"

"The police. The State Police came to the house. They told me. They said I should come to Atlantic City and identify him."

"This was yesterday? About what time?"

"I guess around four o'clock. Bobby said he'd be back around noon. I had started to worry by then ."

"But you didn't come here until today?"

"The first thing I did was call Bobby's parents in New York. His mother said they'd drive me down to Atlantic City - I don't drive. They didn't get to Pennington until around ten last night. They stayed over so that we could come here today. We had to go to the funeral home this morning, that's why we didn't get an early start."

"Did you call anyone at the place where Bobby worked?"

"No. Right after I talked to Joe and Buni, Bobby's mother and father, I called my friend Mary. She told her husband, that's Ruben Winokur, he's got a fellowship at the Institute. I guess he called the Institute to let them know. The Director called me right away, and he offered to get someone to drive me to Atlantic City, but I said that I'd already arranged a ride."

"Did you know why your husband was here?"

"The card game, you mean?"

"Yes."

"Yes, I knew."

"And this didn't bother you?"

"I knew why he did it. It was how he relaxed. It's an old story with him. They expect an awful lot from him at The Institute."

"You mean he could lose his job?"

"No. He worried about doing the job, not keeping it. He was unhappy about the... about what he was doing."

"What do you mean?"

"The consequences. The... horror. He has been having a hard time with it."

"So he gambles?"

"Bobby is what they call a savant; like a genius at one thing. Bobby can... could... calculate things in his head. He loved cards, the probabilities intrigued him endlessly."

"You're saying this was how he relaxed?"

"It was fun for him and just distracting enough that he could forget about his work. And he liked it when he won."

"So he did it for the money?"

"Of course he did it for the money, he wouldn't turn it down. But we have enough. We spend his winnings on the kids or, sometimes, on art."

"You're not in debt?"

"Just for the house, the mortgage."

"You're sure?"

"Of course I'm sure. What do you mean?"

"I'm sorry. He doesn't have another bank account? Just for his gambling money?"

"No. I don't think so. Do you think so? What makes you think that?"

"Nothing. I'm sorry. Men who gamble have been known to lead separate lives. Please forgive me."

"I'm exhausted. This is hard for me. I didn't think it would be this hard. I should go now."

"Of course. Whenever you feel like it. But can you give me a few more minutes? Investigations like this grow stale very quickly; the sooner we have information, the more likely it is that we will catch the killer."

"I understand. What else can I tell you?"

"Had he been gambling more than usual lately?"

"Yes. But it went in cycles. He'd been this way before, over the years. He was not an ordinary person, Detective. Don't you understand? He was special. He was different. He'd get lost in his head. The problems, the science, required him to go down all these mental tunnels, to follow all the mathematical trails. It's a kind of work that requires a level of concentration and discipline I can't even begin to imagine. And, as I say, the consequences were very much on his mind. He cared."

"The hotel has records of him staying over on Friday nights during the summer. Had he spent two nights away before?"

"No. This was the first time."

"So that was unusual."

"Yes."

"And he wanted to spend two nights away to gamble?"

"Are you implying that he was here for another reason? Whatever is on your mind, forget it. Bobby didn't have a girlfriend."

"That's not really what I meant. Forgive me, please. But, right now, we don't know what he was doing on Saturday. If you can think of another reason why he planned to stay two nights instead of one, it would be helpful."

"He was just taking advantage of the long weekend. The girls and I had plans for Saturday. I took them shopping for school clothes in the morning and then to a birthday party in the afternoon, neither of which are Bobby's favorite activities, so we were going to be gone most of Saturday anyway. He didn't have to be back at The Institute until tomorrow. He just decided that he'd stay over the extra night."

"He didn't say anything else?"

"He brought his bathing suit. I know that. He asked me to help him find it. I think he was going to go on the beach."

"Good. Anything else?"

"He said he might try playing someplace different."

These were two discouraging bits of news. There had been tens of thousands of people on the seventeen miles of Absecon Island beach on Saturday, and there were a dozen card rooms. Determining Weber's movements during his last day might prove difficult.

"Did he say where else?"

"Not that I remember."

"Fine. Thank you. Can I ask, did he have any enemies at work?"

"At the IAS? Impossible. It's not that kind of place. The people who work there are friends. They have to be. The whole purpose of the place is collaboration; it's what they sign up for."

"How about rivalries? Academics can be pretty competitive, can't they?"

"That's true, but it's not tolerated at the IAS. Ego? Absolutely. Little princes, some of them; men who grew up as the center of everyone's attention. Their parents, their teachers, everybody catered to them. It's a hard thing to grow out of, I suppose. But they try not to take it out on each other. It's just not the way The Institute operates."

"What about Robert? Him too?"

"No, not really. That was not how he measured people, especially not himself."

"I don't know what you mean."

"Intelligence is not a virtue, Detective. Being smart can mean being clever at the wrong things. Robert had no time for rats, no matter how smart. He liked kind people, sweet people, like himself. Now please, I should go. I have to get home for my girls, get them ready for the funeral. They're staying at a friend's house, but I have to get them home. I need them near me now."

The anger that had coursed through Levitan as he'd sat next to the body in the morgue rose again. Forget the fact that Weber was an important scientist;

someone, some lowdown son of a bitch had murdered a fine man. "When is the funeral?" he asked.

"It'll be Wednesday. His sister is flying in from California, we have to wait for her."

"You'll be sitting *shiva*?"

"Yes, his parents expect it. They'll be staying at our house. But, I have to ask you, can you get our car back to Pennington? I don't drive."

"Certainly. I'll see to it. Do you think I should talk to his parents before you leave?"

"Their English isn't very good. And, to tell you the truth, I don't think this is the time. My mother-in-law has been very emotional."

6

Palermo's was a corner luncheonette on Arctic Avenue where they built a sandwich fit for a king. Levitan, Turner and Staup discussed their approach to the case over oregano-scented hoagies dripping olive oil.

Staup said, "We've got to put everything in the case file. You can be damned sure that people in Washington are going to be looking at that file. Let's load it up."

"People in Washington can kiss my ass," said Turner.

"More likely they'll kick it so hard you'll end up in Camden," said Staup.

"It's a long shot," said Levitan, "But somebody needs to check local directories for a John Smith. Someone using that name was definitely at the table with Weber Friday might."

"John Smith. You have to be kidding," said Turner.

"Just check the phone books, okay Cal?"

"Whatever you say, Dave."

Atlantic City was an easy town to drive around, as most of the population at any given time had arrived by train and was on foot within a block of The Boardwalk - traffic jams didn't happen. They left Palermo's and drove across town in five minutes, to the Indiana Avenue parking lot where Weber had left his car, the same lot where Levitan had left his 1941 *Dodge* before his meeting with Brixton earlier in the day. The lot attendant said the car associated with the ticket in the dead man's pocket had not moved since Friday evening.

Using flashlights, they examined the interior and the trunk, finding nothing of interest - no documents, no blood, no diagrams of mysterious gizmos. They found child debris in the seat cushions and under the front seats: pieces of candy wrapper, a pink barrette, a packet of stale peanuts. But, otherwise, Levitan saw no reason why he shouldn't dispatch the car to its owner as she'd requested. Turner and Staup volunteered to drive to Pennington the next day and return immediately. Levitan discouraged them and suggested that their assistance on the morrow would be more helpful interviewing witnesses, and that transporting a car was not worthy of men in their exalted positions within the ACPD.

"Hard ass," said Staup.

He retrieved his suitcase from his *Dodge* and took it with them in the radio car, an unmarked 1940 *Plymouth*, to *The Traymore's* street entrance a block away. Staup pulled the ACPD car behind the last taxi in the rank alongside the hotel's Illinois Avenue entrance. On their way in, they stopped to interview the door man, Hercules "Urkie" Savarin, who didn't recall the victim, or anything unusual happening on Friday or Saturday.

"Hold onto my suitcase for me, would you, Urkie?" said Levitan, handing the doorman a dollar. "And I really appreciate your help."

"Are you checking in?" Urkie asked. "I can send it up to your room."

Taking a room at an anti-Semitic place like *The Traymore* went against Levitan's grain; he'd sooner spend The Government's money someplace else. "Just watch it for me, would you? I'll be back for it soon."

Inside the hotel, they approached the night manager at the reception desk, a stranger to Levitan who'd taken over for Gerald Percy, the daytime manager.   Levitan showed his credential and explained that he and the Detectives standing behind him were there to investigate the murder of the man who'd been registered in Room 803.

The night man all but clicked his heels and introduced himself as Fred Travis.

"We'd like to have a look at Mister Weber's hotel bill," said Levitan.

"Do you intend to pay it?"

"Absolutely," said Levitan. "Double."

A healthy roll of cash in his pocket was a tool of Levitan's trade; he'd sooner have left the office without his gun than work the streets as a poor man.

"Double?"

"Sure, keep the change"

Travis retrieved the hotel bill from a drawer under the reception desk and handed it to Levitan. The charges totaled a little over fifteen dollars. Levitan took the fold of cash from his trouser pocket, keeping it at waist level. Staup and Turner, standing a step behind him, with Levitan's shoulders blocking the money from their view, looked away, casting their gazes to distant corners of the lobby.

Money did not always work, but in a roaring cash economy like The Boardwalk's, it usually did. Although Levitan's code forbade him from taking money, giving money was righteous. Every place is different, every witness is different, every case is different - money did not always grease conversational gears. Earlier in the day, he'd intimidated Gerald Percy to achieve the same result – cooperation. But Fred Travis, the Night Manager, was not Gerald Percy, nor had he yet pissed Levitan off.

He peeled off three tens and slid them across the desktop under his palm. Travis, standing in the midst of the widest cash river on The Boardwalk, swept the money into his pocket with a practiced motion.

There were only two items on the bill for 803 aside from the cost of the room itself: a ten-cent phone call and a twenty-five cent call, both made on Saturday, August 31st , the day of Weber's death. "Do the operators keep a log of phone calls?" he asked.

"I'll be right back," said the well-compensated Mister Travis, disappearing through a door in a partition behind the front desk, returning after a few minutes to hand a slip of paper to Levitan.

"You're an ace," said Levitan. "Much appreciated."

The switchboard operator log showed two phone numbers charged to Room 803 during Weber's stay.

The first was an AC number, placed at 1:14 PM. The second was a PR number placed at 5:35 PM. Either Weber had been alive to make the second call at 5:35 or the killer had.

Levitan put the slip of paper in his pocket and walked with Staup and Turner to the middle of the lobby.

"You guys ready?" he asked.

"We were supposed to be off shift at four o'clock. It's after seven. What do you think?"

"It's overtime – go for it. We need to talk to people while their memories are still fresh. Talk to the hotel detective, the restaurant people, the bellhops, and room service – anybody working here who might have seen something on Saturday. Give it another hour or two then go on home. I'll see you at the station house in the morning. Let's say eight-thirty."

Using a phone booth in a vestibule off the lobby, Levitan called the local number that Weber had called at 1:14 PM on Saturday. It was picked up on the third ring.

"*The Breakers*. How may I help you?" said the switchboard operator on the other end of line.

"*The Breakers*" had been embossed in raised red script on the matchbook found in Weber's pocket; it was an expensive Jewish hotel.

"Yes, Operator. My name is Weber and I'm staying in Room 803 at *The Traymore*."

"Yes? How may I direct your call?"

"I placed a call from here on Saturday, isn't that correct?"

"I wouldn't know, sir."

"You don't keep a log of calls?"

"No sir. Only outgoing calls. How may I direct your call?"

"Okay. The card room, please."

"I'll connect you to *The Newark Room*."

There was a pause, another ring, and it was answered, "*Newark*, Quincy here."

"Hey, Quincy. It's Bob Weber from Saturday. How you doin'?"

"Yeah? Bob Weber?"

"Yeah. We talked on Saturday. I called you about getting into a game."

"I think maybe you must have talked to somebody else."

"I called in the afternoon on Saturday, about one o'clock."

"Okay, that would not have been me; I don't come on until nighttime."

"Well, here's the thing - can I get in a poker game?"

"It's too late for tonight, all our chairs are booked. Sorry."

"How about tomorrow?"

"What time?"

He would be at the police station at eight-thirty, he had to call Brixton at nine. "Say around eleven in the morning?"

"Okay. I got you down. Weber you say?"

"Yeah. Eleven o'clock tomorrow morning?"

"Gotcha."

He tried the long distance number, the PR number used by telephones around Princeton, and listened to it ring. It was a holiday evening, not surprising that no one answered.

He retrieved his suitcase from Urkie and proceeded up the ramp leading from the sidewalk of Indiana Avenue to The Boardwalk, intending to get a room at *The Breakers*.

7

With the exception of Atlantic City, New Jersey's seashore towns refused to accommodate black people, dark people, and Jews. Most of them excluded Catholics, and definitely people whose names ended with a vowel. But in Atlantic City, anybody could find a place to escape the miserable brick oven summers - you just had to know where your kind was welcome. If you didn't happen to know, if you somehow found yourself asking for a room where you weren't considered acceptable, helpful desk clerks and boarding house owners would cheerfully point you in the proper direction.

Except for the men who pushed the rolling chairs, black people were rarely seen on The Boardwalk. As visitors on holiday, black people could find lodgings a half-mile inland from the surf and The Boardwalk in a sprawling neighborhood of row and frame houses where the maids, cooks, and janitors lived. There was a small beach at the northeast tip of the island on the shore of the Inlet where they would not be chased away. White people assumed that restricting access to the ocean was okay with black people, it being common knowledge that they tended to sink in the water and therefore did not enjoy swimming.

A rolling chair consisted of a carriage seat surrounded by a wicker shell, a floor with three little wheels attached to the underside, and a bar in the back for the pusher's hands. Some of the wicker shells came over the top of the seats to form a canopy, some supported awnings. The Boardwalk had been built with two lanes for the chairs, an upbeach lane and a downbeach lane, constructed with planks laid side by side instead of cross-hatched, smooth roadways that allowed the wheels to glide, making for a pleasant ride and an easy push.

When they had no riders, the rolling chair operators, all of them black men, waited for fares with their chairs backed up to the beachside railing. Levitan spotted a handful of empty chairs when he topped the ramp. One of them was attended by a man he had known since his days on the beat.

"Hello, Mister Eugene," said Levitan.

"Well, look at what the cats drug in! Hello, hello, Mister Dave. I ain't seen you in forever."

"I took a job out of town."

"I think I heard that. Yes indeed. You want to take a ride?"

"Sure do. Take me to *The Breakers*."

The number of rolling chair licenses was strictly limited by an owners' association. The more successful men, like Eugene Gaffney, owned multiple chairs, renting them out to friends and relations. By 1946, some of the operators, like Gaffney, were of the third or fourth generation in the business, their forbearers having worked as rolling chair men on The Boardwalk since the 1880s. In 1946, in town, there were old men and women living with their families who'd been born as slaves.

Rolling chair operators were expected to be part tour guide. Eugene Gaffney, who earned generous tips on the strength of his storytelling prowess, favored removable awnings to wicker canopies on his chairs because they allowed him to converse more easily with his passengers and because the canvas could be taken down, which most passengers preferred when the sun wasn't blazing.

The seven block ride upbeach to The Breakers took ten minutes. At the going rate – five cents a block or a dollar an hour - the ride to The Breakers cost thirty-five cents. When Levitan stepped out of the chair in front of the hotel, he gave Gaffney a ten dollar bill. "Keep the change," he said.

"What's that for?"

"I work for a rich uncle. He doesn't care how much I spend."

§

Levitan's relatives couldn't afford *Breakers'* prices and therefore stayed in one of the thousands of overnight lodgings available for rent in town. Levitan's class of people considered themselves privileged if they could afford a room and a bed above street level. Theirs tended to be basement apartments crammed with beds, places with sandy floors and outdoor showers. For people like Levitan's family, *The Breakers* was way too high class.

He checked in as Commodore David Levitan, showing his Coast Guard identity card. His title impressed the desk clerk as it did most people. It was an exalted-sounding rank bestowed upon civilians working for the US Coast Guard if the circumstances called for it. The title gained him instant respect, even though he was strictly a man of the land who didn't know starboard from port.

"Are you here on business or pleasure, sir?"

It might have been useful to introduce himself as an investigator, but that would have depended on whether the leads panned out – the phone calls and the matchbook. Until then, he'd just snoop. "Got me a few days off... thought I'd get in some time on the beach," he said.

"Let me just see... Ahh, yes," said the desk clerk, "We're in luck. We do have one of the ninth floor balcony rooms available. Very fortunate. It's one of our best rooms - it overlooks The Boardwalk. I think you'll like it."

"I'm sure I will. Let me ask you, might a fellow find a poker game here in your hotel?"

"We do have a card room, yes sir, *The Newark Room,* " replied the desk clerk. "I must tell you that they can only accept cash for the chips. Will that be alright with you?"

Taking it as a cue, he placed a five dollar bill onto the register and saw it deftly removed by the desk clerk.

"And what's your name?" he asked.

"Oscar, sir. Are you interested in playing tonight?

"I wouldn't mind. Do you think there might be a seat open?"

"I'll make sure of it, if you'd like," said Oscar with a friendly smile.

Ahh, the magic of cash - no seats had been available when he'd spoken to the man named Quincy on the phone.

"Well that would be fine," he said. "Thank you. Give me a half hour to get settled in."

"Not at all sir, just part of the job. Shall we say ten o'clock?"

"That would be fine."

Waiting with the bellhop for the elevator, Levitan read the notice board mounted on the wall. Tomorrow, Tuesday September 3rd, The Feldman Cousins' Club would have brunch in the *Perth Amboy Room* at eleven o'clock. There would be bingo all day in the *Million Dollar Room*. Jewish Charities of Patterson had booked a room on the mezzanine until 3 PM. IKOR would hold meetings in *The Vineland Room* at 9AM and 1 PM. The seawater swimming pool would be open from 9AM until 7PM. The Beth Am Sisterhood Luncheon would be at noon in *The Trenton Lounge*.

He was surprised by the notice of an IKOR meeting. The acronym stood for *Idishe Kolonizatsie Organizatsie in Rusland*, a Jewish Communist group that Levitan had not heard of in six or seven years. Perhaps this was a different IKOR.

Even though *The Breakers'* was unabashedly a Jewish hotel, Levitan felt a bit alien. He and his older brother Jack had been raised by an immigrant aunt and uncle to be Americans. He had not gone to Hebrew

School nor had he been Bar Mitzvahed. He understood some Yiddish because it had been spoken at home, but not a word of Hebrew. Just as there were Americans who identified themselves as Italian or Swedish or Negro or Irish, he thought of himself as an American whose parents happened to have been Jewish. He was reasonably proud to be whatever he was, and "Jewish" was part of that, but it was a part of which he had only a vague understanding. If being Jewish was a matter of degree, he was not very Jewish at all.

The Breakers was slightly less pretentious than *The Traymore*: more businesslike, the staff less obsequious, fewer art works in the lobby. He tipped the bellhop a dollar and surveyed his room. As promised, there was a fine view of The Boardwalk from a narrow balcony that he could access through French doors. If he rose early enough, he'd be able to watch sunrise over the sea. In the white-tile bathroom, the oversized tub had taps for hot and cold fresh water and two more for hot and cold seawater. It was the only hotel room he'd ever been in that didn't have a *Gideon Society* bible by the bedside.

He showed up at *The Breakers'* card room, *The Newark Room*, at ten o'clock.

Like *The Traymore's Palm*, this card room was located on the mezzanine, but the *Breakers'* version was decorated differently, with glossy white woodwork and brass sconces. The safe was not visible, he assumed it was under the bar, and there was no hula dancer painted on the wall. Two of three baize-covered tables had games ongoing. There were no women in the room and lots of tobacco smoke – the ventilation system left something to be desired.

He introduced himself to the bellhop/bartender as the ten o'clock player named Levitan.

"I was supposed to meet a friend of mine here. Bob Weber? I don't see him here, though. Do you know him? Bob Weber?"

"Yeah. I just talked to him on the phone," he said, apparently not recognizing the voice he'd heard an hour before as Levitan's.

"Yeah. He says he played here on Saturday afternoon and loved your room."

"Well, that's nice to hear."

"Maybe I'll give him a few minutes to show up. Maybe you remember Bobby from Saturday afternoon? Day before yesterday? He would have been drinking *Pepsi*."

"Sorry. I work nights."

"The dealer too?"

"Yep. We work together."

There was no point in continuing the interview. He had a date to play with the day shift tomorrow at eleven o'clock, the dealer who'd sat with Weber, and the bellman on duty at the time; he'd keep his questions for them. "You know what?" he said. "I changed my mind. If Bob Weber shows up, tell him I went to bed."

Back in his ninth-floor room, Levitan took off his shoes and socks and went onto the balcony, the cement cool on the soles of his liberated feet. The moon above the horizon backlit scattered clouds. Electric signs on the entertainment piers made the sky glow and shimmered off the water. He could hear the surf. He thought of Helen, far away.

TUESDAY

8

Levitan awoke after sunrise and opted for a freshwater shower. He shaved, dressed and gave a dollar to the bellhop who brought him a pot of coffee and a toasted bagel. Sitting at the desk, on hotel stationery, he rewrote the notes he'd taken the day before, adding questions to the bare facts, planning his next steps. He considered placing a phone call to Helen, but decided against it, as she was probably still asleep in her Greenwich Village apartment. Perhaps he'd call later on - just to let her know where he was staying.

He left the hotel at around eight and took a northbound jitney on Pacific Avenue for five blocks to Indiana Avenue, and walked inland for a block to the municipal buildings on Atlantic. Fulton, Turner and Staup were waiting for him.

"Okay," he said. "Let me bring you up to speed." He recounted the facts he'd learned since they'd gone off duty the night before: that Weber had called *The Breakers* and placed another call to Princeton. He explained that there had been no answer when he'd tried calling the PR number the night before. Staup said he'd find out whose number it was.

"So what's our next move?" asked Turner.

Levitan said, "Me, I'm in a poker game with the same crew who were working on Saturday before Weber was killed. I'm checked-in as just another guest at *The Breakers* and I want to feel them out before we come in officially. Look for me on the *Breakers'* mezzanine at noon, okay? By then, I should know whether he was there for sure. If he was, I'll need you to collect information the same as Buster did at *The Traymore* last night."

"Got it," said Staup, his arms crossed in front of his broad chest.

Turner said, "Okay. Besides the PR phone number, what do you want us to do until then?"

"I took the books from *The Palm Room's* safe into evidence. I want you both looking them over. Focus on Fridays, the nights Weber gambled there."

"Concentrate on what? What are we looking for?" asked Turner.

"Look at the player register first. Look at Friday night, the night before he was killed, and see if there are any familiar names, any low-lifes whose names you recognize, any of your old friends who might be the sort to mug a hotel guest and strangle him to death with his bare hands. Compare the names with the people who were playing cards there on Saturday afternoon. See if there are any names you recognize. Then look at the ledger. See if everything adds up. Start with the entries for Friday night, August 30th, and work your way back through all the Fridays during the summer – those were the times Weber played at *The Traymore.* Dawkins, the cashier, claims that Weber never invested more than twenty dollars in chips. Let's see if we can figure out whether that's true. Look for a pattern of big buys. See if they occurred on Fridays."

"You think Weber was laundering money?" asked Turner.

"To tell you the truth, he doesn't seem like that kind of guy. But if he was, it will give us another direction to follow."

"Another direction? What else are we looking at?" asked Fulton.

"We don't know why Weber decided on *The Breakers* when there were so many card rooms closer to *The Traymore* where he was staying. Buster, wait here while I call Brixton with the phone in the conference room. As soon as I talk to him, we'll head out for *The Breakers*. You guys, come on over to the *Breakers* when you finish with the books. We'll be in a card room called *The Newark*."

At five minutes before nine o'clock, Levitan placed a call to the FBI's Philadelphia office through the police station's switchboard and was put through to Brixton immediately.

Brixton asked, "How did it go with the ACPD? Are they going to cooperate? "

"Your agents tried to bully the Detectives on the scene and walked off with the victim's effects. They went out of their way to antagonize the locals. What the hell is the matter with you people?"

The FBI Agent said, "They were doing their jobs. This thing has to be contained. You have no idea what's been going on down in Washington. It's getting vicious. What do you think happens when a guy who keeps atomic secrets gets murdered? Think about all that big fat FBI budget that goes to vetting people in the bomb business, and imagine that Weber's death could be dumped in Hoover's lap. It could be a security failure and an intelligence failure all wrapped into one. If you're one of those who wants to see The Director knocked down a few pegs, then this is your moment. We are under enormous pressure."

"I get it," said Levitan, wondering how his Admiral was faring in the budget wars. "Does this affect the murder investigation?"

"Certain things may be off limits."

"Like...?"

"The Institute for Advanced Study, to be specific. Stay away. Get it? And get a little perspective, okay? Get it into your head that my men are doing absolutely the right thing, and boo-goddam-hoo if the ACPD gets its feelings hurt."

"You know, it's not about hurt feelings, John. Somebody's got to be worried about a murder prosecution."

"Alright. So do it. Let that be your worry."

"Not mine, the ACPD's. They have the responsibility here, not me, not you."

"So, you're our liaison, just like you are with the Admiral. I'm counting on you."

"Did you know that your idiot agents didn't get the stuff that was on his body? There was stuff in his pockets when his body was sent to the morgue. Were you aware of that?"

"Shit."

"I want to examine the effects taken from Room 803."

"Was there anything of interest on the body?"

"Maybe. There was a matchbook for *The Breakers* hotel. And Weber placed a phone call to *The Breakers* hotel from his room at *The Traymore* on Saturday afternoon. And then he called a Princeton number at around 5:30. Means he was probably still alive at that time."

"Okay. That's useful. What number did he call?"

He read the number off the slip of paper the night manager had given him, "PR-2681."

"I think that's one of the IAS numbers. Let me check it out."

"Okay. My guys are on it, too. There's one other thing. Have you ever heard of an organization called IKOR?"

"You bet. They were a Soviet front - Commies. They were active before the war. What about them?" asked Brixton.

"Last night I saw their name on the hotel bulletin board - that they're having meetings today. There might be a Weber connection."

"Really? What makes you say that?"

"Only that he came to the hotel where they happen to be meeting when there are a lot of other places he could have gone."

"I see," said Brixton. "Good work. I'll send a squad to *The Breakers* right away. To tell you the truth, I'm surprised they're still in existence."

"Hold off for a bit, okay John? Let me see if I can find anything out before you muddy the waters."

"We need to know everyone who's at a Communist meeting. It's what we do."

"Do any of your agents speak Yiddish?" asked Levitan. As a way to emphasize that the USSR did not endorse Judaism - they were opposed to all religions - IKOR had been dedicated to establishing a Communist mini-state of Yiddish-speakers, not Jews as a religious group.

"Get serious," said Brixton.

"Well, I understand it, from at-home when I was kid. I might be able to establish a relationship with them. Give me some time to talk to them. Please hold off making your presence known to them, alright? Give me a chance to snoop around before you spook them. I'm sort of undercover, John. I'm registered as myself, but I haven't said that I'm on an investigation. I told the *Breakers'* desk clerk that I was on vacation. Let me keep it that way for the time being."

"How long, Dave?"

"I don't know yet. First, let me see what I can find out undercover. I knew some IKOR guys in Spain. If any of the people at this meeting were there, they might remember me."

"Why didn't I know about this before?"

"You knew I was in Spain."

"Yes, if course I did. But you never said anything about you and the IKOR."

"These were just a couple of guys I met. I don't even remember their names."

"Alright. I'll hold off for a little while. What's your next move?" Brixton asked.

"I plan to have a talk with the dealer who was working the *Breakers* card room on Saturday. Weber's wife told me he was interested in finding a different game and I'm guessing, based on what was in his pockets, that he played at *The Breakers*. The dealer and the bartender who were on duty come on shift at ten o'clock this morning. I'm scheduled to sit-in at eleven. I checked in at *The Breakers* last night."

"When did you talk to the wife?"

"After she identified the body, she came over to the station house to talk to us, her and Weber's parents. We had a nice, long chat. I took notes, so listen up." He went over what he'd learned from Miriam Weber.

"Well, that's a lot more than I would have wanted her to tell you."

"She's not one of your scientists - she's just the widow, and a nice lady to boot. Come on, John, if I'm going to work a murder investigation I have to talk the widow."

"I suppose. You said you've got one of your guys checking the phone number. Somebody with the ACPD?"

"Yeah. I've got a partner to work with me - a guy I used to walk a beat with named Buster Fulton. A good man. And the Chief has assigned the two Detectives who were at the scene to keep working on it, reporting to me. Cal Turner and Lou Staup."

"But they don't have clearance!" Brixton protested.

"We're investigating a robbery murder – they don't need clearance."

"You trust them? Atlantic City cops and you trust them?"

"Yes, John, I trust them. This is why you asked for my help, so's I could get the ACPD working the case."

"Yeah, I guess I did."

"I will come to Philly tomorrow to look at the rest of the stuff that was in his room."

"Let me think about it. The science boys haven't finished with his effects."

"You mean his stuff is radioactive?'

"You know, that hadn't occurred to me. I'll ask if they've checked for radiation. Shit. My men have been carrying the stuff."

"What did the Army take?"

"Some technical journals that your ACPD men shouldn't see."

"Alright, John. We can live with that. But listen, we can't work in a box. We have to have access to all the evidence and you have to let us chase down the leads. We can't just assume it was a botched robbery."

"So?"

"So what do you want from me? Do you want me to solve the case or do you want me to invent a solution? Do you want me to pursue leads other than robbery or not?"

There was silence on the other end.

Evidence and intelligence are not the same thing. As a law enforcement officer, Levitan's purpose had been to put someone inside the frame of a crime. As an intelligence officer, he used information to give substance to shadows, to find out what people were doing. As evidence, his discoveries were often useless, but he was no longer tasked with building prosecution cases. One of the reasons that Levitan liked his job was because the Admiral was an intelligence chief as well as a law enforcement officer.

Brixton's boss had a different style. The Permanent Director of The Federal Bureau of Investigation, John Edgar Hoover, was an obsessively hands-on chief who had seized sole ownership of domestic intelligence during the war, when it had been sensible to streamline counter-espionage and domestic intelligence. The wartime Government had prohibited the uniformed intelligence services from investigations on American soil - other than those conducted on military bases. Thanks to Hoover's ties with the most powerful men in the American government, he'd been authorized as the wartime emperor of domestic intelligence. But, as Brixton was reminding him, now that the war was over, many of the high and mighty, including Coast Guard Admiral Spiegel and his counterparts in the Army and Navy, as well as many influential Senators and Congressmen, were challenging the legitimacy of Hoover's empire. The permanent boundaries of the FBI's authority were uncertain.

Investigations in Hoover's FBI were team affairs lasting months and years. Levitan operated independently and, by the standards of the FBI, with blinding speed. Over the previous two years, in overlapping investigations, Brixton and Levitan had exposed a sabotage plot and an arms smuggling ring. Brixton respected Levitan's investigative prowess, so much so that he'd advocated giving him a Top Secret security classification. With the Admiral insisting that a Top Secret designation was essential for a man he wanted as his investigator on the docks, Brixton had been able to overcome the Bureau's resistance to Levitan's apparently subversive background.

Finally, Levitan tired of waiting for Brixton's reply. "John?" he said, "Are you still there?"

"Well. I guess I trust you."

"You're not sure? Even now?"

"All right. I trust you."

"Well thanks for that," he said. "So you'll let me out of the box?"

"Like what, Dave? What is it exactly that you want to do? Keep in mind that this case is dynamite; there's no way to tell what kinds of destruction it might cause if it blows up. You're going to have to be really, really careful."

"Always, John. I'm always careful. I'll come to Philly to look at his effects first thing tomorrow morning. Please make sure your people know that I'm coming. Then I'm going to the funeral and see if I can find an IKOR connection."

"Stay in the background at the funeral."

"I need to know more about the victim, John. There are likely to be IAS people there, people from his job. Can I talk to them?"

"I don't think that's a good idea."

"You have to trust me, John. I have the clearance, thanks to you."

"Oh boy," said Brixton.

"I'll be as careful as I can be. If you want a solution, you'll have to trust me."

"Alright. You'll report to me later on today about whatever you find out at *The Breakers.*"

"As soon as I know anything, I'll call back," said Levitan.

"Leave a message if I'm out of the office."

"Let me ask you, John... who else is involved besides the FBI? What other kinds of Government agents am I going to bump into?"

"At the moment, no one but us. But this is at The Cabinet level now, so there's no telling. They've just established a new outfit called the Atomic Energy Commission. Them, and maybe Army Intelligence and the OSS and who knows who the hell else."

"Tell them all to cooperate."

Brixton laughed. "Yeah, good luck with that! I've got to say goodbye. It's time for me to call The Director."

9

Buster Fulton signed an unmarked car out of the police station lot. They drove uptown to *The Breakers*, where he'd spent the night, and parked in the no-parking fire zone next to the hotel. It was ten-thirty, a half-hour before his eleven o'clock reservation at the poker table.

"Buster, get yourself a cup of coffee. I have to call my wife."

He went up to his room, removed his jacket, unstrapped the holster, and placed a call to Helen's New York phone number.

"How you doin' Babe," he said when she answered.

"Not bad, Dave. I'm okay. I'm glad you called. I tried calling you all day yesterday, but you weren't home. You went to the *Phillies* game?"

"Nope, I got sent to Atlantic City on a job. It was a rush thing and I didn't have time to call you. I'm staying at *The Breakers,* Room 905. You'd love it."

"Oh, Dave. You know I'd like to."

"Sure."

"*The Breakers*, huh? Very fancy."

"That's me, nothing but the best. The room's got a great view. And seawater for the bathtub, hot and cold."

"I can't, Dave. Tomorrow I'm sitting-in at the record studio. And I'm booked through Saturday night to accompany Warren at the club. I can't. Unless you'll still be there on Sunday?"

"Probably not."

"I'm sorry, Dave."

"It's okay, I understand."

"So, since you're down there, are you going to go see Mom and Dad?" Helen's parents, Al and Ida Rubin, had a photography business in Atlantic City and owned a house in The Inlet neighborhood.

"If I get a chance."

"That'll be nice. They'll be glad to see you."

"Yeah, and maybe your Mom will feed me."

"There's not much doubt about that. So I can reach you at *The Breakers*?"

"Yeah. If I'm not in my room, just leave a message that you called and I'll try to call you back. But I never know for sure where you're going to be."

"That makes two of us, Davey," she said.

"Right, Babe. I'll talk to you soon."

He buttoned the front of the lightweight sport jacket he'd had tailored for his long frame and broad shoulders - cut to conceal the gun on his left side. He kept his notebook and an automatic pencil in an inside breast pocket. When he'd had the jacket made, he'd gotten the tailor to reinforce the hip pockets to carry the weight of the roll of dimes he carried in each one. He patted his sides and felt their reassuring mass. Last, he replenished his money supply from the stash concealed behind the false panel of his suitcase. On the job, he kept the money folded in the right-hand pocket of his trousers so that he could reach for a gun or for cash with equal ease.

§

At fifteen minutes before eleven o'clock, he posted Fulton in the *Breakers'* mezzanine to make sure nobody left *The Newark Room* after he entered. Inside, a four-player game of five-card stud was underway at one of the tables, the other two were vacant. The cashier/bellman's name was Pinky D'Annato. Levitan asked him for a glass of orange juice and slid onto a barstool.

"Hey, I'm supposed to meet a pal of mine here. Bob Weber? Did he leave already?" Levitan asked. He had set up the appointment, posing as Weber, when he'd called from *The Traymore* the day before.

"I don't think so. He was supposed to be here at eleven?" D'Annato replied.

"Yes, that was the plan."

"Let me check."

The appointment book was open at one end of the bar. D'Annato read over the listed names. "Yeah, he's in the book. Probably got tied up somehow."

"That's odd. You probably remember him from Saturday? He played Saturday afternoon."

D'Annato thumbed back a page and ran his finger down the list of names. "Oh. That guy. Yeah, I remember *him*. The *Pepsi* guy. He did good."

Levitan smiled, "That's my Bobby. How much did he win?"

Card room protocol required D'Annato to keep any sums he knew to himself. Players valued discretion in a card room, as many of them were debtors whose occasional wins could prompt unwelcome demands for repayment. Too, there were players to be watched, possibly banned. And for a cashier to admit recalling an amount won or lost would have been to second-guess the fraudulent account book he kept in the safe. For a card room's cash manager, discretion was a fundamental job requirement. D'Annato's face, except for his eyes, remained impassive. "I can't say," he said.

Levitan said, "He doesn't cheat, you know. He sees the deck in his head and has a gift for math."

"I noticed," said D'Annato. "Very smooth, that guy."

Levitan broadened his smile, "He walked out with a bundle, didn't he?"

D'Annato wiped the bar top with a towel. He shrugged. "He seemed to know what he was doing."

"And you remember the guy he was with? *That* guy! He's almost as good." This was a shot in the dark. But Weber must have heard about *The Breakers* card room from someone. Perhaps he'd arranged to meet that person at the game.

D'Annato frowned and tilted his head, puzzled. "No other guy. What other guy?"

Men who play as a team are not welcome in card rooms. If they're honest, partners are no more likely to beat the house than single players, two fools being somehow more than twice as likely to lose as one fool, the laws of probability skewed by greed. But professional dealers can recognize signals and will end a game if they see any sign of cheating.

"I was thinking of Steve," said Levitan, making up a name. "I guess he didn't come. I guess he couldn't make it. make it."

That seemed to satisfy D'Annato's curiosity.

"But, listen. I'm a bit concerned that Bob hasn't shown up *today*. It's not like him. He's a reliable guy."

D'Annato nodded.

"Maybe I'll call his room."

He put a dollar bill on the bar, "Keep the change," he said, giving a ninety-five cent tip for a nickel glass of juice.

"Thanks. How many chips do you want?" said D'Annato, reminding Levitan that he'd come to play cards.

"Can I use your house phone? The switchboard will connect me to Bob's room, won't they?"

"Not a problem," said D'Annato, placing the bar-top telephone in front of Levitan. "But I didn't think he was staying here."

"Really? He *said* he would be staying here."

Making sure that D'Annato overheard, he asked the hotel operator to connect him to Robert Weber's room. "That's funny," he said when he hung up. "I was sure he said he was staying at *The Breakers*."

"I think he said he came down from *The Traymore*."

"Oh, so you got a chance to talk to him?"

"Nah. You know, what's-your-name and all that. But he did say he'd walked from *The Traymore.* I remember him saying how crowded The Boardwalk was. Seems like a nice guy."

"The best," said Levitan, placing two ten dollar bills on the bar. "Let me have twenty worth of chips - maybe Bobby will still show up."

Optimists and pessimists play cards differently; pessimists dislike losing, optimists yearn to win. Levitan isn't sure where he fell on that continuum, but he did enjoy a good poker game.

The dealer introduced himself as Frank. The other players were a Herb, a Daniel, a Gene, and an Arnie. Levitan was a few dollars ahead when Frank called a break shortly before noon. They all trooped out of the card room together and made their way to the men's room on the mezzanine. Buster, in street clothes, was trying to look inconspicuous, leaning against a wall.

In the men's room, after they zipped up, standing side by side with the dealer at the sink, Levitan said, "I hear my pal Bobby Weber was here on Saturday. I think he was at your table."

"Saturday? Bobby Weber? Oh yeah, Bob. I had a Bob that day," said Frank, accepting a towel from the men's room attendant.

"Skinny guy? Curly hair?"

"Sounds like the guy."

"Pretty good player, isn't he?" said Levitan, taking a towel.

"He did alright. Yeah," Frank said, on his way out the door.

"Fast, right?" said Levitan, catching up.

"Yeah, he was fast."

As they were re-crossing the mezzanine, Levitan said, "Listen, can I talk to you for a second? Just for a second. I'm a little worried about him."

The dealer turned to face him. He was a pale, soft man – someone who avoided sunlight and exercise. "Okay. What's the problem?" he said, a busy fellow who was nice to his customers.

"I had dinner with him Saturday night, after he played here. He was acting really odd, as if something pretty serious had happened. He wouldn't say anything, but I could tell he was really upset, like something bad had happened. And now he doesn't show up for a card game – which is also very odd for him. Did anything happen on Saturday?"

"Happen? Not that I remember. We just played cards," Frank said.

"Can you remember how long he played?"

"He left before dinner. Said he was going to another hotel, where he was staying."

"*The Traymore*?"

"I don't remember. Maybe."

"He started around two o'clock, right?"

"Yeah, I think so. Left around five."

"And he was okay when he left?"

"Yeah he was okay."

"Huh!" said Levitan. "Then it must have been something else that was bothering him at dinner."

"Must have been," the dealer said. "He was okay, as far as I could tell, when he left."

"How much did he win?"

"Why? Does he owe you?"

"Nope… just curious," said Levitan.

"He did okay."

The elevator doors opened, and Turner and Staup emerged.

Levitan said, "You know, I think I'm going to cash in. Looks like it's a nice afternoon to be on the beach."

"Oh, okay."

"I may be back. I like the way you run a game," he said, reaching for his cash, and handed the dealer a fiver.

"Well, thanks."

"Don't mention it. Good game."

When the dealer turned his back to go into *The Newark,* Levitan raised a cautionary finger toward the Detectives, signaling them to wait before he joined them.

He followed the dealer into *The Newark Room*, retrieved his chips from the table, took them to the bar and sold them back to Pinky D'Annato for cash, having won two dollars and seventy-five cents. He left his winnings on the bar.

"That's for you, Pinky," he said.

"Much appreciated," said the cashier.

Back on the mezzanine, the two Detectives were talking to Buster Fulton, forming as conspicuous a trio of plain-clothes cops as he'd ever seen. He motioned for them to follow him.

10

An outdoor restaurant on a manicured patio separated the hotel from The Boardwalk. Umbrella tables on either side of the flower-lined patio were occupied with a lunchtime crowd, some in beach attire, as Levitan walked past them to the ramp leading up to The Boardwalk. He cut through rolling chair traffic and people enjoying a stroll, followed by the three cops. He crossed the planks to the beachside railing. A high layer of thin cloud filtered the September sunlight; it was likely to rain.

The Breakers was not as fine a building as *The Traymore*, nor as large. Still, it occupied a half a block of Boardwalk property, a huge wood-frame clapboard structure attempting European elegance with a gray mansard roof surrounding the tenth floor.

Turner, Staup and Fulton joined him at the rail.

"Well?" he asked. "What about the phone number?"

Staup said, "It's for The Department of Mathematics at the Institute for Advanced Study. When I made the call, I got the secretary for some guy named Von Noiman. He's out of town."

"That's the dead man's boss," said Levitan. "Good work. Did you see anything in the books?"

"Nothing."

"No regular big buys on Friday nights?"

"No. I did see twenty-dollar buys on Friday nights, but there's no way to tell for sure whether Weber was the buyer," said Turner.

Levitan said, "Nothing, then. Too bad. How about the register?"

"I seen his name down for last Friday night and for most of the Fridays since June; same time, eight o'clock, every night. And there were also twenty-dollar buys those nights."

"Well, that's good to know. It confirms what the dealer told me. Good work."

Staup said, "Yeah. But, if he was laundering cash, there's no sign of it in the books."

"It was a long shot, anyway. Thanks for your help."

"What's next, Dave?" said Staup.

"For you three, it's *The Breakers'* card room. The last people to see Weber alive were the dealer and the cashier who are on duty now. Go in officially and don't take 'no' for an answer. Same routine Buster used at *The Traymore* - collect their books and get the names and addresses of everybody in the room. Find out if any of them played with Weber on Saturday afternoon."

"Just take their books? That's heavy, Dave," said Sergeant Buster Fulton.

"I'll be nearby, just in case," said Levitan. "If they don't honor your credentials, then they'll for damned sure honor mine. So, if you need me, I'll come in and throw the weight of the Federal Government at them.

But I'd prefer not to. So far, no one at this hotel connects me to Weber's murder. As far as we know, no one at this hotel knows or cares that he's dead. Let's keep it that way for as long as we can."

"Where are you going to be?"

"I've got to give the FBI a report. I'll call them from a booth in the lobby. Then I'll be in *The Vineland Room*, checking out a meeting. If I have to leave to chase something down, I'll leave you a message with the duty sergeant at the station house. Let's use him as our point of contact. If we get separated, we'll call in every hour or so."

"Got it," said Turner. "What room are you in? In case we want to leave you a message here."

"No messages. I'm in 905, and you can knock on the door, but I'd prefer that we not involve hotel people, okay? Let's try to keep away from their switchboard. We'll use the duty sergeant back at the police station as our point of contact. Cal, you call him and set it up. I've got to make a phone call from the lobby. Let's go."

From a phone booth in *The Breakers* lobby, Levitan asked the long distance operator to connect him to the FBI's number at the Federal Building on Chestnut Street in Philadelphia. Brixton was in a meeting, so he left a message, "*The Breakers Hotel* confirmed as victim's location prior to murder. Will call back at 4 PM."

Before he'd gone to Spain, Levitan had worked in the 'boiler room' of an insurance company, making cold calls to prospective buyers. His task had been to probe the defenses of businesses that might be sold a better deal on group life insurance. He'd been pretty good at getting appointments, but had never closed a deal. He'd hated the job, but had learned a useful skill – how to use a telephone.

He dialed the Princeton number.

"Mathematics, Professor Von Neumann's office. May I help you?"

"This is Commodore Levitan of The US Coast Guard. May I speak to the Professor?"

"I'm sorry, sir. The Professor is out of town. What's this about? Maybe I can help you."

"Bob Weber," he said. "I'm investigating the cause of his death. Somebody must be in charge while Professor Von Neumann's away. Who would that be?"

"Well that would be me, as far as you're concerned," said the lady on the other end of the line. "Tell me again who you are."

He repeated his name and the reason for the call. "I'm working with Special Agent John Brixton of the FBI. Do you know him?"

"No, sir," she said. "I will connect you to Professor Gordon. He's taking Professor Von Neumann's calls."

The man named Gordon explained that Von Neumann was on his way back from Chicago to attend Weber's funeral. "This has been a terrible shock for us, Commodore. Devastating."

"Yes. It's a terrible business. I promise you that we'll catch whoever did this. But we need your cooperation."

"I understand. What can we do for you?"

"I'll be at the funeral myself," he said. "Will you let Professor Von Neumann know that I'd like a few minutes of his time?"

"Yes I will. How do you spell your name?"

Buster was waiting for him in one of the lobby easy chairs, waiting for instructions, looking almost ordinary absent the leather and lead of his uniform.

"Let's split up," said the Commodore. "Same drill as at the other hotel - talk to hotel employees about Saturday afternoon. It seems as if he returned to the *Traymore* from here at around five o'clock. See if anybody remembers seeing him - a small, skinny guy with glasses and curly brown hair."

"Do I flash the badge or am I undercover?"

"Show the badge, but don't mention the murder."

"What shall I say?"

"Don't tell them anything unless you have to. If you must, tell them you're looking for a pair of pickpockets. I'm going to crash a meeting in *The Vineland Room*."

"What kind of meeting?"

Levitan said, "I saw something that got me interested on the notice board. A weird organization that I thought had gone out of business before the war called IKOR. I'm going to check them out. It's possible that Weber, who was Jewish, had a connection."

11

Levitan did not talk to people about his service in The Spanish Civil War. He was proud of what he'd done there and certain of his reasons; there had been a call to the barricades and he'd answered. But his memories were emotional and conflicted, so he avoided the subject. Too, he usually abstained from political conversations, having learned to stifle his opinions, not because he doubted their validity, but because he was more passionate than he cared to show.

His last battle had been a skirmish at dusk on one of the twisting mountain roads leading to the city of Teruel. A Nationalist soldier higher up the hill had spotted them and was firing from safety, picking them off. Levitan had dashed for the cover of a ravine, misjudged its depth, and landed badly, heel first on a rock, his shattered ankle bones piercing his skin. The bones shrank as they healed, the reason he'd been denied a GI uniform. He'd resented his *4-F* Draft classification as a scarlet letter stamped by doctor bureaucrats. When the Admiral had offered contract work after the *Wisconsin* case, he'd accepted it gratefully as a way to serve his country during the war.

The IKOR notice on the bulletin board sparked memories of two fanatics he'd met in Madrid in

November, 1937, both political officers, in uniform but not combat soldiers, who'd worked as quartermasters directing the meager flow of Soviet goods to the front. He remembered that one had been an Ohioan, and nothing at all about the other one. But he'd recognize them if he saw them again, if they were at the IKOR meeting in *The Vineland Room.*

The Vineland was a small meeting room in which a half-dozen men were seated in folding chairs facing a table at which a pretty young woman wearing pants sat next to a man with salt and pepper hair. The men facing the table twisted in their chairs to look at Levitan as he entered through the door in the back of the room.

"Yes? Can I help you?" inquired the man with salt and pepper hair.

"You know, I just wanted to stick my head in to see if I know anyone here. I met some of your guys in Spain, back in '37. I'm staying at the hotel and noticed that IKOR was having a meeting. I was really surprised. I just thought I'd see if any of my old friends are here."

"And who are you?" asked the leader.

He took the leader's question as an invitation and walked toward the front. "My name's Dave Levitan. I served in the Lincoln Battalion at Teruel."

He'd volunteered at a rally in the summer of 1937.

In New York, looking for work, having failed as an insurance man, he'd gone to the rally with a cousin on whose sofa he'd been sleeping. Inside the hall, full-throated Communists explained that the Spanish Civil

War was a test of freedom and democracy against tyranny and hate, the critical battleground in the global war against the oppression of the Fascist anti-Semites, a just and vital cause. Without a career, without a girlfriend, without any obligations, and with a simmering hatred for Nazis and their ilk, Dave Levitan had volunteered to save the world.

He'd fought in the mountains northeast of Madrid during the bitter cold winter of 1937 and 1938. The International Brigades, like the Lincoln from the USA, had been pathetically overmatched by the *Fokker* dive bombers, the *Panzer* tanks, the German Army, and the Spanish Nationalist soldiers who'd regarded the ragtag brigades of foreign idealists as despicable invaders. There had been around three thousand Americans, divided into four Lincoln Brigade battalions. A third of the Americans died in action. He'd been in a field hospital during the final retreat of the International Brigades and come home shortly before the Spanish Republicans conceded defeat at the hands of Franco's Nationalists in the spring of 1938.

The IKOR men Levitan had met in Spain were committed Communists from Yiddish-speaking immigrant families, the sons of people who'd escaped the pogroms of the Czarist lands during the decades before 1917. The émigrés from the Jewish Pale of Settlement who'd come to America during the half century before World War I had universally been heartened by the demise of the Romanovs, and hopeful that a new set of governing principles would replace the fallen regime's. At that time, there had been considerable enthusiasm among Jewish Americans for the Russian revolutionary cause.

Dave Levitan regarded himself as distinctly different from the men of IKOR, even though his parents and the aunt and uncle who'd raised him, had also come to America from a Czarist country in Eastern Europe. He spoke English, not Yiddish; he read Raymond Chandler and John Steinbeck, not Karl Marx and Friedrich Engels; he regarded Stalin as a murderous tyrant and the Communist prohibitions against profit, individual enterprise and political freedom as dead wrong. He had not gone to Spain on behalf of the Communist ideal, but to combat the spread of Fascist evil. He had fought on the same side as IKOR, but nor for the same reasons.

And yet, a battlefield comrade is a friend for life.

When he reached the front of the room, he scanned the faces, not recognizing anyone. But they'd been cold, dirty and hungry that year; no doubt he himself looked quite different from the soldier he'd once been. So he scanned the faces more carefully.

"This is a closed meeting," said the leader.

"I'm amazed it's a meeting at all. I mean, I think it's… amazing. You know, after everything that's happened."

"Get out! Leave!" said the leader,

"Please, give me a minute. I know all about you guys. I was *there*. That war, that was *you too*. I *remember* some of you guys."

"I don't remember you," said one of the men. "Who was your commanding officer?"

"At Teruel? That would have been Bill Wheeler, under Herm Seligman."

"You knew Bill Wheeler?" asked the man.

"Of course, he was my Lieutenant. A helluva guy."

"Tell me about Seligman."

"Sure. Captain Seligman. He had an accent, German I think, but he was from California - San Francisco, maybe? He seemed pretty good to me - a good soldier. Do you know him?" As a grunt volunteer with less than a year of college, layers of rank had separated Levitan from the likes of Seligman, but he certainly remembered him.

There followed ten minutes of reminiscence, during which Levitan proved his *bona fides* by exchanging names of people they had known in common, chuckling over remembered personalities.

"Comrade Levitan, we're very glad to meet you," said the leader, who introduced himself as Kalman Savin. "But we're conducting business here. So, would you leave us to it please?"

"Sure, sure. I'm on my way. But are you guys going to be around? How long are you in town for?"

"Awhile."

"So I'll see you around. I'm here until the weekend. Let's get together."

Leave 'em laughing is always a smart move. He would depart before they started to probe for details about him, before he had more chances to say something stupid. He took a step toward the back of the room and said, "Are you staying here at *The*

Breakers? Give me a room number I can call. Let's get together for a drink."

"Why don't I get in touch with you," said Savin, the leader. "Levitan... right? You're staying here? Maybe we can set something up."

"Great," said Levitan at the door. "See ya," he said, and departed, hopeful that he'd established himself as one of those people that J. Edgar Hoover called a "fellow traveler." Maybe he was.

12

After he left the IKOR meeting, Levitan headed downstairs to *The Breakers'* reception desk. Oscar, on whom he'd bestowed a five dollar bill the night before, was not on duty. This fellow's name was Bernard. Levitan slipped him a fiver.

"Listen, Bernard, I may be getting messages here. Is that okay?"

"Absolutely, sir. Are you a guest?"

"Yes, Room 905. Levitan."

"Very good, sir. In fact, you just missed a call," he said, retrieving a folded sheet of paper from Room 905's cubbyhole and handing it to Levitan. It read, "Call Al Rubin, AC-2925."

Al Rubin, Levitan's father-in-law, owned commercial darkrooms and photography studios in Philadelphia and Atlantic City. In the resort, he had a lease on a double-wide stall in the middle of the city's busiest entertainment pier where, during high season, he oversaw the business of taking photographs and mailing them to their subjects. He loved being in the midst of the action on the pier.

Offseason, Al lived in Philadelphia with his wife, Ida, on the second and third floors above *Albert Photography*, a storefront studio near a trolley stop where his employees took pictures for high school yearbooks, weddings, and bar mitzvahs. In both cities, employees did most of the work, freeing Al to spend time on politics. He had a house on North Rhode Island Avenue in the Inlet neighborhood of Atlantic City, where he stayed during the summers and on offseason trips to manage his businesses and to meet with his political cronies.

Levitan returned to the phone booth and dialed his father-in-law. "Al, what's up? How did you know I was at *The Breakers*?"

"I just talked to Helen on the phone, she told me. I'm worried about her."

Levitan had married Helen in 1945 after a long engagement. After they had been dating for a few months in 1939, Al had pulled strings to get Levitan a patrolman's job on the ACPD.

"Really? I just talked to her myself, a couple of hours ago. She seemed fine."

"Yes. But she's in New York. It's not good."

"There's not much I can do about it, Al. It's what she wants."

"You can't let this happen, Davey. It's a big mistake."

"It is what it is, Al. I don't know what I can do about it."

"There has to be something. I'm on the pier. Come. We'll talk. We'll stop this *mishugoss*."

"I'm in town working a case, Al. I don't have the time."

"You don't have the time to save your marriage?"

"I don't know what good us talking about it will do."

"It may be worse than you think. I don't like what I heard."

"What? What did she say?"

"I don't want to talk about it on the telephone. I'm on the pier. Please."

He could not refuse the man who'd provided him with the best things in his life: his career and the woman he loved. "Alright, Al. I'll be there in fifteen minutes. A half hour is all I can spare. Okay?"

"Good."

§

The Steel Pier extended a thousand feet across the beach and out to sea from The Boardwalk at Virginia Avenue. *Steel Pier Memories*, Al's place of business, was located midway between The Boardwalk and the end of the pier, just above the line of surf. The tide was in, the waves swelling in the sea below *Memories*. The hazy sun shone on the beach, an expanse clotted with people as far as he could see, all the way up to the northern tip of the island a half-mile in the distance. Bathers played in the surf: standing, striding, swimming, diving into the waves, riding them to the beach. The faint sound of lifeguards blowing their whistles seemed as natural as birdsong in a forest. The breeze had calmed. Soon, he thought, a storm would arrive.

If you fancied a picture of yourself as a bathing beauty or a strongman standing on the beach with the skyline of Atlantic City behind you, *Memories* had the equipment to satisfy you. The sandwich board advertisement on the midway in front of the stall read,

"Photos Mailed Home: Highest Quality: 50¢." Inside was a small, simulated merry-go-round where toddlers could choose their mounts: a pony, a tiger, or a dolphin. Children of a certain age dragged their parents inside by the hand, so attracted were they to *Memories'* wooden menagerie of painted animals on roller skates. Sample pictures, many of men in uniform with their wives and girlfriends, adorned a post facing the midway.

Al Rubin was an ordinary-looking man, short of stature, bald on top, with a neatly-trimmed fringe of gray hair surrounding his genial head. He wore bifocals. When he smiled, you felt blessed. Levitan's father-in-law, although as innocuous as he was likeable, was a man held in high regard by those who knew him, especially by the ne'er-do-wells, do-gooders, and do-nothings holding political offices in Trenton, Philadelphia, Newark, and Jersey City. He was connected, knowledgeable, and wise in the ways of power.

The politician who had managed Atlantic City's affairs for a quarter of a century, Enoch "Nucky" Johnson, was over a thousand miles away at Leavenworth Federal Prison, serving the fifth year of a ten-year sentences for tax evasion and jury tampering. In a way, Al Rubin had become Nucky's surrogate. He did not wield the power Nucky once had, nor did he desire to do so; Al rarely asked a favor or tried to use his influence. He'd been Nucky's counselor, not his partner. To Levitan, Al Rubin was a mentor, a father-in-law, and a friend.

"You look good, Davey. But you're pale. You could use a little sun."

"That would be great, but I'm usually working inside."

"You been too busy to come spend a couple of days down the shore? Are you staying awhile? How come you didn't call?"

"I'm here on business, Al. Just some government bullshit."

"There's sure a lot of that. So, this government business, should I know about it?"

"No. Except that I'm working with Chief Rafferty and the ACPD. There are some local aspects to it."

"Well how about that! Back to your old stomping grounds, are you Davey?"

"Temporarily."

"For how long?"

"It's hard to say. I'm staying over tonight, at *The Breakers*, maybe tomorrow night too, depending on how things go. How *you* doin', Al?"

"Eh! How should I be? By me, everything's okay."

Al had an accent - New York Bowery with Yiddish inflection. He pronounced "thirty" as "toity." After arriving in America at the age of fifteen, he'd gotten a job sparring with a stable of Jewish prize-fighters, learning English from tough men who said "dese" and "dose" instead of "these" and "those." His nose was bent and his knuckles were outsized and misshapen.

"So tell me what Helen says that got you so upset."

"It wasn't her... I heard a man, Davey. There was a man talking while she was talking to me."

"She's working with a singer, Al. Some guy named Warren. She probably called you from where they were rehearsing."

"Oh. Do you think that's all it is? Just a rehearsal with a singer."

"Probably."

"So I shouldn't worry?"

"I don't know. That's probably all there is to it."

"Well... Maybe I got the wrong idea."

"Maybe."

"But it's still not good, is it Davey? Have you heard from the adoption people?"

"Not yet."

"Do you think it's going to be alright?"

Helen was unlikely to carry a child for nine months without hemorrhaging, her womb having been damaged during an emergency surgery to deliver a stillborn baby conceived on the honeymoon of her first marriage. That marriage had ended when her husband of only three months, Ben Lowenthal, Levitan's battlefield comrade, had been killed at Teruel. Dave had met her on a visit to Philadelphia to deliver his condolences. He'd fallen in love with her the day they'd met.

She practiced strict birth control, primarily out of fear for her life and her health, but also because an artist requires solitude, and because she relished being a free woman who had paths to choose. Enthusiastic about sex, despite the risks, she'd been fully satisfied to have Dave as her only lover, but had resisted marriage to him until the last year of the war. After the reality of the Holocaust became undeniable, she'd had a heart-shift and agreed to marry him so that they could raise war orphans together.

The adoption agency had received their application months before, time enough to have sorted things out, and the opportunity to give a home to a war orphan might soon have become a reality. Levitan expected a letter from the agency at any time.

"You know her, Al. I can't blame her for going to New York. It's where she belongs right now." Opportunities to play with the best musicians in New York for good money had been powerful inducements. Her ship had finally arrived. She'd left on it.

"But what about you?"

"I'm okay. I miss her, but she's doing what she wants to do. I've never been one to stand in her way. She is who she is. She has to be true to herself."

Helen had a gift for the piano. She played popular tunes or Romantic *etudes* with equal skill and enthusiasm, an artist striving for beauty with every note she struck. Recently, she'd accepted a steady job with a recording studio in New York, too far from Philadelphia for a daily commute. And she worked with the singers she met through the studio, providing accompaniment as they perfected their lounge acts.

"Maybe if you two had a house… maybe she'd want to live in a nice house instead of an apartment."

"Probably, so long as it has room for her piano and her music. Are you saying that she'd come home if I bought a house?"

"I can help you out, with the money, no problem. Let me get you a nice house. It would give her something else to think about... maybe help her make up her mind."

"I thinks she's done that, don't you?" said Levitan.

"But nothing's definite yet, is it? She's not gone for good. She's just taken that sublet in The Village on a month-to-month lease, right? She's planning to come back."

"Maybe. But I think the adoption's out."

"Did she say that?"

"No, she didn't, not in so many words."

Levitan thought he'd be happy in a houseful of children. He had been looking forward to the chance to raise at least one. Now, he doubted that would happen. If the agency had moved a little faster, if the prospect of having a child had become a reality sooner, before the record company offer, things might have worked out differently.

"But you're pretty sure, huh?"

"Pretty sure."

"Maybe it's for the best," said his father-in-law.

13

The return rolling chair ride from *The Steel Pier* to *The Breakers* took him through The Boardwalk's high-rent district, eight blocks of *kitsch* and honky-tonk, where you could buy a paper cone of hot salted french-fries or a diamond ring. As a beat cop, he'd learned that crime follows the money and that the money was thickest along that stretch. He could spot a pickpocket from a hundred yards.

Most of the crime took place just off The Boardwalk in the bars, restaurants and rooming houses. His job as a cop had been to ensure that none of the thieves took up residence. There would always be petty crime on The Boardwalk, but the smart thieves stayed off it, choosing to prey instead upon the vulnerable, footsore, inebriated day-trippers and conventioneers who left the planks looking for a good time in town. And those thieves brought their own with them, forming instant neighborhoods where everyone knew that shit was going down, places where little tribes could form in a season.

A seasonal resort that survived the cooler months on convention business, Atlantic City had a permanent population living in segregated neighborhoods on the bay side across Atlantic Avenue. Italians were in the food services. Jews had retail shops on Atlantic Avenue. Black people worked as housekeepers and in the kitchens. At the northeast tip of the island, there was a substantial white middle class neighborhood called The Inlet where families lived year-round. Levitan had lived there during the five years he'd spent on the ACPD, years when he and Helen spent summers together as lovers before they married.

Most of the tables on *The Breakers'* patio were vacant as Levitan, pondering the legitimacy of Al's concerns, walked to the lobby entrance from The Boardwalk. It was late afternoon, the slow time of day when water pressure in the hotels was challenged by guests washing away salt and sand under showers in high-rise buildings. It was the interval of calm he'd learned to expect on high season afternoons as visitors and locals alike prepared for the night ahead. The sky had darkened, and he felt a sudden gust of wind coming off the sea. Waiters were folding the umbrellas to prevent them from blowing away.

Levitan approached the reception desk to check for messages, but found his way blocked by an officious man wearing a fedora of bleached Panama straw. Another man, hatless, stood watchfully to the side, his hands free, but ready. They seemed to have been waiting for him.

"Are you Commodore Levitan?" asked Straw Hat quietly.

"I am."

The man reached for his ID and showed it to Levitan – he was Captain Rudolph Duplessis of U.S. Army Intelligence.

"What can I do for you, Captain?" Levitan asked.

"I've been told that you have a room here."

"Yes."

"Good. I need to talk to you."

§

Captain Rudolph Duplessis and a Lieutenant, the man who'd been with him in the lobby, had been stationed undercover at the hotel for two days, since Sunday afternoon, having followed a man who led them there from New York. Duplessis had taken notice of Turner and Staup in *The Newark Room*, and of Buster Fulton interviewing hotel employees. He had confronted Buster, who'd told him that Levitan was the man in charge.

"What would you like to know?" asked Levitan.

"Why are you here?" asked Duplessis. Levitan pictured him in an Army uniform: summer khakis, a silver bar on each shoulder of his jacket and a strand of brass braid above the leather brim of his hat.

Levitan said, "The FBI, Coast Guard Intelligence, and the ACPD are collaborating on a murder investigation. I am the liaison and lead investigator. I am surprised you haven't been informed about the murder," said Levitan. "Why are *you* here?"

"No. You first. Fill me in on the murder. But start with why the hell you walked into an IKOR meeting this morning. Is that part of your murder investigation?"

"Ahh. So you, Army Intelligence, have been watching the IKOR," said Levitan.

"We'll get to that later. Who's your boss?" demanded Duplessis.

"Rear Admiral Tom Spiegel, in charge of port security for the East Coast. I'm a little surprised that you weren't told about the murder," said Levitan.

"It's a big government, Commodore. Information, is closely held."

"Too true. Well, here's what I know," said Levitan. "Robert Weber, an important scientist associated with The Manhattan Project, was in The *Breakers Hotel* less than an hour before he was strangled in his room at another hotel seven blocks away called *The Traymore*. He'd won two hundred dollars there on Friday night, money that was not in his room when his body was discovered on Sunday morning. We're at this hotel because this is where he came on Saturday afternoon to play in a card room operated by the hotel. An hour or so later, back at the first hotel, he was dead. I'm working the robbery angle. Now it's your turn. What brings you to this hotel?"

"A question… what is your clearance level?"

"Top Secret. Special Agent John Brixton, FBI counterintelligence, is my FBI liaison… and he talks to Hoover. Now it's your turn. What's going on?"

They were seated with Duplessis on the sofa, Levitan in the easy chair, the drapes open to an ocean view. Duplessis leaned forward, and said, "Tell me what you know about the IKOR."

"Well, what I know is probably very old news."

He had not heard of IKOR since before the Second World War. They had advocated a plausible idea when Hitler was a rising power, when only the USSR stood against him. Those were the days when theories of governance were much discussed, even by the middle classes, days when a Catholic priest from Detroit had broadcast the most popular Sunday radio show on the air, telling tens of millions of Americans about secret Jewish power and that the Jews were behind the country's terrible economic problems. Those were the days when many Americans believed that the Jew-hating Ku Klux Klan had the right idea.

"There were a few them in the Lincoln Battalion – my outfit. But I knew about them from before. If you'd been a Jew, you'd have known about them too."

The IKOR had been prominent during the late Twenties and until the Spanish Civil War. American Jews had been frightened by newspaper reports of the Nazi state, built on a foundation of racist rhetoric - inferior races cause all of German society's problems. According to Hitler, the Jews who were victimizing good Germans were the financiers, the media barons, the grocers, the teachers, the Communists, the Capitalists, the lawyers, the factory workers, the crooks, the union men, the artists, the accountants, the neighbors. They had been everywhere, all a German had to do was look.

To Levitan, who'd understood Germany through a cop's eyes, the Nazis had been murdering thieves who'd invented a rationale for using the plundered wealth of Jewish people to finance their conquests. They had identified Jews as the perfect scapegoats and killed them because it was easier than raising taxes and cheaper than feeding them after stealing everything they had. As people bereft of everything, keeping them alive would drain resources from their military – economic expedience required their slaughter. Nazi anti-Semitism was just an excuse for grand theft, mass murder merely a means to steal.

"They're Commies," said Duplessis.

"Not just Communists," said Levitan. "The IKOR is a mouthpiece for the Comintern. But what they were about was emigration. Resettling Jews in the Soviet Union, in their own community, as an alternative to the idea of Israel. They'd reported to the Comintern."

"What's that?"

Levitan said, "The International Communist Party headquarters in Moscow. But this is America, and the IKOR have a right to their opinion. What surprises me is that they still exist. I mean, they were never particularly popular. People always understood that they were being as cynically political as they were humanitarian. Then, when everybody got to see who Stalin really was – the purges and the pact with Hitler – I thought they'd lost the little support they'd had before. And now, with our Army nose to nose with the Red Army in Central Europe, and with so many people going to Palestine, I'd have thought the IKOR would just have disappeared for lack of support. I'm amazed that there are even any of them left.

"Now it's your turn. Why were you watching the IKOR meeting? Who is the man you followed from New York?"

Duplessis leaned back against the sofa cushion and explained that they'd followed a diplomat, a member of the Polish delegation to the United Nations, from Manhattan to Atlantic City.

"Why him?"

"We're thinking that this guy was a Colonel in the Red Army during the war."

"Does the FBI know about him?"

"We haven't told them yet. Last week, we collected information in Berlin that suggests that this guy had been a Soviet Intelligence officer in the Baltic countries during the war. We think he'd served with forward units of the Red Army as they were pushing westward. We'd met him at the border talks in Berlin during the first days of the joint occupation. Then he disappeared.

"Now we get word that he may be a member of the Polish delegation to the UN. So we take a look at the Polish delegation and find this guy, Tomasz Biernacki, who matches up with this Russian Colonel in a couple of ways. So we started keeping an eye on him last week. The other morning he takes a suitcase with him out of his New York apartment and loads it into the back of his car and takes off through the Holland Tunnel. We follow him down the Garden State Parkway and he ends up here."

"When was this?"

"Sunday morning."

"Damn," said Levitan. "Then he's not Weber's killer. What about your Russian Colonel?"

"Valentin Reshetnikov. That's the who we think this Biernacki really is."

Levitan rose and went to the window. People were leaving the beach, walking toward the wooden stairway carrying blankets and beach bags, forming a single file like ants returning to the nest. The sky was dark. A spray of heavy raindrops thudded against the glass.

"Does he know you followed him?" Levitan asked. "You came all the way down the Garden State Parkway without him noticing?"

"We were careful."

"But he may have spotted you?"

"It's possible."

"So, what's he been doing?"

"He's been going to the beach; going to restaurants; walking on The Boardwalk."

"Why were you watching the IKOR meeting?"

"We weren't. I was posted in the mezzanine so's I could watch the lobby and watch the elevators without being seen. I saw you go into and out of the IKOR meeting. But I didn't know what IKOR was until just now, when you told me about them. How were we supposed to know that they are Commies? It's a very Jewish thing, right?"

"Yeah," said Levitan. "But they were never a secret. They were out in the open, raising money, handing out pamphlets. These people are used to being watched – they've probably been on top of Hoover's list of subversive organizations since the Twenties. A guy like Savin, that's their leader, has been looking over his shoulder for twenty years. I'd be amazed if he hasn't noticed that you're in the hotel.

And, if this Polish diplomat is really a trained espionage agent, he would have been watching his back on his way down the Garden State Parkway on a Sunday morning."

"We didn't have any choice," said Duplessis. "We did our best."

"I didn't mean it as a criticism," said Levitan. "I might well have done the same. I meant that they probably know you're here and that you're watching them. They probably think you're the FBI. But you have to tell me about your Russian Colonel. How did he check in?"

"He's registered here as Tomasz Biernacki, and he gave his correct New York City address."

"You realize that this is the FBI's jurisdiction. You're supposed to stay on Army bases."

Duplessis said, "Yeah, we know. But the UN is neutral territory; everybody has agents there. In fact, everybody there *is* an agent. We'll have to hand the Biernacki surveillance over to the FBI at some point. But right now we're waiting for one of our men to arrive from overseas to make a positive identification, someone who met Reshetnikov during the border talks. But tell me something," said Duplessis. "How is it that you had the balls to just walk into a meeting of Soviet agents?"

"I met some of these IKOR characters when I was in Spain. I walked in thinking that I might know someone. If not, I was hoping that they would accept me if I came across the right way."

"And did they?"

"Time will tell. Maybe."

"And you were in Spain with The Abraham Lincoln Brigade. Are you a Communist!"

"I used to be, sort of. More of a socialist if you want to get picky."

"And the Admiral knows about this?" Duplessis challenged.

"Absolutely. And so does J. Edgar Hoover."

"Well I'll be damned."

"Yes," said Levitan. "Do me a favor, give me the quick and dirty briefing on the Polish diplomat. Are you watching him right now?"

"He's in his room."

"And where are your men?" Levitan asked.

"One in the lobby and one outside watching the alley behind the hotel."

"Not enough."

"I know. It's all I've got right now. I've called for more men. They'll be here tonight."

"Give me his description and room number."

"He's staying in *Room 681*. Medium height, about five nine. Hair and eyes brown. Around forty years old. He dresses well. Average build."

"What's he drive?"

"A *'39 Ford*. Parked at a lot on Atlantic Avenue."

"The average guy."

"Down to his shoelaces," said Duplessis.

"I think you need to question him."

"We're holding off, waiting for authorization. He's a diplomat and in a civilian jurisdiction."

"You're right, of course," said Levitan, looking at his wristwatch. "It's five of four. I have to report to Brixton now. Why don't you stick around while I talk to him; let's see if we can figure out if there's a way to do this without shooting each other in the face."

14

Through the duty sergeant at the police station, Levitan had arranged to meet his cohort at six o'clock at *Palermo's* hoagie shop where they were unlikely to be seen by anyone from *The Breakers*. He was in the hotel lobby near the street exit, about to leave and hail a taxi. The rain was coming down hard.

The woman who'd been at the front table in the IKOR meeting was seated in one of the easy chairs, reading a paperback book. She waved at him. He watched her approach. She'd changed out of the slacks she'd been wearing that afternoon into a burgundy dress, a white cashmere sweater, and low-heeled, white shoes.

"Remember me?" she said. Her perfume smelled faintly of flowers.

"Of course," he said. "You were in the IKOR meeting."

"I'm the stenographer. My name's Judith Horowitz. I'd like to talk to you."

"Well, I'm flattered," he said.

"Don't be… Commodore," she accused. Her eyes were dark brown, her lashes long and thick.

"Oh my, you know who I am."

"It's how you're registered."

"It's not a secret. But so what?"

"Why didn't you mention it when you crashed the IKOR meeting this afternoon?"

"I didn't think I had to mention it."

"You work for the Federal Government! Of course you should have said something."

"Miss Horowitz, I was just curious, that's all. I understand how you must feel about the Government. But I'm just a contract employee, a civilian. I'm here on vacation. I work for the US Coast Guard Auxiliary, with the emphasis on 'Auxiliary.'

She didn't appear to buy it. Her eyes narrowed as she said, "How is it that somebody who joined up to fight in Spain has such a fancy government job? Or was that all just made up?"

He said. "I work for a man who's smart enough not to give a damn. He's an Admiral and he sees nothing wrong with my politics. In fact, since a lot of the work I do is with the Longshoreman's Union, he considers my background an asset. I don't have to hide the fact that I went to Spain from anyone. I'm proud of it."

"Well, what kind of work are you doing? Union busting?"

He shook his head. "The opposite. As far as the Coast Guard is concerned, the more organized the dockworkers are, the better. The Union, The International Longshoremen's Association, gives us a way to spread the word when we need to and somebody to talk to when there are problems. There would be chaos on the docks without them."

"You didn't answer my question," she challenged. "What kind of work do you do?"

"Do you know anything about shipping?"

"Try me."

"Well, I'm like an auditor. You know – finances. I look at documents like bills of lading and invoices - that sort of thing." That was true; he routinely examined shipping documents during investigations. "It's just a glorified clerical job with a fancy title. A lot of civilians get to be Commodores. It's like being a vice president at a bank; it helps with the chain of command."

"And you just happened to see our name on the bulletin board?"

"Oh… You think I'm spying on you! Well, I had no idea that you people were here. I did not come to Atlantic City looking for you. And yes, I was surprised to see an IKOR meeting on the bulletin board. So don't you flatter *your*self. The government did not send me to spy on you." True enough.

"And you just wanted to say hello?"

"Damned right. Were you in Spain?" Levitan asked.

"Me? No. I'm not that adventurous."

"Well, then, you don't know what we went through."

"I suppose not. So you're a Comrade. I should call you *Comrade* Levitan instead of *Commodore* Levitan?"

He said, "It was a nasty, vicious war. You make friends in circumstances that you cannot forget. You learn who to trust. I have comrades - guys I'm proud to know."

She was fine-boned, with delicate features. She shrugged her narrow shoulders, "So. Okay then."

"Did you want to talk to me?

"Not me. Comrade Savin asked me to find out your room number so that he could talk to you. You told us you were staying here, remember?"

"Oh. Right. Okay, let's set something up."

"Not so fast. I haven't had a chance to tell him about you. I don't think he'll want anything to do with you."

"Just because I have a Government job?"

"The Government does everything it can to make their lives miserable. They have lots of reasons not to trust them."

"Believe me, I am well aware," said Levitan. "But I would be disappointed. I repeat, Miss Horowitz, I was not sent to spy on IKOR. I just wanted to touch base. I am truly interested in what's going on with you people these days, now that the war is over, now that we know that the Jew-haters want to kill us all."

They stared at each other. He took a breath and continued, "I mean, how does IKOR fit in anymore? What about the Zionists? What about the Soviet Union's autonomous Jewish territory? Seriously, can we talk?"

"We'll see what Comrade Savin has to say. I'll see whether he wants to."

"Listen, I don't need to talk to Comrade Savin. How would you like to have a drink with me later on? I could tell you whatever you want to know about being a Commodore. You'll see. I'm harmless."

She regarded him appraisingly, as if he'd asked her to dance. "Are you married?" she asked.

"Yes. What about you?"

She said, "I have a boyfriend."

"Fine. We know where we stand," he said. "But I'm free as a bird tonight and I intend to hear some good jazz at a club uptown. Why don't you join me?"

Before she'd risen from the easy chair, he'd admired her legs. Bare legs are permissible in the summertime since the war ended. Women who'd grown accustomed to the comfort of unsheathed legs during the war, when nylons were in short supply, chose not to wear them in the warm months, a fashion that was considered racy before the war. Her breasts filled the fabric of her dress.

"I'm on my way out to meet some friends for dinner across town," he said. "But I can be back in an hour or so. Are you free?"

"I can be. I love jazz."

"That'll be great. I'll meet you here." He checked his watch. "Is eight o'clock alright with you?"

"Fine," she said.

§

A cab pulled up to deposit passengers just as he exited through the revolving door. Despite the heavy rain, it only took five minutes to ride across town to *Palermo's* hoagie shop, where Fulton, Turner, and Staup were waiting for him in a booth.

"Buster," Levitan said. "I hear you had a conversation with Army Intelligence this afternoon. And you sicced them on me."

"What else was I supposed to do?"

"You did the right thing. But now our life might get more complicated."

"Army Intelligence!" said Cal Turner. "Are they investigating our murder? Sons of bitches!"

"No. They've got their own thing going. I'm sorry, but I can't talk about it."

"Of course not," said Cal Turner, wiping crumbs from his moustache. "Complicated how?"

"I talked to them. They're going to stay out of our way. Don't worry about it. As of now, there's no connection between Weber's murder and some guy they're watching. We might be okay. And we have to make a plan for tomorrow."

Their sandwiches arrived and the always-hungry cops dug in.

Levitan said, "We still don't know why Weber picked *The Breakers*. We don't know what he was doing before he showed up there for a two o'clock poker game. We need to fill in that period of time on the day he was killed."

"So how do you propose we find that out?" said Turner, wiping crumbs from his mustache with a paper napkin.

"First, tell me about John Smith."

"He's got an alibi," said Turner. "He was at a farm auction Saturday afternoon and evening."

"He's a farmer?"

"Yep. Chickens and eggs."

"And he admits playing cards with Bob Weber Friday night?"

"He does. He remembers the skinny little guy who won all his money. Not that he cares - he's rich all of a sudden. The Army bought his farm to expand the airport in Pomona."

"So... nothing."

"Right. Except that I finally met a real John Smith," said Turner.

Staup said, "What's next?"

"We just have to keep turning over rocks until we get hit by the smell. You've talked to people once? Talk to them again. Go down to another level. And start talking to the staff here at *The Breakers*, anybody who was working on Saturday."

They nodded.

"Should we split up?" Turner asked. "The three of us?"

"Sure, that makes sense. Decide how you'll divvy it up and keep in touch with each other. While you're doing that, I'll be at the FBI's office in Philadelphia in the morning. I'm going to look at what they took out of Weber's hotel room. Then I'll go to Weber's house in Pennington for the funeral in the afternoon. Some of the people there will be from his job. The last thing Weber did before he died was call the place where he worked – on a Saturday afternoon. If we know why he made the call, we might know why he was killed. I'm going to talk to the guy he called, this Von Neumann. Then I'll be back here tomorrow evening. Shall we get together for hoagies tomorrow? We'll fill each other in."

"I the FBI actually willing to let you look at the effects? Are they expecting you?" asked Turner.

"Yep. Okay... Communication. Let's call in to the desk sergeant as often as we can, at least once every couple of hours. Okay? We'll use the duty desk as our link. Got it?"

"Sounds like a plan," said Cal Turner. "You guys want to split another one?"

"We have to be quick," said Levitan. "I've got a date."

"You dog," said Cal Turner. "Why don't I just go ahead and order another one and have Tony cut it four ways. Who's the lady? And ain't you married?"

"That I am. This woman was in that meeting I crashed in the hotel this morning. I'm real curious about these people for personal reasons."

The sandwich arrived, and Levitan forked the onions out of his share.

Lou Staup declared,. "You *do* have a date! You dog!"

"You are one hell of a detective," said Levitan.

§

Judith Horowitz emerged from the elevator in *The Breakers'* lobby ten minutes late. She'd exchanged her white sweater for a thicker black one and her white shoes for a pair of black ones that revealed the tops of her toes. She'd put stockings on, a different perfume, and her lips had been freshly painted. She had small, delicate ears that invited breath and whispers.

"So, where is this jazz place?" she asked.

"Uptown in the Inlet. We'll take the trolley."

The rain had stopped. They left by a side entrance, took to the sidewalk, and headed inland toward the trolley line on Atlantic Avenue two blocks away. They talked as they walked. She told him that she was originally from Connecticut, and that the IKOR was paying her by the hour to take minutes.

"So, you're the real deal," he said. "A genuine, card-carrying-Communist. They're probably going to outlaw The Party, aren't they? Pretty soon, groups like the IKOR will be against the law. Isn't that what they're saying in Washington?"

She said. "Some free country this is."

"Yeah. I'm with you on that. They can't make political parties illegal; it's un-American. But still, The Party hasn't been endearing itself to people, has it? Why won't Stalin withdraw his troops from Central Europe?"

"It's what happens after wars. Why doesn't Truman leave first? Maybe the people in Central Europe are happy to have the Red Army protecting them. Maybe they've welcomed Communism."

"I doubt that. From what I read in the papers, the Russians are running police states."

"The IKOR men say that's propaganda. They say that there has to be centralized control in order to implement reforms."

"Stalin-style control. He's as bad as Hitler."

"Are you sure you were in Spain? You sound like a Republican. Tell me about yourself. Where are *you* from?"

They saw a trolley at the corner as they approached Atlantic Avenue. They hurried, lengthening their strides, but it departed without them. They stood to wait for another one. It was a calm, pleasant evening after the storm passed.

"I'm from Philadelphia," he said. "I never thought about joining IKOR, not even during the Spanish Civil War. But, really, I could no sooner be a farmer on a collective than a pig could fly. I'm a city guy. I love baseball and big cars, an American through and through."

"I've heard a lot of that lately," she said. "It's the anthem of the bourgeoisie."

"Then I guess I'm bourgeois. But it's the socialists who are going to Palestine, isn't it? A lot of the *kibbutzim* are collectives. Socialism is catching on there. Why even bother with the Soviet Union?"

She said nothing, walked to the curb and looked downbeach for the next trolley car.

Levitan had grown cautiously optimistic about the fate of the Jews for the first time in his life. At last the fantasy of a Jewish state could become a reality. Britain was weak. The English had inserted a clause into their mandate - their proclamation of ownership - after they took control of the Turkish Empire following the First World War. The clause, called *The Balfour Declaration*, specifically declared the sliver of coast on the far Eastern shore of the Mediterranean as a place where Jews could go, a place where they had a right to belong. Now, after the Second World War, the American Government seemed sympathetic to a

Jewish insurgency in the Palestinian Mandate. The newly established United Nations would be charged with recognizing postwar boundaries and a State of Israel had been proposed. England, short of food, would probably be happy to withdraw from the mess in the Near East to give their attention to feeding their population and to building a post-war economy with a depleted, rebellious empire. With England distracted, there might be a land the Jews could call their own. Imagine!

She turned away from the curb and rejoined him.

"So what about IKOR? What's their position on Israel now?" he asked.

She said, "I've been taking it all down - these people have a lot to say. According to them, Zionism glorifies an ancient tribe and a religion. Those kinds of definitions are obsolete, they say. The Soviet Union eliminates the old labels, welcoming all peoples as one. There's no need to dispossess anyone; no need to fight the Arabs and the English. There are enormous open spaces in the Soviet Union. They believed that IKOR was the better idea."

"And what do you think?"

"I don't agree. I don't think it makes sense anymore. I'm going to Israel."

"Why not stay here?" Levitan asked.

"You *are* a Republican,"

"Not usually."

Downbeach, from the south, a single disk of light grew as a trolley car rumbled toward them. They went through the accordion doors and sat side by side, hip to hip, shoulder to shoulder, in the light of ceiling bulbs, with the darkness outside.

The photographs of withered corpses piled like cordwood, and of skeletal survivors, were like dirt on a coffin in a shared Jewish nightmare. Wherever Jews were together in 1946, the question of what it all meant was on their minds. Levitan had heard the Zionist argument often; if there are to be Jews, so the argument went, then there had to be an Israel, a place, a land. Once a State of Israel was established, Jews would have a safe homeland, no longer wanderers, no longer Christendom's victim.

But why was it necessary for there to be Jews? He had often wondered, if the anti-Semites rose in America as they had in Germany, whether he would deny his Jewish ancestry. He had blue eyes under dark eyebrows, thick, unruly hair, a square jaw, a straight nose. He believed he could change his name to Jones and no one would know that his ancestors included rabbis. America was a huge country populated by folks who'd moved on, forgetting their troubled ethnic histories.

But the Germans had investigated ancestries and found tens of thousands of people whose Jewish parents or grandparents had tried to assimilate into the German mainstream. The Gestapo had used their ancestry as an excuse to dispossess them anyway. Most of those so labeled were among the millions of Jews killed in the Nazi camps.

"So, what band plays at this jazz place?" she asked. "Anybody I've ever heard of?"

"We'll find out when we get there. It's not a big enough place for a whole band. Usually it's smaller groups, friends in town for the big shows, playing together. At least that's how it was during the war."

"Do you come to Atlantic City a lot?"

"I lived here for five years, up until two years ago. I know my way around," he said.

The Whichway was a restaurant supper club in the Inlet neighborhood that featured crab cakes and live music. It was one of the clubs where Helen used to play. The air was thick with cigarette smoke. They were shown to a tiny table near a wall. He ordered a ginger ale, she a Sidecar.

"You're a teetotaler?" she said. "You don't seem the type."

"It's just that it's hard for me to stop once I start drinking. It's better if I don't get started."

"Good for you," she said.

When their drinks arrived, he said, "It must be very hard being you these days."

"What do you mean?"

"You are a Party member, aren't you?"

"I used to be - before the war," she said.

"Do you still keep the faith?"

"I've lost it now. Never really had it. But it wasn't faith, anyway. It was common sense."

"They're going to ban The Party, I'd bet on it. They'll be illegal."

"Just because they put Communists in jail doesn't mean that they're wrong."

"Why is it so important for them to be right? Why don't they just give it up?"

"Well, that's the question, isn't it?"

"Is that why the IKOR is having this meeting? Are they deciding whether the time has come to throw in the towel?"

"Actually, they've already decided. This is their last official meeting. They're packing it in. There are less than a dozen signed-up left anyhow. They won't be around much longer."

"I see. What will you do when the IKOR is no more?"

"I have a full-time job. This is just temporary. It won't make any difference to me. After I have enough saved up for the fare, I'm going to Palestine... Israel. I've already made up my mind. Who cares what happens to IKOR?"

"I thought you said IKOR was the best idea – an autonomous Jewish collective within the Soviet Union."

"It wasn't a bad idea, but it's a dead one now. Survival is more important than political idealism. That's obvious, isn't it? After Hitler? After Stalin's purges? A State of Israel in the Jewish homeland makes much more sense. How about you? Would you go to live in a Land of Israel?"

"I doubt it," he said. "I love being an American. Being Jewish is not very important to me. I can't see myself wearing sandals and doing folk dances."

"How about being alive? It's not safe to be a Jew anywhere."

"I think it's safe here in America… for now. What will you do in Palestine? Will you join a *kibbutz*?"

"I will. And I'll carry a rifle, too," she said.

"How about your boyfriend? Is he going with you? Does he want to carry a rifle too?"

"He's thinking about it."

"Tell me about him," he said.

"He's still in the Army. He's a Master Sergeant."

"Where's he based?"

"Listen, I don't want to talk about him. Either he goes to Israel with me or he doesn't. It'll be up to him. What about you? Tell me about your wife."

"This used to be one of the places where she played in the summertime. She's a pianist. During the school year, she taught music at a Philadelphia high school. She played every club in Atlantic City in the summertimes during the war. She's working for a record studio in New York now."

"Is that where you live? New York?"

"No. Not at the moment. My work is around Philadelphia, the waterfront between Trenton and Wilmington."

"So you're not living with your wife?"

"That's the way it is."

"How do you feel about that?"

"It is the way it is."

"But how do you *feel* about it?"

"I'm still trying to work it out," he said. "Do you live with your boyfriend?"

It was too warm in the room for her sweater. She hung it over the back of her chair. Her dress was short-sleeved, revealing smooth ivory arms. "No," she said, "Not unless he's on leave."

"He couldn't get leave this week?"

"Yeah, he got leave. I told you... I don't want to talk about him."

"What's his name?"

"George... What's your wife's name?"

"Helen. Helen Rubin Lowenthal Levitan," he said, "Quite a mouthful. She was married before, to someone who was killed in Spain, a friend of mine named Ben Lowenthal."

"So she's a nice Jewish girl."

"Yes, she is. But she's not political. She's an artist. She lives for her music. She votes and that's about it."

Finishing her Sidecar, Judith said, "And here we are."

The waiter delivered another round. The musicians returned for another set. He liked the small ensembles. He liked to hear how the new jazz players were shrinking the harmonies of the big swing bands, toying with the syncopation. He liked to listen, to hear if they got it right, but his mind was on the woman at his small table.

"What do you think of the music?" he asked, leaning toward her.

She met his eyes, leaned toward him, and said, "I like it. Thanks for bringing me."

"My pleasure," he said.

The mixed-race band made fine music, leaving Levitan and Judith in a good mood. She was happy, a little drunk. He wanted to touch her.

They talked about the music; about how the drummer stroked his brushes over the skins to soften the rhythm, how he used his pedal to strike the beat, how the saxophone player sang through his reed; all things that Helen had taught him to hear.

Judith Horowitz seemed interested in what he had to say, as if he knew what he was talking about, which he did not. It was the doing that mattered to him, not the understanding. A person either does something or he does not, he either makes something or he does not - all the rest is noise. Helen is the one who made the music; he was merely the one who heard it.

They decided to walk back to *The Breakers* on The Boardwalk.

He said, "It's about two miles."

She said, "It's a nice night for a walk."

Up at the Inlet, where a gentler tide swept under the planks, the boardwalk was a promenade where you could lean on a railing and watch little waves break on the hard sand of the beach below. There was no honky-tonk, just people walking along and enjoying the blessings of peace.

"You'll be walking into a war," he said. "If you go to Palestine."

"I want to fight," she said. "I'm so... *angry* at what they are doing to Jews. If they have to deal with us as people with a land and an army, it'll be a different story. But we'll have to fight for it."

"That's not so important as peace is it? You'll be starting a war."

"You still do not get it - the war has not ever stopped. It's still the same war it's always been. The War Against The Jews. Always. Anywhere. The Jews loved Germany, didn't they? Just like you love America. But the Germans made war on us, they chased us down, took everything we had, and murdered us."

The moon glimmered silver on the surface of the sea.

He stopped and leaned on the rail. "It's beautiful, isn't it?"

She came to his side and put her elbows on the rail.

"This is peace, Judith. I like it."

She said, "But I don't feel safe here. This is a racist country and you know it. They hate Jews here. And the value system is so... so *wrong*. We can make a better country, one that's safe for us."

Gentle waves broke, the sea rushed, slackened, foamed, and disappeared into the sand.

He said, "You know, you can live an ordinary life if you want to. You can put all the politics behind you."

"Then I'd be denying everything I've always believed in. Unlike you, I think it's important to be right," she said, hugging her arms. "It's starting to get chilly can we walk?"

Had the woman been Helen, he would have put his arm around her to keep her warm and safe. This one is Judith. He wondered about her boyfriend. Was she angry with him?

"Did George come down the shore with you?" he asked.

"He's been around."

"But he left you here on your own."

"He had plans to meet an Army buddy for a drink. Enough already. I don't want to talk about George."

"Is he going with you to Palestine?"

"We've talked about it. He has work to finish here. Listen… I promise I won't ask you about Helen if you shut up about George. Alright?"

They walked well together, easily matching stride. When they were within sight of the hotel, he realized that her shoulder was touching his. He resisted the urge to pull her close.

When they reached the hotel, they stood side by side in the lobby waiting for the elevator. When the doors opened, she went inside and turned to face him.

He said, "Good night. I'll catch the next one."

As the doors closed, she said, "Thanks for the music."

WEDNESDAY

15

Levitan left Atlantic City at six-thirty in the morning to beat the traffic to Philadelphia sixty miles away, with a halfway stop at Hammonton for gas and a pee. He crossed into Philadelphia from Camden over the Delaware River suspension bridge, drove through rush hour traffic, and parked in a lot at Tenth and Sansom Streets.

The FBI offices were on the Seventh Floor of a block-square WPA building that had been finished just before the Second World War. The Federal Reserve Bank was located there as well as the Federal Circuit Court of Appeals and a Post Office. Granite *bas reliefs* of civic virtues, portrayed as muscular people wearing Greek robes, lined the face of the building above the heads of hurrying pedestrians. Armed sentries had guarded the elevator lobby during the war. They were gone now; he didn't show his credentials until he got to receptionist on the Seventh Floor. Brixton was waiting for him in his office with a big window overlooking the rooftops of old Philadelphia.

"The *Phillies* finally won one against the *Dodgers* yesterday," said Brixton.

"I didn't have time to read the paper. Who pitched?"

"Robin Roberts, went nine, only gave up two runs. Hamner hit a triple with the bases loaded in the seventh. A good game."

Levitan nodded, pleased that the *Phillies* had snapped a four-game losing streak. "Where are the effects from Weber's hotel room?" he asked,

"They're here. But we should talk first. This business with the Polish diplomat is creating some complications."

"Why am I not surprised?" said Levitan.

"So," said Brixton, "Yesterday, after you called, I had to tell the AD about another federal presence on our case. He sent word up to Hoover that a foreign diplomat was being surveilled by the Army at a hotel where a Communist organization was having a meeting, where, it just so happens, an atomic scientist had been playing cards just before he got himself strangled a half-mile away. Hoover wants us, the FBI, to take over the surveillance. And he wants permission from State to interview this Pole, or Russian, or whatever he is. The Army, a three-star general, is pissed. It's a mess."

Levitan laughed. SNAFU for sure, 'situation normal, all fucked up'. "Well that's good news," he said sarcastically.

Brixton said, "It's being sorted out, but it's pretty bad."

In the government, conflict between agencies are problems that usually stop projects cold. Or, worse, the issue gets resolved by the White House.

"You can't slow down," says Levitan.

"Of course we can't. I'll let the brass fight it out. What's holding things up is that we now have to get permission from the State Department to question the diplomat."

"I hope the diplomat, or the spy, doesn't know that his cover has been blown. I was not real impressed with the Army guys keeping an eye on him. He drove down to Atlantic City on the Parkway. If he's really a spy, he probably spotted them trailing him."

Brixton said, "It doesn't make much difference. As soon as I hear from Washington that we have been authorized, we're going to question him. He'll know then."

"Yeah, that'll do it. Listen, John, I learned a lot about the IKOR last night. I got lucky and had a chance to talk to somebody's who's been in the meetings. I didn't hear anything that connected that bunch to Weber."

Brixton settled back in his chair, frowning. "What makes you so sure they're not involved?"

"I'm not sure, but I doubt it," said Levitan. He explained how he'd ingratiated himself with the group, and then taken advantage of an opportunity to go on a date with Judith Horowitz. "They're disbanding. That's why they're in Atlantic City, to hold their final meeting. As of next week, IKOR will be history."

Brixton said, "Well, I've sent a pair of agents to *The Breakers* to collect the list of attendees." Taking down the names of people attending meetings is what the FBI did best.

Levitan said, "You have to do what you have to do. But they're finished. They're declaring themselves officially dead."

Brixton said, "It's too good a chance to pass up. These people could lead us to a Russian spy ring. Whether they're closing up shop or not, we need to know who they are."

"I understand. But I get the feeling that these people have been forgotten. Did you see any connection between the IKOR and Bob Weber in his file?"

"No. There have been a couple of real pinkos who worked at IAS and Weber probably knew them, but no mention of IKOR."

Levitan said, "Lots of academic types are Marxist."

"Too true," said Brixton.

"After I look at the effects, I'm driving over to Pennington for Weber's *shiva*. Von Neumann is going to be there. I want to ask him if he knows why Weber called him on Saturday."

Brixton leaned back alarmed. "Not Von Neumann. Please, say it ain't so."

"Do you know him?"

"Not personally. I've been in the same room with him once or twice. John Von Neumann is a genius.

He's not in just one Top Secret program, he's in *all* of them. He's The Man."

"He's on the atomic bomb project?"

"At the very top. And he has meetings with men who're working on every aspect of it. Von Neumann is a mathematician, a scientist, and an engineer. He solves practical problems that Einstein doesn't even try to tackle. He won't talk to you unless he knows that you have clearance, I can tell you that."

"I *do* have Top Secret clearance – thanks to you."

"But Von Neumann doesn't know you. I should come with you."

"You'd cramp my style, John. Could you give me a letter to show him? Make it look official, with FBI stamps and imprints all over it, signed with your full title. The fact that you've met him might convince him. I need to talk to this guy."

"I'll have it typed up for you while we're examining the effects," said Brixton, rising from his chair.

"One other thing, John. Judith Horowitz's boyfriend. I'm curious about him. She absolutely did not want to talk about him. He's an active duty Master Sergeant named George. I'd like to know more about him."

"There are probably a hundred Master Sergeants named George."

"I understand, John. She says he's been in Atlantic City on leave, but that's all I know."

Brixton said, "If I ask the Army for a list of Master Sergeants named George, we'd get it after Christmas. No way."

Levitan said, "I'll have Turner and Staup examine *The Breakers'* register for anyone staying there over the weekend named George."

They went to a conference room to inspect boxes containing what was taken from Robert Weber's hotel room by the FBI. Most of it was clothing, including a still-damp bathing suit. Bob Weber's toiletry kit contained nothing out of the ordinary. Levitan noticed the absence of paper. There was nothing to read and nothing written down.

"This guy was a professor, John. Where are his books? Where are his letters and notes and such?"

"There were a few other items," said Brixton.

"Were?"

"The Army scientists are analyzing them."

"For godssake, John!" said Levitan.

"It wasn't my call. We are outgunned. National security trumps murder every day of the week. Get over it."

"But, John, I can't tell what's *not* here. Where's his wallet? Where's his pocket phone directory? Was there a notebook? Where's his briefcase? This is bad, John."

"There was no wallet or phone list or briefcase, I can tell you that. But there were a couple of academic journals on the floor next to the bed. That's all. The Army has them."

Levitan said, "Why didn't you tell me he'd been to the beach?"

"You mean the bathing suit? It didn't seem important. How do you know he went to the beach and not to the pool at *The Traymore*."

"Why would anyone go to the pool when they have the whole ocean? And look here, grains of sand in this crease. We've been trying to piece together his last day and the morning was a big gap for us. Now, it looks like he'd been on the beach. It would have been good to know."

"Do you have any other complaints? Listen to me, Dave. Stop with this *prima donna* bullshit. It is the way it is."

"SNAFU," said Levitan.

"Exactly. This is normal. So stop bitching about what we can't control and get on with the investigation. Now that you know Weber was on the beach, does it change anything?"

"I don't know. The lifeguards in Atlantic City are actually policemen, so I'll find out if anyone saw anything. But it's unlikely. The beaches were crowded on Saturday."

"Anything else?" asked Brixton.

"Wish me luck at the funeral."

"Just try to stay out of trouble in Pennington. And call me tomorrow morning. Nine o'clock."

Using Brixton's phone, he called the duty desk at The Atlantic City police station and left instructions for the cops to look for someone named George in guest registers at *The Traymore* and *The Breakers*.

16

Pennington is thirty miles to the north and east of Philadelphia, five miles east of the Delaware River border between Pennsylvania and New Jersey where General Washington crossed to attack King George's Hessian mercenaries. It took Levitan almost two hours on two-lane roads to travel there from downtown Philadelphia, the traffic so slow that he missed the burial ceremony. The manager in the cemetery office gave him the address of Weber's house, where, according to the widow, the family would be suiting s*hiva*. It was on Laning Avenue, a cream-colored corner house with blue trim, lots of lawn, shade trees, and a deep porch. The cars of mourners and well-wishers were parked all around the intersection. Before he went inside, he spent fifteen minutes writing all of the license numbers in his notebook, SOP.

The house was crowded. Miriam Weber sat between her dead husband's grieving parents, all three shoeless as was the custom. It was an odd tradition, not wearing shoes when a loved one died. He didn't get the significance. Of course, he knew very little about being Jewish.

Levitan waited until an elderly women who'd been commiserating walked away before he approached them. The elder Webers looked careworn and tired. The father was a tall, heavyset man, surprising given the delicacy of his son's frame. Robert had taken after his mother, a tiny woman, with bloodshot eyes in a pale face.

"Is this normal, Mister Levitan?" the widow asked. "Do the police always come to a murder victim's funeral?"

"It can be a good idea."

"Well, join the crowd. I've never met a lot of these people - Government people they tell me."

"I'm sorry," said Levitan.

"It's just so… so unpleasant."

"Yes, I'm sure it is. My apologies."

"Not that I'm not used to it. Bobby and I have had to deal with people like you ever since the beginning of the war. You should know that he was always very careful; he never talked shop."

"But he was involved with the atomic bomb. You knew that."

"I didn't *know* it. Not until Hiroshima. As I told you the other day, Bobby became very upset after the bombs were dropped on Japan. But all he ever said to me was that it was something he'd been involved with. Even now, I have no idea what he… was… actually doing."

"Nor do I. I doubt that I would understand it if I did."

"The main thing is, do you have any idea who killed Bobby? Have you found out anything?"

"Yes. We know where he spent Saturday before it happened. We think he went to the beach for a swim in the morning. In the afternoon, he went to another hotel, called *The Breakers,* to play cards. Apparently, nothing untoward occurred during the game itself. The Atlantic City Police are trying to find out whether anyone saw anything involving your husband after he left the game."

"Like what?"

"That's our question. We're doing our best to find out."

"That's progress, I guess. Thank you for telling me."

"You have the right to know. I do have one question for you, though. Was Mister Weber ever involved with the IKOR?"

She thought for a moment. "The Communists? Is that who you mean?"

"Yes."

"Absolutely not. The opposite; he thought they were loonies."

"You discussed the IKOR with him?"

"I think we did, way back, years ago. Before the war."

"Can you remember how the subject came up?"

The elder Webers were paying close attention to someone asking political questions about their dead son. The father said, "Bobby's uncle used to be involved and we all talked about it. Bobby thought his uncle was nuts. Why are you asking?"

"Well, there was an IKOR meeting at the hotel where he was playing cards. It's just something we're looking into."

"I can't imagine that it had anything to do with him."

The father said, "Robert didn't like them IKORs. This I know."

"Mister Weber," said Levitan, "I am truly sorry for your loss. We are doing everything we can to catch the man who killed your son. Do you recall your conversations with Robert about IKOR?"

"We talked. Everybody talked. My brother, Gershon, he is a Communist. We had arguments."

"Is your brother here today?"

"No. Gershon is far away by California now, Los Angeles."

"Thank you, sir," he said, and returned his attention to the widow. "Can I ask you to point Professor Von Neumann out to me?"

"He's over there," she said, indicating a short, soft-faced, balding man with dark hair, about forty years of age, nattily dressed, wearing a beautifully tailored pin-stripe black suit. He was engaged in a conversation with two men.

Levitan, aware that he was holding up a line, thanked the Webers and approached the genius.

"Excuse me, gentlemen. Professor Von Neumann? May I have word? Professor Gordon was supposed to inform you that I'd be here."

Von Neumann met his eyes. "You're Levitan?"

"Yes sir. Can we talk outside?"

They went to the porch, saw it crowded with people, continued out to the lawn and stood under an old maple tree.

"This is a genuine tragedy," Von Neumann said.

"Yes."

"You're trying to catch the son of a bitch?"

"I am."

"How can I help you?"

"Sir," said Levitan. "Are you aware that Professor Weber placed a phone call to your office from his hotel room late on Saturday afternoon?"

"No, I am not. I was in Chicago."

"Do you have any idea why he might have placed the call? On a Saturday? On Labor Day Weekend? I mean, was there some kind of emergency situation having to do with the work he was doing?"

"I won't talk about his work. It's a secret project."

"I have Top Secret clearance."

"I don't care. I won't talk to you without permission. Bark up another tree."

"Good for you." Levitan said. He showed Von Neumann his Commodore's ID card and the crisp new letter signed by Brixton.

Von Neumann flicked his eyes to the card, studied the letter, and handed it back. "That's satisfactory. But, the fact remains, Commodore, that I can't imagine any sort of emergency regarding Robert's project. He has been working on the computing machine at Penn."

"Do you know Special Agent Brixton of the FBI? The man who signed the letter I showed you?"

"Yes, I've met him. He's a counterintelligence agent, right?"

"Yes. Agent Brixton knows I planned to talk to you. He told me that the machine uses radio tubes to do math. That Professor Weber was calculating equations about the atomic bomb."

Von Neumann regarded him more closely. "Okay, so you know a little about the project. So what?"

"You see, I'm wondering whether there was money changing hands. A big, secret government project with millions of dollars pouring into it? All that money has got to go somewhere."

"You're not suggesting that Bob Weber was embezzling from the project. That's ludicrous."

"How would I know? Tell me the kind of job he was doing. Did you know that he was a serious card player? A gambler?"

"Serious? Of course he was serious. Why would he do something without taking it seriously? He liked to bet at cards. So what?"

"Well, did he have a money problem? Was he involved with bids and contracts? Did he write budgets?"

"Nothing like that. He wasn't even fulltime on the project. He'd go down to Philadelphia once or twice a week to work with the programmers at Penn. They've built a prototype there."

"Programmers?"

"Programmers are the people who wire the machine and punch the tapes that tell the machine the variable values and what equations to use."

"With radio tubes?"

"Just think of the tubes as thousands of switches, on or off. They can represent numbers and be changed at the speed of light. If we use enough of them we can do complex calculations using very big numbers in minutes. It's been a good project. We think the machine at Penn is only the first. The potential for science of having machines like it, of having such computing tools, is unlimited. With this machine, we do calculations in seconds that would take people months, even years, to perform. Science will leap ahead a hundred times faster than it can today. A new day is dawning, Commodore."

"This is a wartime project?"

"We started during the war, yes. Two men at Penn got funded by The Army to build a computing machine that would speed up the development of artillery firing tables. When the war ended, they'd proven that they'd developed an electronic computing machine that works on any problem. Washington is very excited."

"So you're still funded by The War Department?"

"For the time being. The project managers, Eckert and Mauchly, have decided to apply for patents and want to start a company to build and sell the machines. They're looking for sponsors in the private sector."

"So, these machines, they're not considered secret weapons?"

"So far there's only one of them – the ENIAC at Penn. But some of us think of it as a general purpose tool with scientific and commercial potential."

"Could this have anything to do with Mister Weber's death? I mean, it sounds like this is a big money project. How much is the knowledge worth?"

"That's what Eckert and Mauchly are trying to find out. The patents are, in my opinion, worth fortunes – treasuries should be emptied. But I'm not aware that Bob had anything to do with the money side."

"Had you ever played cards with him?"

"Yes. He loved cards."

"What did you play?"

"Bridge, mostly. He was damned good."

"How about the other players? All friends? They were friendly games?"

"Absolutely."

"Did he have any enemies at work?"

"Enemies?" said Von Neumann. "We don't make enemies. We disagree with each other all the time. There are people who are hard to take, it comes with the territory. But enemies? No. Commodore, I cannot think of a single reason why anyone in our orbit would kill Bob Weber. I think you'll be better served looking elsewhere."

17

Levitan was in a reflective mood after his conversations with Von Neumann and the widow, scarcely noticing the pine trees and traffic during the ride to Atlantic City. When he walked through the double doors of the station house at four in the afternoon, Duty Sergeant Eric Ransom, a patrolman with whom Levitan had walked a beat, informed him that the Chief had a visitor in his office and that they were waiting for him.

"This guy is Army brass. *Big* brass – a General. Watch your ass, okay?" said Ransom.

"Always," said Levitan.

Upstairs, the General waiting for him in the Chief's office was a towering individual with broad shoulders and an enormous belly that strained the khaki of his shirt and the brass of his buckle. Wearing six gold stars, three on either side of a yard-wide expanse of shoulders, and a manner that presumed absolute control of the moment, the general dominated the room

Rafferty said, "This is General Groves. He just flew in at Pomona."

"How do you do, Sir."

"Commodore, I have no damned idea what the hell you are doing. I see no reason to keep you on the case."

"Sir, I'm here by order of Rear Admiral Thomas Spiegel, Sir. I'll be happy to step aside if he so orders."

"That's as it should be," said Groves. "I know Tom Spiegel. I'll see to it. But you'll brief me now. I will get to the bottom of this mess right now. I've been told that you're right in the middle of it. Are you making a mess of things, Commodore?"

"Just trying to make sense of it, Sir. I agree. It's a mess."

Groves turned his attention to Rafferty. "Chief, I'm asking you to leave the room. I want to discuss some sensitive matters. Thank you."

Rafferty was steamrollered by a man with enormous authority. The Chief didn't hesitate, "Yes sir," he said and walked out of his own office.

"Who brought you in?" demanded Groves.

"Special Agent Brixton, FBI, head of counterintelligence for the Mid-Atlantic region. He knows that I used to be an ACPD officer. He asked the Admiral for my help, as liaison with the local police."

"Alright. Tell me where we stand."

"There are several trails, General. First, it's possible, perhaps most likely, that whoever killed him did so after a robbery, possibly to protect the robber's identity. We've been looking for people who dealt with the victim on the day he was killed. We've been questioning anyone who might have seen anything involving Weber at the hotel. Now we are about to focus on the people who had been sitting with him at the card tables."

"You should have talked to them first thing."

"We collected the names of all the players during the initial round of interviews. The names are in a book kept by the card rooms. We're going to track as many of them down as we can. I personally interviewed the card dealer and the cashier; it was the first thing we did. Our next move will be to track down all the players from both card rooms. We've found one of them, a farmer from around here. He didn't do it."

"What the hell else have you been doing in the meantime?"

"Focusing on the victim's last hours. Besides robbery, we're looking at reasons why Bob Weber might have allowed someone into his hotel room, perhaps someone he knew. One possibility arises from the fact that he was playing cards directly across a hallway from a Communist meeting. So far, we don't know why he happened to be in that particular card room on that day. He was Jewish, and a great many Jews had an interest in that particular Communist group, called IKOR, at one time. Their idea was to get American Jews, all the Jews from all over the world in fact, to move to the Soviet Union where they would have a semi-autonomous government."

Groves said, "I know all about Jewish scientists and Communist groups, I've had to deal with the problem for years. But the FBI cleared Weber years ago. And I can tell you that he's been checked on regularly ever since. If Weber was a Commie, we would have known"

"Yes, Sir," said Levitan. "We haven't learned anything yet that contradicts your findings. I've just come from Mr. Weber's house where I spoke to his parents. They're sure he never had anything to do with IKOR. And I had a chat with his boss at the IAS, Professor Von Neumann."

"You have a lot of nerve."

"Yes, Sir. All part of the job. I found out that Weber called Von Neumann from his hotel room shortly before he was murdered. The Professor was out of town. He came back for Weber's funeral. He has no idea what the call might have been about."

"I understand that you had a talk with Army Intelligence yesterday. Is that right?"

"Yes. Your Captain Duplessis came to me and informed me that a diplomat - who could be a Soviet agent - is staying in the same hotel. That's another angle, to go along with the robbery and the Communist meeting. But the espionage angle, the Polish diplomat, well that's probably not anything I'd be allowed to get near.

Groves nodded. "Damn right," he said.

"We've also been exploring two other angles - money angles. One has to do with the large sums laundered through hotel card rooms by hired gamblers. We've looked at whether Weber might have been one of those. And then there's the fact that he was working on very expensive Government projects and we've been exploring whether he had opportunities to divert project funds. And, it seems, according to Professor Von Neumann, that knowledge of the computing machine project might be worth millions. So far, none of these avenues of inquiry have borne fruit, but it's still early days. We're still left with the probability that his murder was simply a robbery gone bad."

"How many men are you working with?"

"Captain Rafferty has put two of his best Detectives and one patrolman on the case to help me."

"You need more men."

"Yes sir. I will need help tracking down the other card players. But shouldn't I be asking the FBI, not the Army?"

Levitan assumed that a general like Groves knew where the jurisdictional lines were drawn. The Army was not permitted to engage in intelligence activities outside of military bases. It was a situation that any General would have despised, one he did not control. Groves had Military Intelligence agents in the investigation, forcing him into a tussle with the bureaucratic titan J. Edgar Hoover. Groves was a powerful man at the center of a morphing, postwar Government, one in which J. Edgar Hoover claimed broad jurisdiction. It occurred to Levitan that Hoover's saintly FBI could end up taking the blame for the loss of a top scientist, which would be a very positive result for The Army.

Levitan watched the big man. It seemed as if his briefing had impressed the General. Levitan had been careful not to make excuses or deny responsibility. He hoped that Groves was not the sort to abide unfinished projects. In this case, the project's objective was to find out who killed Robert Weber.

Whatever his reasons, Groves changed his mind. Perhaps he'd simply wanted to find the killer as soon as possible, and concluded that Levitan was competent to do the job.

The General proclaimed, "I'll talk to Spiegel. Get him on the phone him right now, Commodore."

Using Rafferty's desk phone, after going through two switchboard operators at Coast Guard headquarters in Philadelphia, Levitan was put through to the Admiral.

"Hey, Dave, What's up? What do you need?" said his boss.

Levitan said, "I'm in a meeting with a General Groves, Admiral. He'd like to talk to you." He handed the telephone to the khaki behemoth.

"Tom? Lieutenant General Leslie R. Groves, here. I've just been briefed by your Commodore." He listened for a few seconds.

"I'll have to trust you on that," said the General. "You should know that we have a Military Intelligence presence here on a case that may or may not be related to the murder." He paused to listen to the Admiral. "Yes. Levitan needs to keep his distance from our investigation. Hoover's men, a shitload of them, are all over the case too. We can't afford to let this get out of hand. Do you follow me?"

Groves paused, listening to the Admiral's response.

"I just want you to know that The Army's here and that *I*, *personally*, want Doctor Weber's murder investigation to be given the highest priority."

The Admiral, apparently, asked whether Groves had known the victim.

"Yes I did. His loss is significant, he was a valuable man. My concern is whether he transferred secrets to the enemy." Another brief pause. "The Russians! The Communists! Who else? The point is, Admiral, that the stakes are extremely high. Somehow or other, your man Levitan is positioned at point. I just want you to know that *I* am now involved and that *I* expect him to cooperate. Do you agree?" He paused to listen. "Good. Let's get this done."

Levitan felt as if he was standing on the tracks of a railroad junction listening to train whistles.

THURSDAY

18

Most murders are solved within a couple of days because who dunnit is obvious – someone jealous or angry or greedy is known to people who were acquainted with the victim. That person is soon identified as the prime suspect and the job becomes a matter of tracking him down and building a prosecution file after he's in custody. Police detectives rarely deal with mysterious deaths.

Nor do they give much of a damn. Coming up through the uniformed ranks, they learn to distance themselves from the miseries of people in trouble and, as they accumulate experience, they realize that a goodly percentage of murder victims have criminal backgrounds. For them, distinctions between victims and perpetrators tend to blur.

If, for some reason, as in the Weber case, they are compelled to care, standard procedure dictates interviewing people who saw nothing and know nothing, then talking to them again, asking different questions, trying to uncover another layer. This is usually fruitless and the majority of such cases are never solved.

In Atlantic City's corrupt police department, detectives like Cal Turner and Lou Staup had even less incentive to conduct rigorous investigations. Their perceived worth depended much more upon their ability to keep the politicians to whom they owed their jobs happy than to building cases. They stayed employed and earned promotions based on protecting and lubricating the convoluted status quo. Turner and Staup hadn't had much practice conducting murder investigations – they'd had other priorities.

So Levitan was in a pessimistic frame of mind when he showed up to meet with his team in the police station bullpen at eight-thirty on Thursday morning, at the start of his fourth day on the case. He had no good news for Brixton, whom he would call at nine o'clock. The most likely explanation for the murder continued to be a thief who knew about Weber's wad of cash, followed him to his room, and killed him for the untraceable folding money. The case would remain unsolved without a witness, but the chances of discovering anyone who saw something in a crowded resort hotel on a busy weekend were diminishing rapidly.

The night before, he'd ordered a room service supper of chopped sirloin steak and mashed potatoes, then spent gloomy hours sorting through his notes, pondering possible motives, and trying to convince himself that new lines of inquiry might be productive.

He'd tried calling Helen's apartment in New York, but, as expected, she hadn't been there to cheer him up.

He'd slept badly.

He'd learned something about leadership during his eight months as a combat soldier - negative commanders get negative results. He knows that Fulton, Turner and Staup would allow their cynicism to affect their performance if he did not seem positive. So, despite all the reasons for being in a foul mood, he walked into the Detectives' bullpen with a smile on his face and a spring in his step.

He summarized what he had learned from the effects taken from the scene by the FBI - that the victim had probably gone for a swim in the surf on the morning before he'd been killed. As for his visit to Pennington, Levitan reported that Weber's project was potentially worth millions, but that he hadn't been involved in the money side, and that the man whose number he'd called just before he died had no idea about the nature of the call.

He said, "I think Bob Weber was straight, a scientist with a wife and two kids and a good job. We haven't connected him to anything suspicious, so it's looking more and more like he was mugged in his room by a thief who got away. That's why we have to keep pounding away with these interviews."

"Did they show you everything?" asked Turner.

"Not hardly. The Army took some stuff and they're keeping it secret. All I saw were his clothes, including his bathing suit. That's how come I think he went to the beach for a swim."

"Him and a million other people," said Staup. "Where's that gonna get us?"

"Buster's going to talk to the lifeguards. Right Buster?" said Levitan.

Fulton took a moment, "Yeah. I guess."

"You don't have to check all the stands, just the ones near *The Traymore*. You never know."

"Whatever you say, Dave."

"I know, Buster. But it's the job. It won't take you long. Did you get my message - I left it yesterday - about checking for Georges in the hotel registers?"

All three nodded.

"Well? Did you find a George."

"Yeah," said Turner. "There is a George Koval who checked in at *The Breakers* around four-thirty on Saturday."

"And he's still checked in?"

"Yep."

"Well, that could be her George. Where's he from?"

"Someplace with a screwy name." Turner thumbed through his notebook and read aloud, "He gave his address as 'ORMR-C-699'."

"What the hell is ORMR?"

"Beats me," said Turner.

Levitan said, "I've got to put in a call to Brixton in few minutes. This ORMR place could be a Government address. Sounds like it, doesn't it? It could be an Army base. I'll ask Brixton to check it with the Post Office. Did you guys get anything useful from the hotel staff?"

"I think maybe I got something from *The Breakers'* hotel detective," Lou Staup said. "He was watching the stairs on Saturday, looking out for pickpockets, and he noticed somebody who matches Weber's description."

"Really?" said Levitan. "And?"

"Yeah. Maybe. He said he noticed this guy because he thought he was dipping. The hotel detective, Antrim's his name, he's standing on the mezzanine from where he can watch the stairway and the elevators in the lobby, and he notices this skinny guy with glasses, maybe Weber, zoom in on another guy who's going down the stairs. He thinks the skinny guy may be about to bump a mark. Then he realizes that he's not out to pick the other guy's pocket, but that he knows this other guy who's going down the stairs. But this other guy blows him off, like he doesn't recognize him, and keeps going downstairs. So these two guys attracted Antrim's attention."

"Now we're talking," said Levitan. "Great work, Lou. Does he remember what the other guy looked like?"

"Wait. I'm not done," said Staup. "So the second guy keeps going down the stairs to the lobby, but the skinny guy with the glasses goes back up to the mezzanine. Then Antrim sees the guy who was down in the lobby coming *back* up the stairs. But he doesn't go all the way to the top. He just stands there, a couple of steps down from the mezzanine, and he's looking at something. So Antrim looks at where the second guy is looking and sees that the skinny guy, let's say it's Weber, is with the people coming out of *The Vineland Room*."

"How so? How 'with'?"

"You know, just talking. But real quick, maybe only for a minute or so, maybe less. Then the *Vineland Room* people leave him standing there and they go for the elevators on the mezzanine. The skinny guy, let's say it's Weber, just stands there, watching them. When Antrim looks back at the stairway, he sees that the second guy is gone."

"So what does this second guy look like."

"Mid-thirties, fairly tall. With a buzz cut, dark hair, cut short like he's in The Army."

"He wasn't in a uniform?"

"No. But Antrim doesn't remember what he was wearing."

"Okay. That's really good work. Thanks, Lou."

"Judith Horowitz's boyfriend is in the Army, right? It could be her boyfriend," said Staup.

Levitan remembered his last look at Judith Horowitz, standing alone inside the elevator at *The Breakers*.

"So? Are we going to bring her in?" demanded Staup.

Levitan, after a thoughtful moment, said, "She's in the middle of these IKOR people. If she's involved, then they're involved. Rather than bring her right in, I think we should keep an eye on her and see who she's tight with. But let's not let her get out of our sight."

"So you think this guy on the stairs is George Koval," said Turner.

"Whoever he is," said Levitan, "He's the last person to be seen with Robert Weber before he was killed. He's our prime suspect. She's in her mid-thirties, too. So the age is right. What's good is that we have a description now. We need to talk to this Koval guy and see if he fits the description of the man on the stairs. Does Antrim remember what time it was when he saw them?"

"He says the people in *The Vineland Room* leave it for the clean-up crew at five o'clock in the afternoons."

"So the timing fits. It only takes fifteen minutes to walk up to *The Traymore* from here. Do you have a check-in time for this George Koval?"

Turner looks at his notebook, "Yeah, 4:40 PM."

Levitan thinks aloud, "So the timing fits. Weber left the card game at around five o'clock. He meets Koval on the stairway. But for some reason, Koval doesn't want to talk to him. They separate, but Koval goes back up the stairs and sees Weber talking to the IKOR people, and he scoots."

"So?" asked Buster, "Are we saying that Weber was involved with the IKOR too?"

"I don't know," said Levitan. "He was there to play poker; that's why he came to Atlantic City. His family says that he was definitely not a Communist. But, you make a good point, now that we know he was seen talking to them, we can't rule it out."

He dispatched Fulton to talk to the lifeguards who watched the shoreline in front of *The Traymore,* and asked Turner and Fulton to wait for him downstairs in the bullpen.

§

Alone in the police station second-floor conference room, he dialed the FBI number he knew by heart. Brixton had been waiting for his 9 o'clock call.

The G-Man said, "You've gotten Hoover all excited about this Communist connection. We haven't been watching IKOR since 1939. He's thrilled that they've reappeared."

Levitan said, "I think they believed they weren't being watched anymore. They reserved a hotel conference room for a week and occupied a dozen rooms - no big deal in a place like *The Breakers*. They could easily have gone about their business and no one would have been the wiser."

Brixton said, "If you hadn't spotted the IKOR notice in the lobby the other night, we would never had made the connection in the first place. The only thing is, Hoover's pissed off that the Coast Guard uncovered it."

"He'll claim credit anyway. But listen, I think we're finally starting to get some breaks," said Levitan. "Wait 'til you hear this," and he told Brixton about a hotel guest named George Koval and the encounter that the house detective had seen on the stairway. "We're thinking he could be Judith Horowtiz's boyfriend, whose name is George. See if you have anything on a 'George Koval'. He may be in the Army. And have you ever heard of a place called ORMR?"

"Yes," said Brixton.

Levitan waited for the man on the other end to elaborate. "John? Are you still there?"

"I'm here."

"Well? So? What the hell is ORMR?"

"It's the Oak Ridge Military Reservation in Tennessee. It's where they make the atomic bomb."

"Holy mackerel."

"Yes," said Brixton.

19

The idea, back in 1926, had been to extend the summer season by conducting the Miss America Pageant during the week following Labor Day. In September 1946, Americans were prideful about their victory in the Second World War, convinced that the outcome of the global catastrophe proved the superiority of the American Way of Life. And their women were, *ipso facto*, the most beautiful in the world.

It turned out to have been a solid gold marketing idea. Ambitious young women from every State in the Union came to town to have their pictures taken as they strutted their stuff in bathing suits. Full-page picture displays in daily newspapers across the country invited everyone to participate in selecting the prettiest woman in America. Breakfast conversations across the land were debates about who would win. On the upcoming Saturday night, the 7th of September, a national radio audience would listen to the end of the competition. The Sunday morning editions would feature front-page pictures of the beaming winner wearing a tiara.

Levitan passed the doorway to the Chief's office on his way to the stairway after he finished talking to Brixton. Apparently, Rafferty had been waiting for him to leave the conference room. "Dave," he called,

"Can you come in here for a minute? Tell me what's going on."

Levitan summarized their recent discoveries to the Chief.

Rafferty said, "So that's good. You've done the job. I knew you could do it."

"Done? Chief, we've just started. This is all guesswork. We still have to talk to this Koval. We're only guessing that he was the guy on the stairs."

"Why us? You told the FBI all about this, right? And what about The Army? You think the guy's a soldier, right? You have to make sure General Groves is informed. This is a Federal matter now, Dave. It's way out of our league."

"What are you saying?"

"I'd like my men back. I need them on the pageant. I'm stretched too thin."

"That's a shame," said Levitan.

"The pageant is bigger than ever this year. I need more coverage around the Convention Hall."

"Well, they're yours to command. But the case is nowhere near closed. Don't you think catching the killer of an American atomic scientist is more important than a beauty pageant?"

"A damn sight more important, which is why I'd rather have the important people deal with it. I want to step back."

"Listen to me, Chief. We haven't even started to build a case. Let's think ahead. After the fuss is all over, you're still going to need a case that will stand up in court. Do you want to rely on the Army or the FBI to build it for you?"

"Right now, I have other things on my plate. I'm pulling my men."

Knowing Rafferty's sore spot, how much he loathed the FBI Director, Levitan said, "And you're going to have the Justice Department looking over your shoulder – count on it. Hoover is very interested; Brixton reports to him every day. In fact, he's probably talking to him right now. If ACPD screws this up, it'll be giving Hoover another excuse to come down on South Jersey, and you know he's just waiting for the chance. At the very least, he'll accuse the ACPD of being unpatriotic for refusing to cooperate in the investigation."

"Goddammit! What am I supposed to do? I'm already paying everyone overtime to work the pageant. We can't have anything go wrong this year – the whole country's watching us."

"Sorry, Chief."

"Alright, dammit. You can keep the men."

"Good move."

"You know what worries me?"

"What's that, Chief?"

"Who's in charge? Overall, who's calling the shots for you?"

"I'm handling it myself for now."

"Good. Don't let them get in your way."

20

It was near noon when Buster Fulton returned from the beach, having learned nothing from the lifeguards. The four of them drove to *The Breakers* in two separate cars. Their plan was to locate and interview George Koval, perhaps to arrest him, and to begin a surveillance of Judith Horowitz. But Levitan realized that the plan would have to change as soon as they got to the lobby and saw that the United States Government had come to *The Breakers Hotel* in force: men in dark business suits and others wearing Army dress uniforms were stationed around the lobby. A soldier stood in front of the reception desk. Behind it, a civilian stood next to Oscar, the manager. Others, in and out of uniform, stood by the entrances, the elevators, and at the top and bottom of the stairway to the mezzanine.

The train whistles were shrieking, the wheels were locking up, right there in the lobby of *The Breakers Hotel*.

He'd been expecting to see them, waiting for the minions of the Justice and War Departments to descend on the investigation, lucky to have had a relatively open field for a couple of days. But the presence of his father-in-law sitting in an upholstered chair reading a newspaper was a surprise. Al Rubin glanced up, saw Levitan, smiled, winked, and returned his attention to an edition of *The Philadelphia Evening Bulletin.*

Standing in the middle of the lobby, he gestured for the three cops to form a huddle. He looked into the faces of his team and called the play, "All right," he said. "We're screwed in here. Right now, there are at least three men in this place who think they are in charge, and I'm not counting myself."

"Fuck 'em," said Lou Staup.

"We can't do anything about it, Lou. But stay cool. Relax."

"We should just go ahead and do what we came to do," said Calvin Turner.

"Maybe," said Levitan. "But first, let me find out what's going on. I want to talk to that guy reading a newspaper. That's Al Rubin."

"Nucky's pal?" asked Buster.

"That's him. I'm guessing he's here with some advice."

"He was the one who got you your job on the force. Right?" said Turner.

"That... and he's my father-in-law. Do you guys mind leaving us alone for a little while so's I can talk to him?" They agreed to go out on The Boardwalk and to return in a half hour.

He'd been away from the hotel for a couple of hours, so he needed to check for messages. Four clerks were working with guests at the front desk, two on either side of Oscar, who was pretending that he could run his hotel despite the G-Man at his side and the soldier standing at ease in front of the desk. Levitan caught the manager's eye as he approached.

"Room 905 - any messages?" he asked.

He hoped Oscar would not fuss over him. *The Breakers'* employees, as far as he knew, still had no reason to connect him to the Government's intrusion. The manner of Oscar's greeting would indicate whether his cover had been blown. He was relieved that the manager simply retrieved three message slips that had been placed in the pigeon hole over the empty hook for his room key.

Brixton had left a message, "Will arrive by noon. Meet me in lobby."

Levitan checked his watch - it was ten-thirty.

The Admiral's note said, "Call ASAP."

Helen had called, but left no message.

Al rose from the lobby chair, stubbed out his cigarette in the floor-standing ashtray, tucked the paper under his arm, and said, "Let's go get a cup of coffee. They make it good here."

The Breakers' restaurant was decorated with travel posters. Al chose a table in the farthest corner of the room. The waiter brought a silver pot of coffee, a pint pitcher of heavy cream, a sugar bowl, and dainty china cups with saucers.

"How are things going on the pier?" Levitan inquired. "Any beauties coming in to *Memories* to have their pictures taken on the pony?"

"Not so far. The weather's been too good." The covered stalls on the entertainment piers thrived on rainy days when people didn't go to the beach. "So, *boychik*?" Al said, "Are all these government men here because of the bullshit you were talking about on the pier?"

"Some of them," Levitan replied. "The ones from the Army are here on different business from the ones in the FBI. It's the FBI's case that I'm involved with."

"Is that son of a bitch Hoover involved?"

"Yeah. He gets reports directly from the Agent I'm working with. What brings you here?"

Al said, "I have an interest in the hotel. "

"An interest?"

"A few shares."

"So?"

"So, after we talked the other day, I called Oscar and I told him to take good care of you."

"I wish you hadn't. Why did you do that?"

"Because it's you, Davey. You tell me you're here at my hotel, so I wanted to let Oscar know to treat you good. And also, I admit, since I know what kind of business you are in, it's also true that I have a concern. You get involved in interesting developments, Davey... *kaynahora*." Al took a sip of his coffee, added cream and sugar, and said, "So when a whole big bunch of FBI Agents come to *The Breakers* and say that they are looking for Commodore Levitan, Oscar gives me a call. So here I am."

Levitan liked his coffee unadulterated. "Well. I'm glad to see you Al. And thanks for your concern. But it would have been better if you hadn't done it. It means that the management of the hotel no longer think I'm an ordinary guest."

Al said, "So? Is that so bad?"

"Well, it's not a catastrophe, but I can learn different things when I'm unofficial. I was trying not to attract attention. I thought I'd been completely undercover. But, there's no real harm done. I'd have to drop the cover at some point anyway."

"Good. I didn't screw anything up?"

"No. It's okay."

"So what's with all these Washington types in the lobby?" asked Al.

"I do appreciate your concern, Al, but you have to stay out of this. It's a national security matter and in no way involves local politics."

"Civilians, military. I been watching. These people are not talking to each other. Who's in charge?"

Levitan smiled. "That's a question I'm not going to ask. I don't want to get caught in the middle when they start pissing all over each other. It's going to be a big problem, but it is *their* problem. I have my own squad and we'll just carry on the best we can. And, Al, you can tell Nucky that Francis Rafferty knows what's going on – except for the national security aspects. This is the ACPD's case and I'm watching out for their interests. If you happen to be in touch with Nucky, tell him not to worry."

"This is good, Davey. I'll be sure to let him know in my next letter. So everything is under control?"

"Never," said Levitan.

"Okay, Davey. I just wanted to offer my help."

Levitan said, "Appreciate it. Thanks."

"Did you talk to Helen?"

Levitan said, "She called me a little while ago."

"So? *Nu?*"

"I wasn't here to take the call. But I guess she's okay. Now let me go, Al. I have to call my boss."

So that Fulton, Turner and Staup would be able to see him when they returned from The Boardwalk, he used a phone booth in the lobby instead of going to his room to make the call to Admiral Spiegel.

"Just calling in, Sir. The shit seems to have hit the fan."

"What's going on where you are?" asked the Admiral.

He described the scene.

"Well, that's about what I would expect. I've had calls this morning, Dave. From Director Hoover and from General Groves."

"Ouch!" said Levitan.

"You seem to have kicked over a hornets' nest. It was you who got the Army onto this soldier from Oak Ridge?"

"I guess I did. All I did was ask Brixton if he knew where ORMR was. One of the ACPD Detectives found his name and address in the hotel register."

"These ACPD Detectives are not authorized for access to secret material, are they?"

"No. But they've been working the robbery angle. There's been no need."

"That line of investigation may no longer be necessary. It may be time to break up your team. Groves is on the warpath. I can't talk about it over the telephone, but this soldier, Koval, is very highly placed."

"I understand, Admiral. John Brixton is on his way from Philadelphia. I'm sure he'll fill me in."

"I want to talk to you about your role on the investigation."

"Yes sir. It might get problematic. What is it you have in mind?"

"It seems to me that you're doing the job."

"We've had a few breaks, that's true."

"Call it what you want. Brixton's boys couldn't have done it and The Army wasn't investigating the murder – they didn't even know about it until you and your cop friends started interviewing hotel people. So it's been you."

"Us. I've got a good team."

"Good, I'm glad it's worked out. Hoover and Groves can't figure it out, so we get to be the best option. Are you okay with that?"

"Not really. You got them to agree to that?"

"I did. It's a sensible option. They know that if they keep butting heads, blood's going to flow. So, for now, they're okay with leaving it up to a neutral party - us. And you made a good impression on Groves. And Brixton swears by you. So it's your baby. What do you need from me?"

"Besides getting Hoover and Groves to love each other, I don't know. I'll let you know if I run into any trouble."

Levitan said goodbye and hung up the phone.

He walked to the front desk and showed his Commodore's credential to the federal man wearing the dark civilian suit, "Do you report to SAIC Brixton?" asked Leviatn.

"I do," said the G-Man, impressed by Levitan's rank.

"Good. Please ask him to give me a call in Room 905 when he arrives at noon. He'll be looking for me." He faced the hotel manager and said, "How's it going, Oscar?"

"Fine, Commodore." Said the desk manager. "Are all these Government people here for the same reason you are?"

"More or less. There was a crime at *The Traymore* involving a man who was playing cards in your *Newark Room* just before an incident. We would greatly appreciate your cooperation. Will that be okay?"

"Certainly. But all these men... they will disturb the guests."

"Sorry. Maybe I can get them to back off a little."

"That would be appreciated."

§

When Fulton, Turner and Staup returned from The Boardwalk, he led them to the elevator to the 9th Floor..

The housekeepers had tidied room 905. Mutt and Jeff - mustachioed Turner and muscular Staup – sat down side by side on the couch. Fulton sank into the easy chair. Levitan opened the French doors and stood on the balcony. People were coming onto the beach.

The sky was clear. High above the surf, a slow biplane dragged an advertising banner, "*TONIGHT-MARTIN & LEWIS-500 CLUB.*"

He came into the room and stood facing them. "I can't tell you much, I'm sorry. This case has half the Federal Government worried about atomic secrets because of the victim's work. You know I can't tell you about that, but it's the reason why the lobby has turned into a cluster fuck. Because we found his name and address in the hotel register, the Army and the FBI know about our best lead, this Koval character. It turns out that his top secret work is connected to Weber's."

Staup asked, "So they've picked up Koval?"

"I'm guessing that they haven't, otherwise they wouldn't be hanging around the hotel. But we'll get the story when my FBI guy gets here. He's due at noon and I've sent word for him to meet us here. "

As if on cue, the telephone rang. It was Brixton. He said, "I'm down in the lobby."

"John, I'm in the middle of a tactical meeting. Why don't you come up. The team would like to meet you."

"Goddamit, Dave. They don't have clearance."

"They'll leave whenever you say, John. I just thought it would be good if you got a chance to say hello to the guys who did all the work."

"Well, all right, I suppose. Stay where you are."

§

When Brixton arrived, Levitan said, "Lou and Cal are the Detectives who were working the crime scene

when your agents came to *The Traymore*. And this is
Sergeant Fulton, who's been assigned as my side
man." "

"Pleased to meet you," said Brixton. "You two
detectives made quite an impression on my men."

"Glad to hear it," said Cal Turner. "They are
assholes."

The boxcars were pushing into each other, about to
jump the tracks.

"They were doing their jobs, Detective. I won't
apologize for their behavior," said Brixton.

"They should know better than to mess with a
crime scene," said Lou Staup.

"They do know better, Detective. But this is a
special case. They were doing their jobs."

The policemen were not mollified, but they were
smart enough to keep quiet.

Levitan said, "Cal, Lou, Buster - get back to work.
Lou and Cal, start interviewing hotel people about
George Koval, same as we did with Weber. We have
his description from the Hotel Detective, so describe
him to everyone you can. We know he checked in at
four-forty on Saturday afternoon. Let's see if we can
find out anything about what he's been doing in the
meanwhile. Let's keep each other posted by calling in
at the police station as often as we can. Go to it.
Buster, would you mind waiting for me in the lobby?"

"Don't go far away," said Brixton. "We'll have
some news for you after I talk to Commodore
Levitan."

The three ACPD cops looked to Levitan, who shrugged.

§

When he was alone with Brixton, Levitan asked, "Let's get to it, John. The Admiral told me that the Army's hair's on fire about Koval. How did that happen?"

Brixton said "We asked them for his service record. They wanted to know why. This is looking like a straight-up national security matter, Dave. Which means that the ACPD has to get off the case."

Levitan said, "Those agents in the lobby? You sent all those men to get the list of IKOR attendees?"

"We completed the list yesterday. Today, we're going to interview the ones who are still in the hotel; half of them checked out last night and this morning. We've deployed agents to the home addresses belonging to the one's who've checked out."

"What's The Army doing? Have they questioned this Polish diplomat?"

"The Army isn't allowed to because he's a civilian and because of his diplomatic status. Now, after we asked for his Service Record, they're looking for Koval *and* because he's checked in to the same hotel as a Polish diplomat who could be a Russian spy. This case is being watched at the Cabinet level now, Dave."

"So? What about Koval? Have they talked to him?"

"It looks like he skipped without bothering to check out. There's no clothing in his room, not even a suitcase."

"Did anyone check the woman's room. Judith Horowitz's?"

"Yes. Her stuff is still in the room. But she's out. We're looking for her. "

"Do you know what she looks like?"

"No."

"So how are you going to find her?"

Brixton cocked his head, "What's she look like?"

"Very attractive: petite, dark hair, well built."

"We wait for her to come back to her room."

Levitan thought for a moment. "She's probably on the beach. I might be able to find her. I don't get why your men are still here. If the IKOR meeting's over, why are your men all over the lobby?"

"They aren't my men," said Brixton. "They are with the State Department, because of the Polish diplomat. That's why I'm here. Hoover doesn't want State or the Army interfering with our Commie investigation. We're interested in Judith Horowitz and IKOR. As of now, the Army and State don't know about her."

"Jesus! When's the Department of Agriculture going to show up?" Levitan said. The Admiral had ordered him to stay on the case as the neutral investigator. There was nothing Levitan could do about the collision between the three most powerful Departments of the Federal Government – War, State, and Justice - except try to keep from getting maimed.

He said, "The woman might be on the beach. Let me go find her. She doesn't know that I'm associated with you. As far as she knows, I'm a harmless bureaucrat on vacation."

Brixton asked, "But you think she's involved."

"She's certainly involved with George Koval, and Koval might have been the last person to see Weber alive. The hotel detective was keeping an eye out for pickpockets when he spotted a man who looked like Weber in an encounter with someone of military age on Saturday, right before he left *The Breakers* to return to *The Traymore*. Weber confronted this guy on the stairway to the mezzanine after the IKOR meeting broke up, and then the guy disappeared."

"What makes you think the guy was Koval?" Brixton asked.

"Just a guess. Based on my conversation with the woman, I had my guys check the register for someone named George. Koval checked into the hotel at 4:40 and wrote down the ORMR address in the register. The rest is all supposition, which is why I want to talk to him."

"And this Horowitz woman is his girlfriend."

Levitan said, "Yep. I gave you her name yesterday. Do you have a file on her?"

"Yeah, but there's nothing in it except her name and an address that's almost ten years old. We established a file after she attended an IKOR rally back in 1937. But nothing since then. We got her current address off the hotel register - she lives in The Bronx. I've put a squad on it and right now they're up in New York collecting information about her. By the time we're done, we'll know everything about her down to the color of her panties, but I'm pretty sure they're red."

"Let me talk to her first. She is not at all fond of the FBI, but I think she likes me. I gave you Koval's name, too. What about his file?"

Brixton nods. "We did a background check on him in 1943, when the Army asked us to give him a Top Secret clearance. I got a summary of what's in the file over the phone."

Brixton opened his briefcase and took out a yellow notepad and read from his notes, "He's thirty-three, born and raised in Sioux City, Iowa. He graduated at the top of his high school class at fifteen years old. That's impressive. He registered for the Draft right away, as soon as it became mandatory in 1940. By then, he was working on a Bachelor's degree in chemical engineer at CCNY and living in Brooklyn. He was drafted in the winter of '42 but didn't enter the service until 1943 because he was given a one-year deferment at the request of his employer, *The Raven Electric Company* in North Jersey - they have government contracts. That's as far as our file goes; I can't tell you anything about what he's been doing since then, not since we gave him clearance to work at Oak Ridge. During our investigation, we interviewed his landlady and a couple of his neighbors, a couple of his professors, and people from his work. No red flags - there is nothing unusual in his file. Nothing political."

"He's Jewish?"

"Yes."

"I didn't know there were any Jews in Iowa."

"Apparently so."

"So he graduates from high school... what year?"

Brixton looked at his notes, "1928."

"Then, twelve years later, he shows up in New York?"

"Right."

"So? What about all the years in between?"

Brixton stared down at the legal pad. "I don't think we have anything about him during those years."

Levitan said, "You probably ought to check."

Brixton nodded and made a note on the top of the page. "Yeah. You're right. I'll send some agents from our Sioux City office to see what they can dig up."

"And you asked the Army for Koval's service record?"

"We did," said Brixton. "That's what got them all agitated. But, because of his classification, and because he's posted to Oak Ridge, I doubt they'll give it up."

"But your Koval file has two huge gaps: 1927 to 1940, and 1943 to now."

The phone rang. It was Buster, calling from the lobby. "Dave," he said. "You better get down here."

"What's the matter? What's going on?"

"The Army is getting out of hand."

"We're on our way."

21

The confrontation at *The Breakers* was the Washington power struggle in miniature. America was invincible, with armies occupying Western Europe, Japan, and Pacific islands. Its Navy was the greatest the world had ever known, with fleets of warships above and below the surface surrounding aircraft carriers in the Mediterranean, the Pacific and the Atlantic. Tens of thousands of American planes dominated the skies wherever they chose to fly. And America alone had the ability to destroy any city on the globe with a single flash of atomic fission. Except for the Soviet Union, no country on planet Earth challenged American dominance.

And the American government chose to dominate, for to have behaved otherwise would have been to squander an unprecedented opportunity to impose its will on the world. But, maintaining invincibility while absorbing a militarized labor force into a peacetime economy was a challenge. To win the war, the government had assumed absolute power over the economic activities of the country, directing inexhaustible sums of money into factories in every corner of the land, spectacularly invigorating an American economy that had been stagnant and struggling for the decade preceding the war. In 1946, the government was reorganizing in a way that perpetuated military dominance while freeing the economy to develop without centralized control.

The men in Washington had learned that constant government funding of the military offsets the vicissitudes of an undisciplined economy. Prosperity, it seemed, depended upon government spending at a level that had been unthinkable before the war. Managing that great economic force while allowing free people to participate in their own economy was the government's core challenge. Key to accomplishing the balance was reorganization of the government, deciding who was in charge of what.

Levitan and Brixton emerged from the elevator into the lobby where Captain Rudolph Duplessis confronted them.

"We need to talk," he said.

"Hi, Captain. What's the problem?" said Levitan.

"Your man, that fellow over there… he put his hands on me."

"Which one was this?"

Fulton, Turner and Staup were standing near the patio doors, watching them. "It's that chubby guy," said Duplessis. "The one with the mustache."

"Let me have a word with him. I'll be right back. Do you know Mister Brixton?" he said, and stepped away to find out what had compelled Cal Turner to manhandle an Army Captain.

Turner was clearly angry. He said, "The son of a bitch. I go to the desk clerk and ask him to show me Koval's hotel bill. This soldier standing there, he hears me asking, and he tells the clerk not to let me see it. And I tell him to back off. And he goes into the office behind the desk and out comes that character you were just talking to."

"That's Captain Duplessis of Army Intelligence. He says you touched him."

"Well, he says we can't see the bill. So I say he should shove it up his ass. He comes right up in my face and asks me who I am. And I tell him, but he won't say who *he* is. So I decide to go behind the desk and get it myself and he tries to stop me. I guess I grabbed him."

Buster Fulton said, "So that's when I called you. What the fuck, Dave."

"Don't worry about it. You didn't do anything I wouldn't have done."

"What the fuck is he doing here?" said Turner.

"They're here watching a man from New York, and now it looks as if they're looking for Koval too."

"Shit, Dave," said Staup. "They can't do this. They can't just bust into our case."

Levitan smiled. "Sure they can."

"Sons of bitches. What are we supposed to do?"

"Let them have their way."

"But what about our investigation?"

"From what Brixton tells me, this is looking more and more like an espionage case. The FBI wanted your help on the robbery angle. But now it's looking like it's something altogether different. It's time for the local police to back out. You did your jobs."

"So that's it? We're off the case?"

"Be happy. There are forty-eight bathing beauties who need you now. The Chief will be delighted to have you guys working the pageant."

"Damn," said Staup. "This has been good, Dave."

"That it has. You guys have been terrific."

"So The Army's taking over," said Turner.

"Well, that's a different question. The FBI has something to say about it. And the State Department too. Count yourselves lucky to be out of it."

22

Levitan hadn't packed a bathing suit, but *The Breakers* had a shop where he grabbed a pair of navy-blue trunks and a Hawaiian shirt, paying with a twenty dollar bill. As he changed in Room 905, Brixton insisted that he come along. Levitan refused. They agreed to have two men follow him onto the beach, but to keep their distance. They were to remove their shirts and jackets, to walk barefoot and to keep at least fifty feet away. Less than a half-hour after he'd sent the ACPD cops back to the station, with a hotel towel draped over his shoulder, he was walking down the steps from the Boardwalk onto the hot sand.

The Atlantic City Beach Patrol was an arm of the police department. Rookie policemen had to be strong swimmers in order to serve as lifeguards during the summer months. Levitan had done his time in the platforms and the rowboats before the war. Then he'd been promoted to Detective to fill a wartime manpower gap. He'd not been on a beach during the five years since he'd worn a whistle..

He was fascinated by the ocean. When he'd lived in Atlantic City, he'd gotten into the habit of watching the tide tables and organizing his spare time to coincide with the hour after low tide when the fishing is best. He'd enjoyed the solitude - an excuse to be alone by the sea. He was fascinated by the sand, the wondrous countless particles that had once been rock and shell.

He found Judith Horowitz lying on a blanket reading a book. He admired the curve of her buttocks and the shape of her legs. She was on her stomach, holding the book in one hand, her chin in the other, the side of her breast swelling around the top of her two-piece bathing suit.

"Hey, Judith," he said.

She looked up from the book and shaded her eyes. She smiled when she recognized him. "Hi," she said.

"I thought you'd be working. What are you doing on the beach?"

"The conference has been cancelled. I'm a free woman."

"Well good for you. So you're sticking around?"

"My room's paid for. Why not? I don't have to check out until tomorrow."

"Good for you. It's nice to see you. Are you alone? Where's your boyfriend?"

"Not here."

"Can I sit with you?"

"Why not?" she said. She rolled over and shifted to the side of the blanket, making room for him. Her long, brown hair was wet at the ends.

"Is the water warm?" he asked.

"Perfect."

"What are you reading?"

She showed him the cover of the paperback, a Rex Stout mystery story about Nero Wolfe, the fat detective who never left his New York brownstone.

"I haven't read that one. Is it good?"

"I like it," she said. "So, do you like mysteries?"

"I love them. Who else do you like?"

"Oh, Agatha Christie, Ellery Queen, Erle Stanley Gardner. Do you read those?"

"I do," he said. "So, you're not staying for the Miss America contest?"

"They only booked my room through tomorrow. When is the contest?"

"Saturday night is when they pick the winner. Who do you thinks is going to win?"

"I haven't even looked at the pictures. It's a stupid business."

"Well, you could be in it."

She chortled, "No doubt. A Jewish Miss America! That'll be the day."

"How come your boyfriend isn't here? Doesn't he like the beach. What's his name... George?"

"He had to go back to base this morning. Some kind of emergency."

"Where's his base?"

"I don't know."

He tried to look surprised. "Really? He's stationed at a secret base?"

"It's a secret from me. He won't talk about it. And, really, I'd rather not talk about him."

"So, you're on your own again?"

"That I am."

"Why did the IKOR cancel their conference?"

"The FBI showed up all of a sudden."

"You're kidding me! They shut the meeting down?"

"No. A couple of them were waiting outside the room when we broke for lunch yesterday."

"So? What did they do?"

"They took names and addresses. But the message was clear. So the IKOR decided to call it off."

The IKOR convention had been the swan song of obsolete dreamers, a frayed thread in the fabric of history. He said, "So it's over now. The IKOR is finished for good."

"I suppose. To tell you the truth, I thought they were finished years ago."

"They? You're not a member?"

"I'm a stenographer. They're paying me to take the minutes and type them up. But I'm not one of them. They offered me the job because I used to know them. I went to a couple of meetings with my fiancée. This was years ago, back in the mid-Thirties. He was the real believer. I don't much care for them at all, as a matter of fact."

"George is your fiancée?"

"No. That was some other guy."

Levitan said, "So why did you take the job if you don't like them?"

"Because they're paying well. And they're paying for my room and my meals. And it's in Atlantic City, and George had leave coming, so why wouldn't I take the job?"

He nodded, and said, "But George keeps leaving you alone."

"You noticed that, did you? He had to get back to base – some kind of emergency. So? What about your wife? Have you heard from her?" she asked.

"Sure. She's fine," he said.

"You don't think she's coming back from New York, do you?"

"What makes you say that?"

"It's just a guess," she said.

"So... Are you going to be alone tonight?" he asked.

She lifted her chin and stared at the ocean horizon, peering through the shifting crowd for a glimpse of the sea. They sat, silently side by side. The sun and ocean breeze felt good on his skin. Above the crowded beach, gulls circled, looking for treasures carried in the surf or discarded on the beach. Hungry sandpipers attacked the wet margins where the waves retreated, probing for little sand crabs. Bright white terns wheeled and skimmed the surface, dipping for baitfish.

The ocean is always there but never the same. It moves. The light changes by the hour and by the season. The weather changes. The sound of it varies from place to place; the waves splash and gurgle through the rock jetties up at the Inlet. In the back bay, the stilled sea makes little lapping sounds around hummocks of tall grass. Waves crash onto the beach during storms, but roll so quietly against it on calmer days that you can hear the cry of gulls far away.

"Terrific weather."

"Great," she agreed.

"Let's take a swim."

She turned to face him. The sea had washed her makeup off and stiffened her long, dark lashes. "Okay,"

She slid her book inside a canvas bag. He took off the beach shirt and dropped it onto the blanket. They asked a family camped under a nearby umbrella if they would be so kind as to watch their things for just a little while. He let her lead the way down to the surf.

He glanced over his shoulders and saw the FBI agents in dress pants keeping their distance.

He stood next to Judith for a minute or so, watching the people playing in the surf. Where the wavelets reached their farthest extent, three heavyset women sat with their legs outstretched, waiting for the waves to cool their crotches.

He waded in and waited for her: the water swirling around his knees, his feet sinking into the sand. When she reached his side, he grinned, turned, and bounded away toward the breaking waves. He hollered a whoop, dove into the face of comber, and powered through with rapid kicks and long, underwater strokes. He surfaced in shoulder-deep water, turned, and saw Judith striding toward him, twisting her narrow waist from side to side. She leaped up as a wave broke over her, ducked into the backwash, and swam toward him with awkward strokes.

"You're right," he said. "The water's perfect."

She bobbed, dancing off the bottom, smiling. "I'm not a good swimmer. I can't go out any farther."

"This is fine," he said. He turned away from her and looked back toward the land and the big hotel two hundred yards distant. A large wave covered Judith's head. When it passed, she bobbed up, sputtering. "It's too deep for me. I'm going back." He followed her in, resisting a temptation to pick her up and help her as she struggled toward the shore.

They toweled off at the blanket. She was not the sort who minded tousling her hair. She said, "About tonight…"

"Yeah. About tonight."

"What did you have in mind?"

"I hadn't thought that far ahead. I don't know. How about a walk on The Boardwalk?"

"That sounds nice," she said.

"Great. Do you think George will mind?"

"I don't think so. I can take a walk on The Boardwalk. There's no harm in that." She took a wide-toothed comb from the bag and pulled it through her hair.

"Exactly," he said, settling his butt on the blanket. "So the IKOR's finished once and for all."

"Yes. And about time. The only reason they wanted to have this conference at all was in case they get prosecuted. A couple of them are lawyers, wouldn't you know. There is so much talk in Washington these days about outlawing The Communist Party that they want to have a good story ready for when it happens. This conference was meant to establish their defense. So that's my job - to copy down what they're saying. They don't want to hear what I think."

"So what would you say?"

"I told you, I'm not a member. Whatever I have to say would be just my personal opinions, and who cares about them?"

"I'm interested," he said.

"My opinion is that it can't be about talking anymore. It has to be about doing. They talk and talk, on and on, just to make sense of the incomprehensible. Talk, talk, talk. Decide already."

"Decide what? They've always known that they were considered subversive. Hasn't the government been all over them from the beginning? If they get arrested, it's because they brought it on themselves."

"They want to be ready when the other shoe is dropped."

"So they're nervous."

"God yes. Wouldn't you be? But do you want to know the real reason they're having this conference?'

"Other than preparing their defense?'

"They could have done that in New York. No - their wives wanted a holiday in Atlantic City."

"Really."

"I know it. That's how come I was asked to do the job. I'm friends with a couple of the wives. Having a convention down here was their idea."

One of the FBI watchers beckoned to Levitan.

He stood. "So we'll get together later?"

"You're leaving?"

"I hate to go… But I promised some relatives that I'd go to their house for supper. Sorry."

"Oh."

"So it might be late before I can get away."

"Sure," she said. "How late?"

"Not very. I'll try to get away as soon as I can. I'll call you from the lobby this evening, as soon as I get back to the hotel."

He put on the shirt and trudged back through the sand, crossed The Boardwalk and spotted Brixton eating a hamburger in the patio restaurant.

23

Brixton was seated under an umbrella. He'd removed his tie and jacket, loosened his collar and rolled up his sleeves in an unsuccessful attempt to blend in with the vacationers. A waiter arrived and took Levitan's order for a *Coke*. The people around them were intent upon their food and drink, paying no attention to barefoot Levitan wearing a bathing suit and a beach shirt, in conference with an agent of the FBI.

"What's up?" asked Levitan.

"Captain Duplessis is about to start interviewing the Polish diplomat. Apparently, Groves told the State Department to fuck off."

"Has The Army identified him? Is he really a Russian Colonel?" he asks.

"Possibly. They had a guy come in from Berlin yesterday. This guy met Reshetnikov once, last year, for fifteen minutes. It was a crazy time, everybody in uniform, everybody under orders that changed by the hour. The Army guy gets to look at Biernacki in the hotel lobby last night. He says 'maybe,' but he can't be sure. So, for now, he's still Tomasz Biernacki, assistant Polish Ambassador to the United Nations."

"Why are they messing with him? Why don't they just watch him?"

"I think it's just political; the Army's staking a claim because they don't want State or the FBI involved."

"That's stupid," said Levitan.

"That's The Army. Duplessis just went up to Biernacki's room."

"I want to meet this guy. Do you want to come with me?"

"Standing orders still apply: until I hear officially that the Polish Embassy has given its approval, I'm not allowed to talk to him."

"Well no one has told me to back off," said Levitan. He rose and threw a wet dollar bill onto the table. "I'm going to see what's going on. Are they in his room?"

"Yeah, 681. Good luck."

"See if you can get a room key for 905. I'll meet you there after I get done talking to Biernacki, or Reshetnikov, or whoever the hell he is."

§

Levitan took the bathers' elevator to the Ninth Floor, changed into his street clothes, and took the regular elevator to the Sixth Floor. A Military Police Sergeant answered Levitan's knock on the door to 681.

He showed his Commodore credential. "Would you ask Captain Duplessis to give me a minute of his time here in the hallway? He knows who I am."

"He's in the middle of something," said the Sergeant. "He's busy right now."

"I understand. He's talking to Mister Biernacki, the Polish diplomat. Please let the Captain know that Commodore Levitan has some useful information for him."

The sergeant closed the door. A minute later, Duplessis came into the hallway. "Commodore? What do you have for me?"

"I'd like to talk to him. Did General Groves tell you that he talked to my Admiral? The Admiral says that the General has agreed to allow me to continue my investigation."

"Yeah I heard that. I don't like it."

"So sorry."

Duplessis straightened his shoulders. "So? What's the information?"

"I'm on good terms with the IKOR secretary – I just left her on the beach. I think I know why Biernacki came to Atlantic City."

"Tell me."

"I think he came here to shut them down."

"So?"

"You told me that you don't know a damned thing about IKOR. Wouldn't it be better if I was the one to talk to him about it?"

"Why's that?"

"Because I know the background. It shouldn't take me long."

Duplessis thought it over. "All right, Commodore," he said.

"Would you mind waiting for me out here in the hallway?"

Duplessis looked unhappy.

"He's not going anywhere, Captain. There's nothing to worry about. Just give me a few minutes alone with him."

Tomasz Biernacki, or Valentin Reshetnikov, was seated in the reading chair of his hotel room, one laid out identically to Levitan's three floors above. The "diplomat" had a narrow, ruddy face with high, Slavic cheekbones, dark-blue eyes and straight brown hair. He was wearing a lightweight shirt without a tie or jacket and tan trousers.

Levitan said, "Mister Biernacki? My name is Commodore David Levitan, an agent of the United States Government. I am investigating a murder that might involve agents of the Soviet Union. Do you understand?"

"Murder? Who was murdered?"

"An American. Someone who was in Atlantic City to play cards. He was seen talking to the people leaving a meeting of people with associations to the USSR. He was seen talking to them shortly before he was killed."

"This is why you've interfered with me, a diplomat? I have immunity." said Biernacki, speaking English with only a slight accent.

Levitan said, "Yes sir. I understand. We just want to talk with you. You can be very helpful to us. What we're trying to do is keep this at a low level, without getting the State Department or your Ministry involved. Is that alright with you?"

Biernacki spoke carefully, "I think that's reasonable, but I insist upon speaking to my embassy."

Levitan responded, "Let's give that a moment's thought, shall we? That might be ill-advised."

"And why would that be?"

"It has to do with men who used to be sponsored by the Soviet Union. They are the *Idishe Kolonizatsie Organizatsie in Rusland,* IKOR. They are openly supportive of the Comintern's Party line. They sponsored emigrants to the Jewish autonomous *oblast* in the Far East, near Vladivostok. Does that sound familiar?"

"It sounds vaguely familiar. What about them?" said Biernacki.

"Are you aware that they were having a convention in this hotel until yesterday? You might have seen their notice on the bulletin board in the hotel lobby?"

"In this hotel? That's interesting."

The Soviet Union and America were the last two Powers standing. Europeans had capped centuries of warfare by using enormous quantities of high explosives to kill each other, destroying the great cities, depleting the farms and the mines, eviscerating a generation of humanity. Now America patrolled the Pacific and The Atlantic with awesome warships able to wreak airborne destruction on the continents from five hundred miles at sea. Russia had soldiers in great number and a vast, rich territory. They were two great powers vying for position on a new board.

"Perhaps you ought to be speaking to someone from the Soviet Union's embassy. I represent Poland," said Biernacki.

"No doubt. May I inquire about where you received your education? Your English is excellent."

"I went to the State University of Wisconsin for graduate school."

"In what field of study?"

"Civil engineering. Please, my background can be the subject for another discussion. You were speaking of a murder? And this group? This IKOR?"

"They are the last people to have seen him alive – they were standing with him on the mezzanine of this hotel. An hour later he was dead, strangled in his hotel room about a half-mile from here."

Biernacki remained impassive, considering Levitan's revelation. At length, he said, "In what way is the Polish delegation to the United Nations connected? I'm not sure why you're talking to me."

"Aren't you aware of The State Department policy about traveling diplomats? You have an obligation to inform them if you plan to travel around the country. Don't you know that?"

"I suppose I do,"

"So? You packed up and left New York without notifying anyone. It's a problem."

"I see," said Biernacki. "Well, I'm sorry for the oversight. My mistake. I am here vacation... *on* vacation. I decided to come at the last minute. I left on the weekend, and I guess I forgot."

"You could be expelled for it," said Levitan.

"Surely not. But, to show our good intentions, I will see to it that you receive a formal apology from my government."

"Well, we can avoid that."

"How would we do that?"

"By settling the matter right now. I'd like to speak hypothetically."

"How so?"

"I'd appreciate hearing your opinion about Soviet Union policy. You need not protest any lack of expertise, as we both know that Poland is a Russian satellite state. I'd like your opinion about what you think the Soviet Union's policy is with regard to IKOR."

"Speaking hypothetically?"

"Of course. What do you think the Soviet Union would think about an IKOR meeting? Just give me your opinion - as a diplomat."

"My opinion is that they would not like it. The Comintern is quite strict. There is only one legitimate Communist voice. They do not appreciate the idea of a group meeting without their authorization."

"Why wouldn't they simply disavow any connection."

"They would, if the matter ever came up."

"And have they endorsed this meeting? Are they sponsoring it? Speaking hypothetically, of course."

"No they have not endorsed it. They are not well pleased."

"Because? Why don't they like it? Good Communists have a meeting. So what? What's wrong with that?"

"It's wrong because the IKOR is behaving badly. Speaking hypothetically, it's possible that the Comintern has explicitly forbidden the IKOR from holding any more meetings. Moscow no longer supports them. They are rogue."

The Communists sent by Moscow to Spain had been committed to the struggle for control, not to the people of Spain or to the idea of a functioning socialist state. Their purpose had been to seize control of the nascent elected government of Spain in the name of the Soviet Union. They had betrayed and killed revolutionaries – good men, good soldiers – all under orders from Josef Stalin. Levitan despised them.

"So, what do you think the Soviet Union would do in such circumstances?"

"They would send somebody to the convention. Somebody who could deliver the message."

"Do you think so?"

"I am certain that's what they would do."

"I see. And what if the IKOR defied the man from Moscow?"

"From what I know about the IKOR, that's entirely likely," said Biernacki. "They are aggravating - a stubborn bunch of diehard idiots."

"And what would the man from Moscow do in such circumstances?"

"He would make sure they knew that their behavior would have consequences."

"They cancelled their meeting. Right in the middle of it. Two days early."

"They must have gotten the message," said Biernacki.

"And why would the man from Moscow kill the card player?"

"He would not. I can tell you, without any shadow of doubt, that he has no idea what you're talking about. Who was killed?"

"A man with lots of cash in his pocket."

Biernacki-Reshetnikov thought it over. "The Jews. It's always money with them, isn't it?"

"No. That's insulting. I am a Jew."

"I am not surprised."

"Now you've made me angry. I think you've just created a diplomatic incident."

"I apologize, Commodore. I meant it as a joke."

"I am not amused."

"I think it's time you let me call my embassy," said Biernacki.

"Check that with Captain Duplessis. Me, I'll inform the State Department to expect your letter of apology for violating travel rules, you prick. Goodbye."

§

Brixton was waiting for him Room 905. Out the window, the beach was emptying, the sunburned vacationers returning to their rented rooms to clean themselves up for supper.

"How did it go with the diplomat?" asked Brixton.

"He did come here to shut the IKOR down."

"That's why they cancelled their meeting?"

"That's what he thinks. But that's not it. You did it, John."

"Me? How did I do that?"

"Your agents came in yesterday and took names and addresses. Very subtle, John."

"The woman told you this?"

"Yep. As soon as the FBI showed up, the IKOR decided to call it quits. You spooked them."

"Well, so what? Good riddance. I don't mind at all. J. Edgar Hoover will say 'well done.' But this guy, the Russian, he thinks he shut them down?"

"That's what he thinks."

"What about Weber? What's Biernacki's connection?"

"I don't think he has one. He claims to know nothing about the murder. Of course, the man's a trained liar."

"Do you think he's the Russian, Reshetnikov?"

"Very possibly. Did you tell the Army that their Sergeant Koval has been sleeping with a Communist sympathizer?"

"Yes, we told them. We're trying to be good partners. We're telling them everything we know."

"Well, how did they react?"

"It's got them worried."

Levitan said, "Did you ask the Army whether Koval returned to base?"

"I asked. No. But he's on leave until Friday at midnight, so he might still report for duty. Let me ask you this – was he with the woman last night?"

"I didn't know how to ask that question," said Levitan. "I should be able to find out, though. I have a date with her tonight."

"Tonight? I want to question her today. Right now."

"I understand, John. But she's not hostile. She's either a terrific liar or completely unaware of the murder or Russian spies. If I were you, I'd treat her nicely."

"Why's that? Because she looks like a pinup girl?"

"She is something to look at," said Levitan. "Gorgeous, in my opinion. But I think she would want to be helpful. I don't see any reason to intimidate her... yet."

Brixton cocked his head and regarded the Commodore. "What's going on, Dave? You getting sweet on her?"

He did not reply.

"So I can't trust you. We'll come at her head on."

"Please don't. Trust my instincts on this, John. Judith Horowitz seems to be a decent woman with a problematic boyfriend."

"Or she's a murderer and a spy, and definitely a woman of low moral character."

"Fascinating woman, wouldn't you say? All of that could be true. But if she is merely a bystander, then she could give us our best chance to find Koval. Besides, she's not real pleased with George Koval right now. If I can gain her trust, I think she would be helpful."

Brixton knew that Levitan's unorthodox methods worked. In past cases, the gimpy Commodore had shown an instinct for finding the keys to the puzzles. Whatever it took – fists, money or charm – Levitan had gotten people to open up. But this gigolo approach was something new.

"I don't know, Dave."

"We have a date for a walk on The Boardwalk tonight. I don't believe that she knows anything about Weber's murder. As far as she's concerned, I'm a bureaucrat on vacation. She's probably still in touch with Koval. I think watching her undercover will give us our best chance to get him."

"What else did you find out from her?"

"She claims to be a hired stenographer, good at shorthand, known to them because she used to have a fiancée who was an IKOR member before the war. They're here, she says, to prepare their defense for the time when the Communist Party is outlawed. And also because their wives wanted to get together down the shore."

"Like a family gathering," said Brixton sarcastically.

"It would seem so," said Levitan.

"These people are weird."

"Not so much. You see them as a bunch of subversives, sneaking around, trying to overthrow the government. They see themselves as high-minded people committed to upholding a proud heritage, to staying alive, and to fighting injustice. After what the

Jews have been through, I think they're anything but weird."

"But they're Commies."

"They don't think that's a crime. To them, it's standing on the right side of history. Put yourself in their shoes."

"No thanks."

Levitan said, "But, about tonight. I want you to stay away from the woman. If we want to find Koval, I think using the woman as a lure is a good idea."

"A lure?"

"She's not easy to pass up, is she? He's been in her bed. They arranged to be together during this holiday week. For all we know, he's madly in love with her. And she with him, although she's sending signals that she's ready to drop him."

There was a knock on the door. It was one of Brixton's Agents. Levitan let him in. The man was clearly agitated.

"Mr. Brixton," said the Agent. "We just got word from Sioux City. About Koval."

"That was fast," said Brixton. "That's good work."

"But it's terrible news."

"Shit. What about him?"

"He emigrated to Russia in 1932."

"You've got to be kidding me. And we didn't know this?" said Brixton, stunned.

"I'm afraid not, sir. We were doing a whole lot of clearance investigations in 1943, as you'll recall. We followed standard operating procedures."

"Have a seat, Winston," said Brixton. "Dave, I'd like you to meet Special Agent Winston McCorry."

Levitan rose to shake McCorry's hand.

"The name on Koval's birth certificate is genuine," said McCorry, now seated. "His parents had a little farm just outside of Sioux City. When we went to the farmhouse, we found out that the place was sold in 1932. The current owner knows all about the Kovals."

"Goddamit. How could we miss this?"

"Like I said, sir. SOP. We just didn't have the resources to investigate that far back."

"That's just what The Director wants to hear. He's gonna love this!" said Brixton. "All right. Tell me what you know."

"Koval's father was a Russian immigrant. He came over in 1910. And get this, his mother was a big time Communist. They both were, both of his parents. And Georgey boy was one too; he was in a Communist Club in his high school. Then, in 1932, they all go back to Russia: Georgey, his parents, and his brother. That's all we know so far."

"That's enough. Jesus Christ," said Brixton "Could this be any worse? We gave this guy a Top Secret clearance, for godssake. Then the Army posts him to Oak Ridge!"

"Yes sir," said McCorry.

"Alright," said Brixton. "I want the whole damn Omaha office in Sioux City. Send a team from St. Louis, too. I want to know everything there is to know about the Kovals. And how did George Koval get back into the country? See if you can get Customs to search arrival records going back from when we know that he was in New York working for that telephone equipment company. What year was that?"

"1940 - *Raven Electric*."

"Alright," said Brixton. "Ask them to start in 1940 and work backwards to 1932. And send some people to *Raven Electric*. Jesus Christ. What a nightmare."

24

Thousands of people had taken to The Boardwalk on a pleasant evening in early September. The establishments that lined the landward side sold hot food, ice cream, souvenirs, imitation luxury items, kitchen gadgets, and fake antiques. Entertainment piers, spaced a few blocks apart on the seaward side, were like permanent State Fairs swarming with families. The electrified signs mounted on the flanks of the piers lit the night sky and glittered off the sea. Every now and then, as Levitan walked with Judith, he caught a whiff of mentholated sunburn balm.

She glowed with sunburn. She was wearing the same maroon dress, with the low-heeled white shoes and the white sweater she'd worn when she confronted him in the lobby of *The Breakers* forty-eight hours before. She wore lipstick, but no other makeup.

"How was dinner with your relatives?" she asked.

"It was fine. I got away as soon as I could."

"Who are they?"

He lied, "An aunt and uncle, and their kids, my cousins, and their kids. It was fine. But I didn't eat much. I wanted to save room in my stomach for The Boardwalk."

She said, "This *chazzerai*?" Yiddish for "pig feed".

"I love it," he said. "Hot dogs, French fries, frozen custard, popcorn, saltwater taffy. You name it and I'll eat it. I lived on this stuff when I worked here."

"You worked on The Boardwalk?"

"For a couple of years. I was a police patrolman, this was my beat."

"You were a cop?"

"Yep. Right here in Atlantic City. Then I was a detective. Then I got this job with the Coast Guard two years ago."

"A detective? Like Nero Wolfe?"

"More like Lieutenant Kramer, the dumb cop that Nero Wolfe is always explaining things to."

"Are you still a detective? For the Coast Guard?"

"You could say so. I do investigations for them."

"So you don't just look at invoices and bills of lading."

"Oh, I do, I do. And I talk to people. And I write reports. It's not glamorous, let me assure you. This place makes the best French fries. Come on, let me buy you some."

"Sure," she said.

They stood with a bunched crowd, eating the hot potatoes, watching a pitchman demonstrate the wonders of a chopping gadget, until there was nothing left in the paper cone but grease stains.

"So, your job is temporary," he said. "Do you have another one lined up for after the IKOR conference is over?"

"I have a regular job. I work for a Jewish social services agency in Midtown. I'll go back to work on Monday."

"Have you typed up everything from their conference already?"

"I haven't even started. I'll do that at night next week. I have a typewriter at home for that kind of work."

"You're a go-getter."

"That's me," she said. "So, do you ever get up to New York?"

"From time to time. Should I call you the next time I come up?"

"I wouldn't mind."

"What about George?"

"What about Helen?"

"You know, the ball's in her court. She knows where I am."

"Would you take her back?"

He said, "If she decides she wants me. But what about George? Tell me about him. What's his last name?"

"Koval."

"And he's in the Army."

"Right."

"But you don't know where he's stationed?"

"It's a secret. That's all I know about it. George never talks about it."

"Have you known him for a long time?"

"Since last Christmas."

Benches were installed along the beachside railing. He saw one vacant. "Let's sit for a spell," he said. "I'll show you how to spot pickpockets."

He explained that pickpockets work in pairs, timing their thefts so that the second thief can immediately receive the items taken by the first thief, who bumps into his targets where the crowds are thickest.

The FBI watchers were also paired, men in sport jackets without ties. He spotted one pair inside a souvenir stand, the other about fifty feet behind them, leaning against the railing.

"How did you meet George?" he asked.

She sighed. "It was a blind date. This friend of mine, Arlene Shapiro, the same one whose husband talked Comrade Savin into offering me this job, she set us up."

"So George is connected to the IKOR?"

"No. Nothing like that. George isn't political at all. He's just a soldier. He was on leave in New York last year and my friend Irene, who knows him from when they were in night school together, she knew that he was in town and looking for a date. So she thought of me – poor, sad Judith, the spinster."

"I can't imagine you that way. You don't seem sad to me."

"I have my moments. I was engaged to be married once. He was in medical school. Then he found someone else. And, just like that, ka-pow, it was over. I guess you could say I was pretty sad after that."

"He sounds like a real *shmuck*. This was last year?"

"No. We split up right around the time of Pearl Harbor. Then everybody went off to war, all the men. So, I didn't really go out much during the war. I didn't really want to, to tell you the truth. Then I met George."

"But you're having second thoughts about him, aren't you?"

"It's him who seems to be having second thoughts. He's been acting funny since he got here on Saturday. And then, yesterday, he just left. He said he had to get back to base. Some sort of emergency."

"That's too bad."

"It depends on how you look at it."

"What about the night before last? When you and I went out to *The Whichway*? You were by yourself that night too, weren't you?"

"I was. George all of a sudden told me that he was going out for drinks with an Army buddy. He said not to wait up for him. I told him not to bother knocking on my door when he came back."

"And then, yesterday, he just cuts his leave short and goes back to base?"

"Maybe. Or maybe that was just an excuse to say goodbye. Truthfully, I think I'm glad he's gone. He was really getting on my nerves."

"So he re-enlisted after the war?"

"He did. He likes The Army. He's in until '48 on a four-year hitch."

"He's Jewish?"

"Of course."

"Of course," he echoed. "Were you going to get married?"

"We were not officially engaged. But... you know..."

"I understand," he said. He doesn't, really. She seemed like a nice girl. Why would she agree to spend a week in a hotel room with a man without a commitment of marriage? He must have charmed the pants off her.

"I know, I know," she said, as if reading his thoughts. "But I haven't really seen that much of George. We only get together every couple of months or so, when he has enough leave to make a trip to New York worthwhile. Until a few months ago, when he had leave for the 4th of July, we weren't all that serious, if you know what I mean. I see it was a mistake. Boy, am I sorry."

"Well, it seems you're rid of him now."

"I don't know. I mean, he was in such a hurry to get back to base, we didn't have a chance to talk. I really don't know what's going on with him. He said he'd give me a call."

"Why don't you call him?"

"I don't have his number. It's a secret."

"What about his family? Have you met any of them? Where's he from?"

"From Brooklyn. His parents are dead and he's an only child. Nope... I have no way to get in touch with him. He's just gone."

"Well, good luck."

"Whatever that is. You know what I like?"

"What's that?"

"Frozen custard," she said. "Let's see if they have peach. I love peach ice cream."

During the war, The Boardwalk had been closed at night because of the blackout restrictions. Throughout the winter and spring of 1942, German submarines had used the glare of American coastal lights to silhouette their targets to devastating effect. Dozens of ships had been sunk close enough to the coastline that sailors who survived the attacks had been able to row to shore. Eighty ships went down, hundreds of merchant seamen died horrible deaths. Boardwalk hotels had been rented out to the Army Air Force as barracks for thirty-thousand men in training at the Convention Hall and the Pomona airfield. The Boardwalk had been patrolled by the Military Police. At night, the strolling soldiers and their girlfriends had nothing on which to spend their money. Now, the nighttime Boardwalk is much the way it had been before the war, a thronged promenade with people looking for ways to indulge their more wholesome appetites.

After they finished the frozen custard, he suggested that they leave The Boardwalk and find someplace to have a drink. Zoning regulations forbade saloons on The Boardwalk.

"I thought you didn't drink," she said.

"But you do."

"Are you trying to get me drunk?"

"Absolutely," he said.

At a booth in a crowded bar on Pacific Avenue, he ordered ginger ale, she a Sidecar.

"I thought cops were all Irish," she said. "You're the only Jewish cop I've ever heard of."

"Go figure. I needed a job. Helen's father has a lot of pull in this town. I met him after Helen and I started going out. He didn't like the idea of his daughter dating a bum, so he got me a slot in the Police Academy. And, it turns out, I liked it. So that's all there is to it."

"Suppose that didn't happen - what would you have done? What did you want to be when you grew up?"

"You know, I can't remember wanting to be anything. I never looked ahead very far. Kind of drifted along. I'd had a couple of sales jobs before I met Helen. But I'm not very good at selling stuff. I was lousy at closing – you know, getting people to sign on the dotted line. There's an art to it that I was never able to master."

"It sounds like you've got a great job with the Coast Guard."

"How about that? Yes. I like it a lot."

It was a noisy place, with people shouting to be heard above the din. The jukebox was playing *A Doin' a What Comes Naturally*, from *Annie Get Your Gun*. Their booth was across a narrow aisle from the bar, where one of the FBI watchers stood holding a beer.

"I have to tell you something," he said. "It's been bothering me. I haven't been completely honest with you… I'm not here for vacation."

"Oh? Really? Are you doing an investigation?"

"Yes, I am. I'm here helping the local cops on a murder."

"Wow," she said. "Like Sam Spade. Now I see it - you're Humphrey Bogart."

That made him laugh.

"Why did you tell me you were on vacation?"

"It's kind of a secret. The victim is involved with national security. I have to be careful."

"You and George. You and your secrets. Why can't I meet a normal person?"

"You can, I'm sure. But, I think, you made a really bad choice with George."

"I'm starting to think so myself. But you're nothing like him. You laugh. You make me laugh. It's hard to get George to smile."

"A serious fellow, is he?"

"Very. But he looks like Tyrone Power with a crew cut. What can I tell you?"

"An attractive man."

"I thought he was a catch. He only needs a few more credits to get a degree as a chemical engineer. That's why he's not an officer – he doesn't have a college degree. He's got a good future. But he's a jerk."

"Is that what he's doing for The Army? Chemistry?"

"I guess so, but I really don't know. I may never know. I don't think I care anymore."

"Maybe you shouldn't be so hasty. What if he comes back and hands you a diamond ring? What would you say then?"

"I'd say, 'Find some other girl to put it on'.'"

"Well, what if it really is an emergency? What if they need him for some really important work? Maybe he didn't have any choice. You can't blame him for that."

"That doesn't make him any less of a jerk. I made a mistake - this week was a bad idea. I see that now. On the other hand, I got to see his true colors. It's better I get it over with sooner rather than later - I've been down that road before. No. I'm done with George."

They left the bar after their drinks and walked back onto The Boardwalk to continue their stroll, heading northeast, upbeach, toward The Inlet. The Boardwalk crowd was mostly couples late in the evening, children having been taken to their rented beds. The honky-tonk thinned to nothing when they left the heart of the Boardwalk behind them, the electrified glare replaced by the softer light of street lamps burning gas.

They were at the tip of the island, where the shoreline bent sharply west. A jetty of quarried basalt rocks a quarter mile long protected the north shore. Far out, at the end of the jetty, he could just discern pale sea spray where a navigation beacon illuminated waves breaking on the rocks.

"I used to fish on this jetty," he said.

"You? Really. Did Helen come with you?"

"No. It's not her thing."

"I can understand that. The thought of killing fish doesn't appeal to me either."

"You throw a lot of them back. A lot of times, you don't catch anything at all."

"So you just sit around and wait. Sounds boring."

"I like being near the ocean. It's not just about the fish."

"That I can understand."

"Does George have any hobbies?"

She thought about it. "Not really. He reads the sports pages. He roots for *The Dodgers.*"

"You?" he asked.

"Me? *The Yankees.* You?"

"*The Phillies*, I'm sorry to say."

Who do you root for? He believed that people were born as tribal creatures, with an imperative to recognize their protectors from infancy, exquisitely sensitive to the most trivial differences between us. We acquire more tribal traits year by year, holiday by holiday, lover by lover, to become more like the people we trust. Could you really trust a *Yankees* fan?

The Boardwalk narrowed where it crossed over the base of the jetty, where the rolling chair lanes ended and the capitalized Boardwalk ceased and became just an ordinary small 'b' boardwalk. It bent to the left, following the placid shoreline of The Inlet. They walked slowly. There were clouds and it was warmer than when they had come along the same stretch the night before last, going in the opposite direction. The tide wais fully out; soon it would turn and the fish would start to feed.

"You know," she said, "I think I had a little too much sun. Can we take a jitney back to the hotel? I'm really tired all of a sudden."

Their watchers had been able to blend with the crowd. Here, there was more open space, making it harder for the FBI to follow without attracting Judith's attention.

"I think that's a good idea," he said.

They took the next ramp down to the sidewalk and crossed the street to wait for a jitney.

A silence came over them. Their mood, like the mist, was quiet.

The little jitney bus soon arrived. He consciously avoided meeting her eyes as they sat side by side on the ride back to the hotel. Were he to look into them, he thought, he would see a yearning there – poor, willing, spinster Judith.

Special Agent Winston McCorry, wearing the same business suit that he'd worn that afternoon on the patio, was sitting in a lobby easy chair reading a *LIFE* magazine. As Levitan and Judith entered, he rose and met them before they reached the elevator.

"Commodore," he said.

"Yes? McCorry is it?"

"Yes sir."

"What can I do for you?"

"Mister Brixton needs you."

"Judith," he said. "This is Mister McCorry, working late. He's involved with that investigation I was telling you about. It seems as if something must have happened."

"Yes sir," said McCorry, "There have been developments."

"Oh," said Judith.

"Give me a minute," he said to McCorry, and led her to the elevators.

"Judith, I have to say good night."

"I can see that."

"But, thank you. I had a nice time."

"Me too," she said.

"It's too bad that you're leaving tomorrow."

"Yes. But I've got a lot of work to do and my room's only paid for through tonight."

"Why don't we get together for breakfast tomorrow? I don't even have your phone number."

"That's true."

"And I'll give you mine," he said

"Well that'll be nice for a change."

"So? Breakfast?"

"Okay."

"What time?"

"Eight o'clock?"

"Great. I'll meet you at the hotel restaurant at eight."

The elevator arrived and she boarded.

"Sleep well," he said.

"You too," and she waggled her fingers as the doors closed.

He rejoined McCorry. The FBI Agent said, "There's no need for you to go up to your room.

Mister Brixton's been waiting for me to call him and let him know when you arrive. He'd like for you to wait for him here."

25

McCorry used the lobby phone to call upstairs. A few minutes later, Brixton emerged from the elevator, beckoned to Levitan, and headed toward the street-side doors. "Jesus," he said. "I thought you'd never get here. I was starting to think I'd have to go without you."

"What's going on?"

"We've been summoned to Pomona. General Groves wants to talk to us."

Levitan checked his watch as they got into the backseat of a waiting government car. It was after eleven o'clock. McCorry sat in the front seat next to the driver. The entrance to the Pomona airfield was a twenty minute drive from the hotel, the last mile would be through pine woods over a narrow road.

"Has Koval shown up?" asked Levitan, watching the sunburned pedestrians returning to their rooms.

"Still no sign of him. How'd you make out with the woman?"

"I still think she has nothing to do with this."

"Come on, Dave. She's been sleeping with a Russian Communist spy. And you're telling me she's innocent?"

"Pretty much. And she might hear from Koval. She says he left in a big hurry, claiming that he had been commanded back to his base to deal with some kind of emergency, but that he'd call her. She has no idea about the kind of work he does. He never even gave her his phone number. She knows he is on a secret project and that's it. I think she's a bystander with lousy taste in men."

"You seem to be getting along with her just fine."

"Like I said."

"How's Helen doing, by the way," asked Brixton. He'd been a guest at their wedding.

"I haven't talked to her in the last few days. I've been busy."

"Give her my regards, would you?"

"Will do," said Levitan, looking out into the darkness. "Did Groves say what the meeting is about?"

"He's been told about Koval's emigration to the Soviet Union. I'm assuming that did not come as good news."

"Tell me about Groves. What do you know about him?" Levitan asked.

"He's got as much clout in Washington as anybody in any branch of government. You've never heard of him?"

"I'm a civilian, remember."

"Okay. Leslie R. Groves was the officer who ran the project that got all the Army training bases upgraded and built after Congress opened the purse strings in 1940. After that, he was in charge of construction of the Pentagon, which he finished in sixteen months. Imagine! But what gives him the most clout is that he's been in charge of The Manhattan Project from the beginning.

"Manhattan is helluva big deal, the Government's most expensive, most secret program - and he's been the boss of the whole thing. He had to coordinate scientists and engineers from all of the Allied countries, to say nothing about the labor of over a hundred thousand workers. They built three complete towns in places where no infrastructure had existed before 1943. It's a major industry now, a totally new nuclear industry, that didn't exist four years ago. And Groves has been in charge of all of it from the beginning. The fact that he was able to keep it all secret until the end of the war is amazing, and it means that he obsesses over security. He can't be liking the possibility that Weber had been compromised, not at all. And he certainly can't be pleased about the fact one of his own is a Communist who used to live in the Soviet Union."

"Have you talked to Hoover?"

"Yeah. He wants us to cooperate with Groves, so I have to go. I'm to be the sacrificial lamb."

"I expect he'll have a little something to say to me, too," said Levitan. "But we need to forget about all that. That's what people in charge are for, to sort out the bullshit. Our job is to understand Weber's murder, and our prime suspect is missing. It would be useful to know why Koval is so important to them. What's he been doing at Oak Ridge? And what's his connection to Weber?"

The resort city was behind them. They turned off the four-lane road onto a narrower, unlit track built by the Army.

The Pomona airfield was a submarine-hunting base from which bomber crews patrolled the New Jersey and Delaware coasts. It had been middling farmland in the pitch-pine forest before the war. The base had been used as a test site for new-fangled electronics that can see in the dark to the far horizons.

The sentry must have been told to expect them; he raised the barricade as soon as Brixton showed his badge.

Groves' uniform – all of that fabric, the multi-colored campaign ribbons over his heart, all of that brass – was quite a piece of work. The overly air-conditioned command center he had commandeered was a divided space, half of it lit by shaded lamps on Groves' desk and in the corners, the other half illuminated by a fluorescent tube that cast blue light onto a conference table with chairs for six. Both halves were squared-away.

Groves led them to the conference table. Levitan and Brixton sat across from each other. The General, tight-lipped, said, "Weber's murder is bad enough. If Koval did it, it's a catastrophe. He lived in the Soviet Union for eight fucking years and nobody knew anything about it! How the hell could this happen?"

"We followed standard procedures," Brixton said. "There didn't seem any reason to check beyond the people we talked to. And we were getting thousands of requests from The Army to issue clearances in

1943, as you no doubt recall. We were under a lot of pressure to issue them and had nowhere near the manpower to check every man's complete history. We confirmed his birth certificate, talked to his classmates and neighbors, and cleared a thirty-year-old engineering student from Brooklyn. This is just one of those things."

"Goddamit," said Groves. "Well, if he's a Soviet agent, which he appears to be, he could not have been better placed."

"That bad?" asked Brixton.

"As bad as it can be. We sent him through special training and posted him to Oak Ridge in 1944. He is the ranking non-com in the labs – a Radiation Health and Safety Officer for godssake. Do you understand what that means?"

"Not exactly," said Brixton.

"He enforces the regulations for handling radioactive material. He travels to every facility at Oak Ridge. He understands the physics and the chemistry. He knows as much about our atomic program as any man alive. And you're telling me he's an enemy agent! Jesus God."

Levitan said, "He may just walk back to the labs at Oak Ridge assuming he's in the clear. He doesn't know what we know. He's not exactly missing - he's on authorized leave. There are other reasons he could have chosen to cut short his week in Atlantic City other than Bob Weber's murder. It could be that his romance had gone sour, and that's all there is to it."

"Do you really think that's so?" asked Groves.

Levitan, feeling sorry for his friend, said, "It's possible. The woman seems pleased that he left. But it's equally likely that he left for the same reason half the IKOR left town – the FBI showed up. Or he might have left because he saw a chance for a better way to spend his leave than with a serious woman who wants to plant cabbages and carry a rifle on a *kibbutz*. But here's the thing, when he does turn up, he could prove immensely valuable."

Groves leaned back in his swivel chair.

"Are you saying we can turn him?" said Brixton.

"We certainly ought to try," said Levitan. "What if he reports for duty at Oak Ridge on Saturday morning as if nothing has happened? He doesn't know that we're onto him. He left before we even knew who he was. I think, at this point, we have the edge on him."

"So what are you suggesting?"

"I'm saying that he can be looked at as an asset rather than a liability. He's got another two years to go on his hitch. Those would be years when the Soviet Union would be expecting him to provide them with atomic secrets. It would give us a chance to screw up their program. And he must have contacts here in the States. If we can find out who those people are without raising an alarm, we may be able to unravel their whole network."

"So? We just wait around for him to show up?"

"Not at all. Look for him, but tread quietly, if you know what I mean."

Groves and Brixton stared at Levitan.

"What are your other options?" he asked. "I might be able to find him myself. We have some things in common."

Groves said, "You're both Jewish. That's what you're saying, isn't it?"

"Yeah. It's a tribal thing," said Levitan.

FRIDAY

26

He was awakened by the telephone in his hotel room at seven o'clock in the morning. It was Helen.

"Hi Davey," she said. "It's me. Where have you been?"

"Just working," he said. He pulled the blanket off the bed and draped it over his naked shoulders with the phone to his ear. "This is a complicated case, and I've been off in all different directions. I'm sorry, Babe. I've been too busy to call."

"That's okay, then. As long as you're okay."

"It's good to hear your voice," he said. "How have you been? How's the job?"

"Which one?" she said.

"See. That's what I was afraid of – that you'd try to do too much. That you'll exhaust yourself. Tell me about it. What have you been doing?"

"Last night I worked at a little, local place. Like a little lounge. I was accompanying this crooner who wants to be Frank Sinatra."

"Please. Tell me he's ugly."

"Cute as a button, *mon cheri*."

"Wonderful," he said. "And what else?"

"The studio. You know, great musicians. These guys are a pleasure, a piece of cake after West Philadelphia High School Orchestra, let me tell you."

Helen became a music teacher in the Philadelphia school system after she graduated from Temple University. The club work started to happen during the summers, when word got around Atlantic City, where she lived with her parents, then with Dave, that she was available for spot work, to fill in between acts in the big rooms, playing in the bars and lounges where beverages sold at triple the prices charged in places without live music. It got to the point that she'd been able to work as the pretty piano player in any one of a half dozen Atlantic City nightspots whenever it suited her. And from there, word had spread to New York, where she showed up for recording sessions with friends she'd made over the summers.

"So, they're treating you well at the studio? It's working out."

"Too well, Davey. I'm really enjoying it."

"Well, good."

"You don't mean that."

"I do. It sounds like a great gig. I'm glad you're enjoying it. I really am. Of course I want you to come back, but I want you to be happy."

"I wish you weren't so nice about it."

"Me too," said Levitan.

"So? Has there been anything in the mail for us? About the adoption?"

"I haven't been home for almost a week, Babe. I don't know what's in our mail. I'm thinking you've decided to give up on that."

"I don't know what to do, Dave. I really don't."

"What if I said they'd found a kid for us. Suppose it was in this morning's mail. What then? You'd come rushing back to Philadelphia to raise a child? You can't have it both ways, my dear."

"But it's about you, too. Davey. What do you want me to do?"

"I want you to be as happy as you can possibly be. This is your choice, Helen."

"Maybe I wouldn't be such a good mother."

"Is that what this about?"

"A little bit."

"I think you'd be a great mother. He, or she, will be the luckiest kid in the world to have you for a mother."

"But I love the music,"

"I know, Helen. And that's a great thing too."

"I don't think I could do both," she said.

"It would be real hard, I know."

"Don't you need me, Davey?"

"I miss you all the time. Especially at night."

"This can't go on forever, can it?"

He said, "Probably not. At some point, it will either be over or it won't. We won't know until someone decides."

"I want you to decide," she said.

"But it's your decision," he said.

27

He liked room service. He liked his hotel room overlooking the sea and the empty morning beach. He was to meet Judith for breakfast at eight and with Brixton at the local IRS office at nine. He showered and wrapped a towel around his middle. He wiped a circle off the steamy mirror so that he could see to shave. As he worked the new blade across his cheeks, it occurred to him that he didn't mind being alone. He could live without her.

He spent fifteen minutes on his notes. His mission had changed. He'd been working to discover the killer's identity, now his focus was locating George Koval.

Koval must be an extraordinary individual, he thought. He'd obtained the trust of fanatically secretive government agencies both in Russia and the United States. What kind of man could master atomic engineering while convincing spymasters on both sides of his trustworthiness? How had he managed to do that? And why on earth had he felt compelled to strangle Bob Weber?

The phone rang. It was Brixton. "Pack your bag. We're going to Philly," he said.

"What happened?"

"Koval will be at *30th Street Station* at noon. He called the woman last night, after she got back to her room, and they set it up."

"How do you know this? Oh… silly question. You're eavesdropping on the hotel switchboard."

"You're damn right we are. So, if you want to be there, you'd best come downstairs now and we'll drive to Philly."

"I'm meeting her for breakfast," he said. "She can't be in two places at once."

"She told Koval that she would take the train leaving at ten-fifteen. He'll meet her at the station. What time are you supposed to meet her?"

"Eight o'clock. Let's see if she shows up. If she's there, keep your distance while I talk to her."

"This has got to stop, Dave. This is a bad woman."

"We don't have time for an argument, John. If she comes to the restaurant, leave us alone. Pick me up outside the hotel at eight-thirty. And don't approach her until I say so. We'll go in your car?"

"Like a bat out of hell," said Brixton.

"We should take the train, avoid the traffic."

"Why can't you ever do things my way?"

§

Judith was waiting for him at the hotel restaurant reception desk. They were shown to a table in the center of the busy room. They both ordered a toasted bagel - something else they had in common.

"Well," he said, taking the notebook and automatic pencil from his jacket pocket, "Here's my phone number." He wrote the number of his West

Philadelphia apartment, tore off the sheet of notepaper and handed it to her. She took it, folded it, opened her purse and dropped it in. Pencil poised, he asked "What's yours?"

She seemed distracted.

"Is something wrong?" he asked.

"George called me last night. Woke me up around midnight."

"So? What did he say?"

"He said he wants to ask me something."

"And you said?"

She shrugged.

"He didn't say he was sorry for leaving you stranded? For being a jerk?"

"He has something he wants to ask me. He says it's important."

"He wants to propose. Is that it?"

"Maybe."

"Well... I'm sorry to hear that. So I guess this is goodbye"

"No. I've had enough."

"Well, that's good news for me. For us."

She smiled and placed her hand on the white linen. He put his on hers. It was the first time he'd touched her, and it felt good.

"Yes," she said. "Good for us."

"So... it's over."

"Almost. I'm going to see him today and tell him."

"You didn't tell him last night?"

"I sort of did. But he thinks he can change my mind."

"He's back in Atlantic City?"

"No. Philadelphia."

"But you're going to New York."

"I can take the train from Philly. It's a couple of extra hours, but it'll be worth it. He has to understand that it's over once and for all."

"Why Philly?"

"He didn't say. I assume it has something to do with his big-secret project. I said I'd meet him at the train station and we'd go out for lunch. He said I should plan to stay over in Philly. I told him that was out of the question."

"Well, good for you."

"I suppose," she said.

"What time are you leaving?"

"There's a ten-fifteen train. He's going to meet me at *30th Street Station*."

"Would you like me to come with you?"

She laughed. "A knight gallant, are you?"

"At your service, my lady."

"Well, that would be a very bad idea," she said. "But it's nice of you to offer. I have to do this myself - in person, face to face."

"Well, you're right. I have work to do, anyway."

"Yes. Your mysterious murder. Sam Spade on the job."

He liked the sound of that. He smiled, "That's me. And I do have things to do." He took the napkin from his lap and put it on the table.

"Why can't I meet a man who's not keeping secrets?" she said.

He put down a five dollar bill and stood up. "You didn't give me your number."

"I'm in the phone book - Judith Horowitz, Holland Avenue, the Bronx."

"I'll call you," he said, resisting an urge to put his lips on her cheek.

§

The government car sat parked at the back of the taxi rank outside *The Breakers Hotel*. McCorry and the driver were in the front seat, Brixton alone in the back. Levitan got in next to him, but left the door open. He said, "I'm taking the train. I'll meet you at the station. Have you dispatched a squad?"

"Six men from the Philadelphia office are on their way to the station. The Army gave us a photo of Koval and we've made copies to hand out at *30th Street*. Which is why I have to be there. Let's go."

Levitan looked at the photograph, a head shot of a pleasant-looking dark-haired man with regular features: a dished nose, large and thoughtful wide-spaced eyes behind wire-frame glasses, a pronounced upper lip, and a sturdy neck.

He said, "Come with me on the train, it's faster and more reliable. And it will give us a chance to talk this over."

Brixton sighed. "Alright," he said. "We'll take the train."

§

The eight-forty-five train was three-quarters full. Brixton was in a seat by a window, Levitan next to him as the train rolled west across South Jersey's flatland of orchards and farms.

Levitan asked, "Does the Army know that Koval will be at the train station?"

"I didn't want to complicate matters any further."

"General Groves will be pissed."

"He'll have to talk to Hoover about that. Right now, things are moving a little too fast to try to coordinate operations with the Army. Besides, they're busy watching Reshetnikov."

"This little oversight could get you fired."

"So be it," said Brixton.

"Have your men in Iowa found out anything else about Koval?"

"Yes indeed. His family was involved with IKOR. Their emigration was handled by the Chicago chapter."

"Hot damn!" said Levitan. "So we have a connection between Koval and the IKOR other than the woman. This is very good information, John."

"But the Chicago chapter no longer exists. I don't know whether we can learn anything else about the emigration. More than likely, those eight years he spent in the Soviet Union will continue to be an unknown."

"Any word from Customs about his re-entry?"

"Get serious," said Brixton "They probably haven't started looking yet. It could take them months. Don't hold your breath."

"I suppose you talked to people in Sioux City who knew the family."

"We're working on it. We have learned that the Kovals wanted other families to come with them, but there were no takers. So, off they went and nobody's heard a word from them since."

"What about George Koval personally. What were you able to find out?"

"Not much more than we already knew. He was an outstanding student who was active in the Communist Party, a member of Iowa's *Young Communist League*."

"What else?"

"What we get is that young George was well-liked, an all-around guy."

"He was nineteen years old when they left. Did he have a job? Was he in college?"

"It seems that he worked in his mother's grocery store and that was it. They were poor - their land wasn't much and the mother supplemented their farm income with a little corner grocery in town. It turns out that there are a quite a few Jews in Sioux City."

The only Jews Levitan knew were East Coast city people, like himself. "Really? Who knew? Synagogues in Sioux City!"

"Yeah, but the Kovals didn't belong to any of them - godless Communists, I suppose. But, they were involved with the community even if they didn't belong to a synagogue. A couple of people remember his mother from her pestering them about emigrating to Russia and handing out Communist literature. As for George, he was President of his high school's

Young Communist chapter. He was on the debate team and the shortstop on the baseball team."

Levitan said, "So he's a good athlete. And a debater. Sounds like quite a guy."

"And a ladies' man," added Brixton. "The women remember him well. This Horowitz woman is at his beck and call, and she's some woman."

"I have another name for you to check out," said Levitan. "She's the friend who set Judith and Koval up on a blind date last year. Her name's Arlene Shapiro. She was the same person who suggested Judith as the recording secretary for the conference. I'm guessing she lives in the Bronx. I think she may be married to an IKOR member. Is there a Shapiro in attendance?"

Brixton extracted a folder from his briefcase and checked the list of IKOR attendees. "Bingo," he said. "Jeffrey Shapiro."

"According to Judith, Arlene Shapiro was a classmate of Koval's at CCNY and knew that he was in New York on leave and looking for date. That's how she met him."

Brixton wrote down the name, "You could have told me about this last night," he said.

"It slipped my mind, what with being a little bit distracted by General Groves. Have you got people looking for him in Tennessee?"

"We're watching train stations in Washington and Knoxville. He'll have to change trains in Washington. But it looks like we can grab him in Philly before he even starts south."

"Are you sure that's a good idea?"

"A bird in the hand, Dave. We can't let this son of a bitch get away."

"But what if you could turn him into a double-agent?"

"You mean a triple-agent, don't you."

"This is a talented man, John."

"And a murderer.

"Maybe he thinks he's a soldier," said Levitan.

"You mean killing Weber was his duty?"

"Could be. Truthfully, we don't know what his motive was, do we?"

"How about removing a top scientist from the atomic bomb program? Isn't that motive enough?"

"Perhaps. But it attracted an awful lot of attention. He's a deep-cover espionage agent in a sensitive and scrutinized position. I would think that he'd want to avoid anything that might attract attention."

"I guess we'll find out when we have him in custody."

"What about the woman?."

"Her too."

Brixton turned his head to look out the window, ending the conversation. The train stopped in Camden to pick up passengers before crossing the suspension bridge to Philadelphia. He enjoyed the view from the crown of the bridge, the familiar docks, wharves, and warehouses lining the banks on either side of the mile-wide Delaware where he plied his trade.

28

The city of Philadelphia was established on the land between two rivers: the mighty Delaware, named for an English lord, and the smaller Schuylkill, dubbed by the Dutch who'd maintained a struggling colony in the swampland where the rivers converged seventy years before the English took over late in the 17th Century.

In the early 1800s, a great steam engine used to pump Schuylkill river water to the heights overlooking Philadelphia, to the top of the hill called Fairmount. It had been a marvel of steam technology - a filthy, coal-fired contraption enclosed within a Greek temple. In 1946, the old pump was long gone, the small temple's columns now enclosed a public aquarium. Gone too were the water tanks atop the hill. The Museum of Art, a yellow sandstone replica of the Parthenon covered the summit.

Across the Schuylkill, on a lesser hill, was *30th Street Station*, the main junction of *The Pennsylvania Railroad*. The architects had failed in their attempt to imitate the elegance of the temples across the river, the station's columns were ill-spaced and graceless. But the inside, rendered in the same golden stone as the museum's exterior, was a vast *art deco* rectangle under a soaring ceiling. At platforms underneath the station concourse, trains left and returned from Atlantic City every half-hour.

Levitan and Brixton came up on the escalator to the concourse. They both knew the station well; Levitan used the trains to get to port facilities in Baltimore, Wilmington and Trenton; Brixton used them to get to Washington and New York. The schedule of trains was displayed on a flip board above a circular information booth in the middle of the expanse. Judith's train would arrive on Track 4 in an hour.

Levitan immediately recognized the FBI contingent – they carried no luggage, wore dark suits, and stood together near the information booth in the middle of the concourse. Brixton motioned for them to follow him into a side hall, a banquet-sized room with phone booths on the back wall.

Brixton handed out the copies of Koval's Army photograph. He deployed his men, scattering them in three pairs to watch the entrances. They were to maintain visual contact with each other, converge on Koval and Horowitz when they met, then apprehend both of them before they could exit to a commuter train, a bus, a taxi, or a car parked in the underground garage. Brixton stationed himself with McCorry in the side hall so that he could easily get to a telephone. Levitan took up a position inside a little shop, a newsstand, on the other side of the concourse with a good line of sight to the stairway to the platform used by the Atlantic City trains.

At eleven-forty-seven, Judith Horowitz, carrying a small suitcase, arrived with several dozen other passengers. She checked the big clock over the information booth, looked around, and went to a bench to wait for George. She took a paperback book from her purse and read. She looked up and checked the time every few minutes. When the hands came together at noon, she stood to look around, and sat back down.

At five minutes after twelve she closed her book, put it in her purse. She crossed and uncrossed her legs, stood, looked around, sat again. At ten minutes after twelve, she stood once more and fixed her eyes on the ticket booths opposite the newsstand. Levitan assumed her patience had been exhausted and she intended to buy a ticket to New York.

Two FBI agents moved in her direction.

She looked over at the shop on her way to the ticket counter. She paused, and started walking toward him; perhaps she wanted a candy bar or another paperback to read on the journey north.

Levitan hid behind a shoulder-high, spinning rack of magazines.

Another pair of FBI agents were taking long strides toward the woman.

She was looking into the newsstand. She slowed, looked puzzled, stopped, frowned. She'd seen him. She continued toward him. She stood outside the little store, staring at him.

George Koval entered the station through double doors on the east side of the concourse. The FBI agents, intent on Judith, missed his entrance. Judith was only a few steps away. The FBI would have her in custody within a few seconds. Koval, scanning dangerous territory, stood a few feet inside the station entrance, saw Judith standing outside the newsstand, and the four men in dark suits heading in her direction. He pivoted and pushed back through the door.

Levitan gave chase.

"Dave! What!..." she said as he rushed past her.

He burst through the doorway and saw Koval a little ahead of him, approaching the first cab in the row.

"George!" shouted Levitan. "Stop!"

Koval looked over his shoulder, saw Levitan, and took off running.

Levitan was fast, Koval faster. But the streets and sidewalks outside the station were congested. Koval made the mistake of running southward, toward Market Street, the busiest street in the city, where six lanes of traffic were moving too fast for him to dare crossing. He veered to his left, but found the 30th Street traffic, backed up to enter the station, equally daunting. Unsure of which way to run, he slowed and looked behind him and saw that Levitan was too close to evade. He decided to stand and fight. Levitan reached into his jacket pockets, grabbed the dimes, stepped forward, and launched an uppercut.

The trick to knocking someone out is to connect to the chin with sudden, concentrated force. The dimes multiply the power of the blow. If the punch connects, the fist has the effect of a mallet, the opponent's jelly brain overloads for an instant in response to the shock of the punch before it smacks against the bone of the skull. An uppercut has the added advantage of being unseen, so that the opponent's neck and shoulder muscles are not clenched in anticipation of the blow.

George Koval's head snapped back and the lights went out; he collapsed, face down, onto the concrete sidewalk like a sack of meat.

29

Philadelphia police radio cars were referred to as *red cars* because they were painted like fire engines. One of them led a motorcade followed by a paddy wagon with George Koval and Judith Horowitz inside, followed by three sedans occupied by FBI agents. Levitan and Brixton sat in the passenger seat of the last car of the procession. The red car, bubble light flashing, siren wailing, cut a path for them through downtown traffic.

When they arrived at the Federal Courthouse at 2nd and Race, Levitan could tell by Koval's posture, as the FBI escorted him into the building through the side entrance, that the man was still dazed by the knockout blow he'd suffered from Levitan's loaded fist. Too, his life had changed dramatically while he was unconscious. He was a Soviet spy who'd been undercover since 1940, who was suddenly in the custody of the American Government. One moment he'd been in a train station, and the next he was regaining consciousness and being marched to a jail cell, a stunning turn of events.

Judith was furious, her posture taut, her jaw clenched. She shot Levitan a lethal look as she walked past him in handcuffs.

"We'll slap Federal charges on them, but I want a Judge in on this," Brixton said.

"Now?" said Levitan.

"The sooner the better. I'm calling Judge Stacy. Remember him?"

Agents had Koval empty his pockets. They took Judith's handbag and suitcase. The captives were escorted down a stairway to the basement lockup. Among Koval's items was a key for a room at *The Benjamin Franklin Hotel* on 7th Street. Brixton dispatched a pair of agents to go there and bring back everything they found.

The Judge had chambers in a study behind a courtroom. Waiting for him, Brixton said "What I want is ruling that gives me jurisdiction over the prisoners."

"You have them. What more do you need?"

"Koval is in the Army. They can claim him, there's no doubt about that. I'd much prefer that he stay in the custody of the FBI. The Army would swallow him up and we'd get nothing. I want Judge Stacy to rule that the Army has to wait until we say they can have him. I think the Judge will go for it; he and Hoover are old pals."

Phillip Stacy of the Federal District Court for Eastern Pennsylvania was a Philadelphia Quaker who lunched at the Union League. Two years before, Stacy had authorized the warrants Levitan requested to aid his investigation of a Nazi spy, a man Levitan had identified during his work on the murder of a soldier in Atlantic City. It had been Levitan's final case with the ACPD and the beginning of his association with John Brixton, the FBI, and the US Coast Guard.

Stacy walked in wearing his black robe. "I'm in court, Mister Brixton. Make it snappy – and it better be worth my time. Mister Levitan," he said. "I didn't realize the Coast Guard was involved."

"Agent Brixton asked me to liaise with the Atlantic City Police, Your Honor. This business started out as a murder investigation."

"That sounds familiar. Alright," Stacy said. "Let me hear it."

After Levitan summarized the case, the Judge said, "So you're telling me that you have no hard evidence linking these people with Professor Weber's murder. Everything you've told me is circumstantial."

"That's right, Your Honor," Levitan said. "But it's compelling. He's a chemical engineer in charge of lab safety at Oak Ridge. He was registered as a guest in the same hotel where Weber played cards on the day he was killed. Weber was seen talking to him. He's a Russian. George Koval left for the Soviet Union with his parents' family in 1932 and then reappeared in New York and New Jersey in 1940. We're almost certain that he's a Soviet agent."

"Does the FBI have evidence that he's a spy?" the Judge asked.

Brixton said, "What more do you need? Just let us interrogate him and we'll fill in the gaps."

"I have a concern about the atomic science. Are you qualified to interrogate him?"

Brixton replied, "It's about the espionage network first, Your Honor. We need to start working on that immediately. At the moment, the Communists don't know that he's in our custody. The sooner we crack these two, the better. We might be able to destroy the entire Soviet spy apparatus in America if we can act quickly."

Stacy asked, "What's the Coast Guard's concern?"

"The Admiral has no stake in this, sir. I'm just helping out."

"So The Government has an espionage concern *and* a scientific concern, is that right, Mister Brixton?"

"Yes sir," said Brixton. "But we need to focus on first things first. We'll turn these two over to the Army scientists once we know how they operate. But the Government's priority has to be their network. And we need to start right now."

"And the ACPD needs to build a case for murder?"

"Yes, Your Honor," said Levitan.

"Alright," said the Judge. "The Army's not going to be happy about this. They will raise hell. You've put me in the middle of a holy mess, let me tell you. I can see it coming - this case is going to go all the way to The President. Here's what I'm prepared to do. I'll talk to the Attorney General and explain the priorities. It will be him who has to fend off The Army - not me. In the meanwhile, what are the charges against them?"

"Espionage," said Brixton.

"And murder, pending extradition to Atlantic City," added Levitan.

"Okay. If anyone asks this Court for a ruling, I'll rule in your favor. The espionage charge has precedence."

"Thank you, Judge," said Brixton.

§

Brixton led Levitan to the attorneys' lounge on the third floor of the court house, a spacious room with low tables. They sat in a facing pair of upholstered wing chairs.

"I want to question him," said Levitan.

"Dream on," replied Brixton.

"Listen to me, I know these people better than you or any of your agents. Before you go in with Koval, let me talk to him. Let me try to gain his trust. And the woman... We are friends... sort of."

"Friends? You just got her arrested. Do you really think she considers you a friend?"

"In a way, I do. I like her. And I respect her. And, until a little while ago, she liked me. She may have nothing to do with any of this. Or, she may be the one behind everything. I don't know. Probably, it's something in between. But I think I know how to talk to her."

Brixton valued Levitan's judgment. During the cases in which they'd collaborated over the previous two years, Levitan's insights had proven crucial. Too, Levitan's flexibility, the way he understood the motives of the people involved in their cases, was unusual. In Brixton's circle of G-Men, there was an unimaginative style of interrogation, a method drilled into them at Quantico. Levitan was different, somehow able to turn the locks that people use to keep their secrets.

Aside from all of that, in this particular case, Levitan could claim standing based on his assigned role; The Army, The Coast Guard, and the FBI had given him their full authority. He could claim top dog status. He'd discovered a connection between the victim and a Communist group. He'd identified the suspects. He'd captured Koval. So, for these reasons, and because he had Top Secret clearance, and because Levitan was his friend, Brixton relented - the Commodore would interrogate the captives.

30

He entered the interrogation room and sat opposite Master Sergeant George Koval, whose right wrist was handcuffed to a ringbolt in a table leg. A microphone sat on the table connected with wires to a speaker in a nearby office, where Brixton sat with two Agents, each of the three with a legal pad and pencil, transcribing the confession of a murdering spy.

Levitan was aware that he represented the Government of The United States of America. Ideally, the spy would provide the Russians with false information. Other results would be far less valuable to The Government. If Koval returned to Oak Ridge before his Russian handlers suspected that he'd been compromised, his value could be incalculable.

Koval was a fit, handsome man - a soldier in his prime. He was dressed in a summer-weight sport jacket, blue trousers, and brown shoes. He looked as if he could still do okay on the baseball field.

"How are you feeling?" Levitan asked.

Koval stared back, slack-faced.

"Glad to hear it. Can we get you anything? A cup of coffee? A soda?"

Koval did not reply.

"I am Commodore David Levitan. I am a civilian investigator working for The United States Coast Guard. I must urge you to tell me the truth… right here, right now. I promise you, you won't get another chance. The Army and the FBI want you for espionage and treason. You wear an American Army uniform that you've betrayed. The Atlantic City Police have you on a murder charge for which you will be sentenced to the electric chair. There has never been a man in deeper trouble than you… right here, right now. Tell me that you understand," said Levitan.

They looked at each other, two Jewish American men born in the year 1913, as different as they were alike.

Levitan said, "We know that you spent the years between 1932 and 1940 in the Soviet Union. You cannot deny it. We have no doubt whatsoever that you spy for the Russians."

He watched the Sergeant as he absorbed the information. The wheels were turning. At length, Koval nodded, very slightly.

Levitan repeated, "Tell me that you understand."

"I do," said Koval.

"And I know about the IKOR, The *Idishe Kolonizatsie Organizatsie in Rusland,*" said Levitan. "I met two of them in Spain when I was soldiering in the Lincoln Brigade. I am Jewish. I understand why your family went back to Russia. If there is anyone in this government who might have any inkling whatsoever of who you are, it's me." He added, "The only way this can go well for you is if you cooperate with me - personally. What's it going to be?"

Koval said nothing.

"Time counts against you. America wants to feast on your bones. The hounds are outside this door right now."

Koval said. "Let them loose. I don't scare."

"If you talk to me, you could be spared a world of pain. There's absolutely no point in withholding anything at all. The sooner you talk to us, the better it will be. Remaining silent will only give your interrogators cause to torture you."

Koval said, "I can be of great value to America."

"No doubt," said Levitan. "But that would depend on whether you could be trusted."

Koval surprised Levitan by smiling. Then he chuckled, shaking his head. And then he laughed. Were he not chained to the table, he would have been rolling on the floor. "That's a good one," he said. And then he allowed himself a final laugh, savoring the joke.

Levitan regarded Koval's laughter as instability. He had no doubt that Koval was cold and calculating – his duplicity must have required tremendous resolve – but even a master spy would be knocked off balance by a murder and its aftermath. And his behavior toward Judith since Saturday night had been erratic, completely unexpected by her, as if the person who'd showed up for a week of sex at the seashore was not the person she'd allowed into her bed earlier in the summer.

Levitan stared at Koval, who returned the look. If ever there was a man caught between a rock and a hard place, it was George Koval. But he was certainly smart enough to realize that he had great value as a double spy. Levitan, despite his loathing for the man's deeds, understood that a Koval working for the United States was worth far more than a Koval carcass.

Koval nodded. "Okay. Let's do it."

"Let's try. No bullshit. Everything straight and true."

"I said okay. Ask away."

"We'll see," said Levitan. "Who is your handler?"

"I have three ways to communicate with Moscow. I have a telephone number in Washington that I can call in an extreme emergency, but I've never made a call, There's a restaurant in Knoxville, and a man in Hoboken, New Jersey named Bannerman. He's the lab director at *Raven Electric Company* where I worked before the war."

Levitan tore off a notebook page and handed it and a pen to Koval. "Write down the Washington number."

Without hesitation, Koval wrote the number and slid the page back to the Commodore.

"And the restaurant?"

"*Joyners Restaurant* in Knoxville. It's next door to the *Andrew Jackson Hotel* and only a few blocks from the train station. We're not allowed to take anything from the labs, not even a scrap of paper. So, when the time comes for me to provide a report, I write one out by hand at a hotel where I stay in town. I take leave, take a room in the hotel, and spend a day or two writing the report. Then I go to *Joyners*.

"I make sure I take a table serviced by a waiter with two red pens in his shirt pocket. That's my signal. He is someone named Earl. If Earl is replaced, it will be by someone who will also keep two red pens in his shirt pocket. So far, it's only been the one man. I order a meal and leave the report on the chair. I take nothing out of Oak Ridge but what's in my head. I suppose you could say Earl is my handler, but he works for Bannerman."

Levitan said, "And Earl conveys your instructions?"

"When he puts the tab on the table, he leaves other pages from his pad with questions on them. I answer the question in my next report. It's a very simple system, as it should be. I don't know whether there's anyone else in the restaurant who is connected to Moscow, but I'm sure you'll verify that."

"How often do you write the reports."

"I keep it to a minimum. Every couple of months, sometimes more, sometimes less."

"So you don't make appointments?"

"No, that would be foolish. I do it when I feel I can, and I do it as infrequently as possible."

"Tell me about Bannerman."

"*Raven* is a Soviet front. Bannerman is my escape hatch. If the time ever comes when I have to, I will go to New York, call Bannerman in Hoboken, tell him where to meet me, and he will bring me enough cash and whatever else I might need to effect my disappearance. Most likely, I will be given a seaman's berth on a freighter, but I might choose another method. Everything is always up to me. I prefer to keep things as simple as possible."

"What have you told them? How much of the atomic program have you given away?"

"As little as possible."

"Really? Why? Why not as much as possible?"

"Insurance. I've been working on a plutonium trigger - a very big deal. I want to have value when I return to the Soviet Union. I've given them enough to keep them satisfied, just hints, but no more. I have omitted things in some of the formulae. When I go back, I want to keep doing the science."

Levitan's mathematical training had ended with elementary algebra; he was not qualified to determine whether Koval was lying. The man seemed willing to go down the scientific paths, but that would have been a waste of his time. He would leave it to the people who knew what Koval was talking about. But the fact of the matter was that Koval was willing to deceive his Russian masters as well as the US Army.

Now he understood Koval's laughter. Trust him? What a joke.

Brixton, scribing in the next room, must have been happy. In ten minutes, Koval had given up three connections to the GRU.

"What else can you tell me about your network."

"That's about it. We can talk about Bannerman, if you'd like. He's a lousy chemist, I can tell you that."

"First, talk to me about Bob Weber. You were the last man to be seen with him, and that was less than an hour before you killed him."

Koval tightened, looked inward, blinked, and said, "He recognized me, and I mishandled it. At the time, I didn't think I had any choice. I knew that he was obligated to inform Army Intelligence that he'd seen me with a group of pro-Soviet Communists."

Koval's speech was even-toned and thoughtful. He said, "I'd come for a vacation with my girlfriend. I caught an earlier train from Washington to Philadelphia and arrived in Atlantic City an hour sooner than I had expected. I had planned to meet her in the lobby at six. When I checked in, I saw the IKOR schedule on the notice board near the elevator, that their meeting was scheduled to break up at 5 PM. So I went to my room, dropped my suitcase on the bed, and decided to surprise my girlfriend by starting our holiday an hour early. I took the elevator to the mezzanine, hoping I'd catch her at five." Koval shook his head. "I don't usually do that." he said.

"Do what?"

"Act on a whim. I should have known better. Idiot."

"All right," said Levitan. "Tell me about what happened."

Koval took a deep breath. "Right on schedule, at a couple of minutes before five, the attendees came out of the *Vineland Room*. Judith was the first one to leave, carrying a stack of folders. I was really glad to see her. I'd been looking forward to it for weeks. I said, 'I got an earlier train,' and gave her a kiss. And she was real glad to see me.

"Then everything went crazy. One of the IKOR men came up to her, saying that he wanted to make sure that she had properly recorded something he'd said in the meting. Then, all of a sudden, I was surrounded by the whole damned meeting, as if they all wanted to make sure that the man who was confronting Judith wasn't trying to pull some kind of fast one. So there I stood, surrounded by Communists. That, by itself, wasn't good. And that's when I saw Bob Weber. He was standing at the doorway to one of the other meeting rooms, looking in my direction. So I just left, hoping he hadn't recognized me."

"Would he recognize you? How well did you know him?"

"Very well. We had worked on some of the same test projects, but on different teams. I'd been in a couple of meetings with him. My team's job was to measure radiation and then compare the results with Weber's equations, testing the metals. We had only the tiniest quantities to work with at first, micrograms of polonium, uranium 237, and plutonium extracted from millions of tons of ore. Yes, we knew each other. We'd been inside the same bunker at the Alamogordo test. But I hadn't seen him in over a year."

"Do you have any connection to the IKOR? Did you know any of the men who came out of the meeting?"

Koval said, "No. Well, not directly. I know Judith who's working for them this week. And we have a mutual friend, the woman who introduced us, Irene

Shapiro. Her husband is one of the attendees. But neither of them have any idea who I am."

"And that's it? You have no connection to IKOR?"

"Not anymore, not since they arranged my family's emigration to Birobidzhan in 1932, but I have no connection to them now. I knew Judith took a job with them. But I should never have gone anywhere near them - I realize that now. It wasn't even a miscalculation, I hadn't even considered it as a possibility. I acted on the spur of the moment... stupidly. But I wanted to see my girlfriend."

"How do you know Irene Shapiro if you're not connected to IKOR?"

"We were classmates at CCNY. One night, I noticed her reading *The Daily Worker* as we waited for class to start. I asked her if I could have a look at her copy when she was finished with it. And after that, we started talking. She is a good lady to know, a *shadkhin*. She has the phone numbers of all the nice Jewish girls from the Bronx who are looking for husbands. When I take leave in New York, I give her a call and ask her to introduce me to girls. That's how I met Judith... through Irene."

"Did you know her husband was IKOR?"

"She'd mentioned it once, that they used to belong. But that didn't matter. I thought they were defunct, that she was talking history."

"She knew about you?"

"Not at all. She thought I was from Brooklyn."

"Are the IKOR people Soviet agents?"

"That could be. But the apparatus is compartmentalized, so I don't know. I wouldn't be surprised," said Koval.

"All right," said Levitan, "So you saw Bob Weber and Bob Weber saw you. Then what happened?"

"He followed me down from the mezzanine, blocked me on the stairs to the lobby, stood in front of me. He said, 'Aren't you George Koval from the mountains?' I should have said, 'Hey Bob Weber fancy meeting you here.' But I didn't. Instead, I said, 'Sorry,' and I tried to get around him. And he said, 'Amazing. You look just like this guy I know. Exactly.' I said, 'That happens,' and went past him.

"But then I realized my mistake. I turned around at the bottom of the stairs, intending to go back and say, 'Sorry Bob. Security you know. You startled me that's all. You know how it is. How are you? What are you doing here?' But I didn't get a chance because Weber had turned around and he was heading up the stairs. I was concerned that it would prey on his mind, so I followed him up the stairs to correct my error. That's when I saw him talking to the IKOR."

Koval's hands were folded on the tabletop. Levitan was captivated by the spy's manner, his perfectly formed American sentences that flowed as if released from a bottle, as if pouring out his secrets satisfied a long-felt need.

Koval said, "Weber had seen me with Judith and with a group of Communists. That was very bad. Making it worse was that he was talking to them too, as if he already knew who they were.

"You couldn't just let it slide?"

Koval said, "The intelligence people control us. A lot of people at Oak Ridge are paid informants. It's part of the security apparatus, to make us unsure of the people we work with. The regulations are strict. Army Intelligence preaches at us all the time: we can't mention Oak Ridge or anything having to do with the work. Everything must be kept secret from everyone, even from wives and husbands. We are to report vague suspicions about anyone who might be trying to penetrate security. Intelligence officers interview us at least once a month, just to keep us on our toes. Weber had been trained, just as I had been, to inform the authorities that he'd seen an Oak Ridge scientist standing with a bunch of Commies. Also, I thought it was possible that he was there under someone's orders, that he might be there officially, that it might have something to do with me. In either case, it was troubling in the extreme. When I saw him go back up the stairs and talk to the IKOR people, I knew that I was in serious, serious trouble. Even if his being there was only a coincidence, he would have ruined everything.

"I didn't know what to make of it. I guess I was stunned. Maybe I panicked. I went down to the lobby. I was by the elevator and I looked across the lobby to the stairs, and there he was, starting to come down, so I ducked into an alcove to the bathrooms before he saw me. Then I peeked out and saw him standing in the middle of the lobby, looking around, looking for me. I stayed in the alcove. When I looked out again, I saw him walking out the front doors to The Boardwalk. So I went after him."

"So that's when you decided to kill him."

"I don't think it occurred to me, actually. I just didn't want to let him out of my sight. I mean, it had been so unexpected, so... out of context. Why was he there? Would you tell me? Was he there for me? Had he been sent? I didn't know. I needed to know. I still don't know."

"He'd come to play cards. He was leaving a card room when he saw you on the mezzanine."

Koval said nothing. He sat, distracted.

The ticking of the wall clock was the only sound in the room.

Koval said, "So? It was an accident?"

"Pure coincidence," said Levitan.

"My God, that's sad," said Koval.

"Finish the story."

"I followed him, staying as far back as possible, stayed small, but I think he spotted me anyway. He kept looking behind him. He kept stopping to look at postcards, but not really. Then he climbed up onto the railing by the beach and looked back, looking for me. I think he spotted me. Whether he did or not, the fact that he was looking for me meant that he was going to report what he'd seen – Sergeant Koval with a bunch Communists."

"So that's when you decided to kill him."

"No. I don't think so. It just sort of happened accidentally."

Levitan said, "An accident? Please."

"Well, I wasn't planning anything. When he left The Boardwalk and walked down the ramp to the entrance of *The Traymore*, I followed. But he wasn't in the lobby; he must have walked right into an elevator. I went to the front desk and said I wanted to call a guest room please, to use the house phone. So the clerk told me that Bob Weber was in Room 803. I took the elevator to the eighth floor and stood at the door."

Koval paused. Until then, he'd been fluent. Levitan waited. Koval stiffened, his shoulders hunched.

"How did you get into his room?" Levitan asked again.

Speaking more slowly, he said, "I put my ear to the door and I heard his voice, like he was on the phone, placing a call through the switchboard, not wasting any time informing on me. I knocked. He said, 'Who is it?' I said, 'Maintenance. Hotel maintenance.' He said, 'What do you want?' I said, 'I need to check your pipes. There's a leak downstairs.' 'Everything's okay in here,' he said. So I said, 'Sorry... I gotta check... Water's pouring into the room below yours...'

"He didn't say anything. I said, 'I can unlock the door if I have to. It's better if I don't have to. Sir? Please let me in. This is an emergency.'

"When I saw the doorknob begin to turn, I used my shoulder and pushed the door as hard as I could. It caught him by surprise."

Levitan heard voices in the hallway, then a quick knock on the door, and John Brixton stepped into the interrogation room. "Let's have a word," he said.

Levitan shot Brixton an angry look, letting him know that he resented the interruption.

"Outside. We need to talk."

Frustrated, Levitan with his eyes locked on Koval's, rose from the table and followed Brixton out of the room, into the hallway, and into the next room, where Brixton, McCorry and another Agent had been listening to the conversation over a desktop loudspeaker.

Levitan said, "Dammit, John. What now?"

"They're overturning the Judge's decision."

"That was fast," said Levitan.

"I told you. This is coming from very high. We have to back off."

"Says who?"

"Says J. Edgar Hoover, my boss."

"I don't work for him. I told you that. When this whole business started, when we were standing together in front of *The Traymore Hotel*, I told you that I only take orders from Admiral Tom Spiegel. I am not backing off."

"It's not your call," said Brixton. "Or mine. This is the Attorney General, who answers only to The President, telling the Director of the FBI to back off. Koval belongs to the Army."

"I have to get in touch with the Admiral," said Levitan.

"But no one is to speak to Koval until the Army collects him. Am I clear?"

"The President? Harry Truman is making this call? Do you know that?"

"Yes. So I've been told."

"All right. Who's going to watch Koval until the Army arrives?"

"We'll put him in a cell downstairs."

"What about the woman?"

"I haven't been told."

"So we are still allowed to interrogate her."

"You are out of your mind," said Brixton. "Why would you take the chance?"

"What chance? I'm investigating a murder. Those are *my* orders. You're assuming the worst, but let's treat her fairly. We can't just assume she's a spy or that she has any knowledge of the murder. We have no indication of either one."

"How about that she's been sleeping with a Soviet Agent and working for a Soviet organization? No evidence? Are you serious? She sure as shootin' looks like a spy to me," said Brixton.

"Let me talk to her, John. I'll get the truth."

"Can you hear yourself? You have a thing for her. You can't see straight."

"Bullshit," said Levitan. "I'm going to check in with the Admiral. Then I'd like to talk to her."

Coast Guard Rear Admiral Tom Spiegel was a widower who had lived alone for ten years. He'd lost a son fighting the Japanese in the Pacific. He owned a red brick row house in the Queen Village neighborhood, close to the waterfront, a house where Levitan and Helen had enjoyed roast beef suppers with other members of the Admiral's senior staff and their wives.

Levitan had a desk at The Port of Philadelphia Coast Guard Station: a repurposed warehouse on Delaware Avenue for offices and radio equipment. The Station was staffed by uniformed men who did their jobs with fewer numbers and less urgency than they had during the war. Until a year before, the place had been overburdened by the demands of dock and ship inspections and with manning a dozen patrol boats. Half the boats had been idle since the war ended, soon to be retired or sold. The major activity at the station in September of 1946 was filing the paperwork accumulated during the war and outfitting the boats with new radio equipment and radar sets. Spiegel preferred fighting a war to cleaning up after one.

It was almost six o'clock. Levitan knew the Admiral was often at his desk into the night. The Coastguardsman at the switchboard put him through immediately.

Levitan said, "Admiral, I've been told that the President wants us to hand Koval over to the Army. Have you been made aware?"

"No. Who told you this?"

"Brixton. Apparently, Hoover's gotten direct instructions from the Attorney General. So, it would seem, the President thinks this is a military matter.

Does my Commodore's commission permit me to stay involved?"

"It could. Tell me what's going on."

"Our suspect, George Koval, is a Master Sergeant in The Army, so they have a claim on him. He has a girlfriend who's been taking the minutes at a Communist meeting. She's a civilian. Do I have your permission to talk to her, sir?"

"Yes. Until I hear otherwise from General Groves, you are in charge of the investigation. Absolutely, you have my permission. If someone tells me otherwise, you'll be the first to know."

"Does that mean I can talk to the man? Brixton says that he's been expressly told to isolate Sergeant Koval until the Army takes him away."

"When's that going to happen?" the Admiral asked.

"I don't know. Soon, I think. But it's the Army, so it might take a week."

"All right. I'll find out what's going on. I'll try to talk to General Groves. Concentrate on the woman until you hear from me."

31

Night had fallen outside the barred window of the interrogation room, a ten-by-ten space near the stairway leading up from the cells, where Judith Horowitz had been trying to comprehend her situation. Now, she sat handcuffed to the oak table.

He sat down across from her. She turned her face away.

"I understand your confusion," he said. "Judith, believe me, I was as truthful as possible. But the stakes here are so, so high, that I had to bend the truth a little. I was not out to get you."

"Why have you arrested George?"

"He killed a Government scientist. Strangled him with his bare hands."

"That's ridiculous."

"I'm afraid not. He is a Soviet spy who was afraid that the victim would blow his cover. George knew him from an Army project and bumped into him accidentally on *The Breakers'* mezzanine. You were there."

"On the mezzanine? Do you mean the first day? After the meeting? He'd gotten an early train and wanted to surprise me. That's all."

"But you were talking to the IKOR men when they came onto the mezzanine. And he was there, right in the middle of it."

"Yes. So?"

"Do you remember someone coming to talk to you? Someone who hadn't been in the meeting?"

"That little man? The one with glasses?"

"Yes. He's the one. What did he say to you?"

"He wanted to know who George was. He'd seen him with us. It was odd, him asking about George."

"Did you tell him?"

"Sure. He asked me if that was George Koval. He sounded like he knew George, the way he said it. I said yes, it was. Who was he?"

"The man George murdered."

"My God."

"What about the men who'd been in the meeting? Did the little man talk to them?"

"He did. He wanted to know if they knew George, like he was trying to make sure that it was *really* him. But those men don't know George. Only me."

"Then what happened?"

"I don't know. Nothing. I went up to my room. I was a little bit confused by George. You know, about how he had shown up then immediately disappeared."

"But you were expecting to see him, weren't you?"

"Not until later. He said he got on an earlier train. Then he just ran off."

"He didn't say anything?"

"No. He just ran off. It was upsetting. Then that man started asking about him. I guess that got me upset too."

"When did you see George after that?"

"Just a little while later. An hour or so? Maybe less."

"He came to your room?"

"No. We went out for dinner, just like we planned. He met me in the lobby."

"And after dinner?"

She paused. "Guess."

"In your room?"

She said nothing.

"This is difficult, Judith. I understand. But it's alright. You took your boyfriend to your room, or you went to his room. I don't care. It was probably happening in a thousand other rooms that day. It's what people do in hotel rooms, isn't it?"

"I wouldn't know."

"Come on, Judith. I am not judging you. I know that George spent a lot of time with you last week. You told me."

She cast her eyes to the table. "You lied to me."

"Only once – about having dinner with my relatives last night before we walked on The Boardwalk. Other than that, I have not told you a single lie. I'd like us to be friends. Think, Judith. What have I said that was a lie?"

"You told me you were just here on vacation. You didn't say anything about George being a murderer. A spy!"

"The reason I was here was a secret. At first I didn't think it had anything to do with you or with George. I didn't even know anything about him until you mentioned his name."

"But why did you talk to me in the first place?"

"I didn't. You spoke to me. Remember? You were waiting for me in the lobby."

"I wasn't waiting for you. I was waiting for Savin."

"But you'd looked me up in the hotel register. Why did you do that?"

"They were curious about you. After you walked out of the meeting, they talked about you, about whether or not they should do what you said, you know, meet for drinks. They decided to do it. Savin said that, even if you were a fake, it's better to know your enemy. So he decided to meet with you and see if he could trust you."

"And he told you to get my room number from the desk clerk."

"Yes. Then they started in again on their defense. Actually, they forgot about you and didn't remember until they were all out with their wives at *Teplitsky's* for borscht and blintzes after the meeting. I didn't go with them. I was exhausted and didn't feel like listening to another word of their politics. It's bad enough I have to pay attention to every word they say in the meetings. I was taking a nap in my room when Savin called me from the restaurant and said I should look you up for him. I didn't like that. I was just there to be a stenographer, not to run errands for him. But I did it anyway. I was waiting for them to come back so that I could tell them that you were a Commodore when I saw you in the lobby. And that's when you started lying. Why am I locked up? I didn't do anything wrong."

"Tell me about you and George. How could you *not* know?"

"Because he never told me anything."

The handcuff on her wrist seemed wrong; he pitied her when they took her back to the cell.

32

While he was Interrogating Judith, Admiral Spiegel had left a message for Levitan to call him at home.

"You are authorized to continue interrogating Koval," said the Admiral.

"Hot damn. How did you swing that?"

"I talked to General Groves. I told him that you get top marks in interrogation. He likes what you've done so far, and you're not FBI. So he's willing to give you access to Koval until they pick him up."

"When's that going to be?"

"Tomorrow morning, first thing. Groves wants to turn him. Do you think that's possible?"

"Sure. Koval will jump at the chance."

"But?"

"I don't know," said Levitan. "I don't trust him in the slightest. He may agree to be turned, but he'll turn back again the instant it suits him. He's a snake."

"The consensus is that the Government's interests are best served by putting him back in play. This comes from the President. Just get back to the interrogation. What are you trying to find out?"

"There are gaps of time between the murder and when we picked him up. He disappeared two days ago. I think we should know how he spent the time."

"Is he forthcoming?"

"Extremely. He wants to talk. He wants us to trust him."

"Well, let's not waste any more time. Get back to work."

"What about Hoover? Is he okay with this?"

"The Army's beaten him this round. He has no choice."

Levitan found Brixton sitting at a table with McCorry in the attorneys' lounge, eating sandwiches that must have been brought in. It was midnight.

"So?" said Levitan, "Are you going to release the woman? You heard her story."

"Release her?" said Brixton. "I don't think so. Don't tell me you believe her."

"I do," said Levitan. "She's telling the truth. She's just a bystander."

"Your problem is that you can't see the truth because you're smitten. I think she's lying, and we'll prove it. We're digging into her activities in New York. I think we'll find evidence that she's a Soviet agent."

"That's doubtful. You should release her."

"Well, that's not going to happen. We're just starting with her. She's going to remain in our custody until we squeeze her dry. Then – who knows? – we may strap her into the electric chair."

"You can't do that. There's no evidence against her. This is outrageous."

"Settle down, Dave. You've allowed yourself to get emotionally involved."

"Goddamit, John. You have no grounds to hold her."

"She's a Communist!"

"Even if that's true – which it isn't – there's no law against being a Communist."

"That law's about to change. Drop it. She's in our custody and that's a good thing. I hope she spends the rest of her life behind bars. Now, let's move on."

They glared at each other. Levitan was angry with Brixton, disappointed by his stupidity.

"All right," Levitan said. "Let's move on. I've talked to the Admiral, and he talked to Groves. George Koval is all mine until tomorrow morning when they come and take him away."

"Well let's get to work," said Brixton, and got up from the table, a half-eaten sandwich in one hand and a bottle of soda pop in the other. McCorry sighed, rewrapped his sandwich, and followed them out.

SATURDAY

33

At one o'clock on Saturday morning, Levitan sat opposite a chained George Koval in the interrogation room. The color had returned to his face and he seemed more energetic.

"Have they gotten it all straightened out?" he asked.

"That's not your concern," said Levitan.

"The matter of what to do with me? Have they made a decision?"

Koval knew his worth. Of course he did. "Nothing has changed," said Levitan. "You're facing a firing squad, the electric chair, and torture. Your only chance is to tell us everything."

"I'm doing that."

"Let's get back to what happened after you went into Weber's hotel room – the *accident*."

The spy clamped his lips, looked at Levitan, breathed deeply, and said, "I caught him by surprise and he stumbled into the room. The telephone was on the desk, off the hook. He grabbed it, and I said 'put it down.' But he didn't. So I went after him to get the telephone away from him. But he wouldn't let go of it. He tried to push me away, but he was short and skinny and I was able to get it away from him. He knocked things over trying to get away, the desk chair and the lamp."

"I wasn't thinking. I lost my temper. I put both of my hands on his little neck and I squeezed. He fell backward onto the floor, and I jumped on him, I straddled him, and I grabbed his neck again. He tried to pull my hands away. Then I felt his Adam's apple snap and he started turning color. I let go, but it was too late. I'd done something to his throat, and he couldn't breathe."

Levitan imagined Bob Weber breathless, gasping, writhing, as his killer watched.

Koval said, "But he had blood on his hands. Didn't he? Me too. Hiroshima and Nagasaki. Both of us had a hand in it."

"A lot of people have blood on their hands," said Levitan. "There was a war."

"For me, it's still a war, and I am a soldier. It was either him or me; one of us had to be dead for the other one to be alive. I was bigger and stronger. It was as simple as that."

Levitan asked, "Then what did you do?"

"I looked at my wristwatch and saw that I'd lost hardly any time. My hands were shaking. I hadn't touched anything except the telephone, which was on the floor, giving a busy signal. I wiped it off and hung it up. There was a briefcase next to the desk. When I opened it, I saw some papers and a textbook. It occurred to me that I might confuse matters if I took his identification with me. So I took his wallet and put it inside the briefcase. I took a last look around and walked out the door.

"I took the elevator to the lobby, walked out of the hotel, up the ramp, and into the crowd. The Boardwalk was really crowded. Nobody paid any attention to me. When I got back to my room, my fingers were only vibrating a little bit."

"His wallet and a briefcase... where are they?" Levitan asked.

"I got rid of them."

"Seriously? There wasn't anything in the briefcase worth handing over?"

"The briefcase could connect me to Weber. Keeping it was too risky."

"What, exactly, was in it?"

"A notebook, an electronics textbook, a few decks of cards, and some correspondence: bills and a letter about a conference in Philadelphia. He was on the agenda to deliver a paper."

"What was in the notebook?"

Koval said, "Really strange math, which I didn't understand. Ones and zeroes. Most of it was hand-written tables, only zeroes and ones. In a few places there were lists of constants. Whatever he was working on was completely outside my area of expertise. I work with quantum physics: mass and energy, temperature and quantities. And I couldn't get anything from the textbook, either."

"What was it about?"

"Electronic valves."

"What are they?"

"Vacuum tubes. Anyway, I sat there trying to make sense of Weber's math. But then I thought, what of it? If I was to give the notebook to the Russians, how would I explain how I'd come to have it? I could think of nothing good that would result once the GRU knew that I'd killed Weber, nor could I think of a plausible explanation for having the notebook in my possession. I decided to dispose of the briefcase and everything inside it, the only things that could connect me to Weber in Atlantic City.

"I took the cash. There was a lot, almost three hundred dollars, and I put it in my pocket. I put the wallet, the books and the papers back inside the briefcase and slid it under the bed of my room at *The Breakers*, where it would be out of sight until I decided how to dispose of it.

"I put my things away and changed out of the clothes I'd been wearing since I'd left Knoxville in the morning."

"And then what did you do?"

"I went to my girlfriend," he said.

"How did that go?" Levitan asked. "You talked to her on the mezzanine and then you disappeared. How did you explain that?"

"I told her that I had suddenly remembered that I had forgotten to do something at work and had to make a phone call. And that was that. We went out for dinner and the subject never came up again."

Despite the spy's coolness, it seemed to Levitan that Judith Horowitz was a tender subject, perhaps a soft spot. Koval didn't know that Judith spent an afternoon on the beach and two evenings with Levitan, that the Commodore had a pretty clear sense of the Master Sergeant's odd behavior since the murder.

"When did you get rid of the briefcase?"

"I disposed of it after Judith fell asleep that night."

"How did you that?"

"I'd put it under the bed in my room when I got back from *The Traymore*. Afterwards, after we had dinner, we went back to her room. Later on, after she fell asleep, I got dressed and went down to my room and got the briefcase. I took it outside and walked around to the alley in back of the hotel, found a half-full trashcan, and put the briefcase under the trash."

Levitan says, "You just threw it out? Even the notebook? Certainly it had value. You're a spy. I don't believe you would just throw it away."

"I did. It was meaningless to me. I don't know enough about binary mathematics to know whether it had value or not. The briefcase and what was in it could connect me to Weber."

"So? What then? Did you go back to your girlfriend's room?"

"No, I hadn't taken her key with me. I went back to my room."

"And had yourself a good night's sleep," said Levitan sarcastically.

The spy took awhile to respond. "No. I couldn't sleep. I was so wound up, I didn't even try. I sat in front of the window until the sun came up. By morning, I had decided to call it quits. I had pretty much decided not to return to base when my leave was up. It was time for me to start over again. You know, watching the sunrise, sitting on the edge of a whole continent with a thousand towns like Sioux City where it would be easy for me to disappear."

This made sense to Levitan. Were he in Koval's shoes, he would surely have concluded that disappearing was the best option. Too, the violence must have been traumatic, a jolt to his identity. But which identity. Russian? American? Jewish? Scientist? Soldier? Colleague? Lover? Clearly, George Koval was capable of extraordinary self discipline. And, as a field agent operating undercover in a top secret military installation, he had a lot of guts.

"So?" Levitan asked. "Why didn't you? Why didn't you just go to the train station and head West?"

"Because I wanted Judith to come with me. I was going to ask her to come away with me. From Saturday on, the whole time I was with her, I was trying to figure out how I could tell her. I thought she would do it if I could explain everything the right way. I was going to tell her on Wednesday, but I didn't get the chance. I had to leave the hotel in a hurry."

"Why? Why did you have to leave the hotel?"

"When I woke up on Wednesday morning, I was going to tell her about me. Not about Weber, but about being an agent, who I really am, that I couldn't do it anymore, that I wanted to start a new life in another city, in another part of the country, that I wanted us to get married, which I knew was what she wanted, and we would take a road trip for our honeymoon to explore the possibilities.

"So on Wednesday morning, the day before yesterday, I started calling her room, hoping to catch her on break. I wouldn't go anywhere near the IKOR meeting – I'd learned that lesson the hard way. She answered at around eleven. She was angry with me and didn't want to see me. I asked her when the IKOR was going to break for lunch so that we could talk alone and I could apologize. And that's when she told me that the rest of the IKOR conference had been cancelled because the FBI had shown up. That meant I had to leave the hotel immediately."

"Did you think they were looking for you?"

"I didn't know; that was a possibility, but not a very strong one. I hadn't left any evidence. There was nothing I knew of that connected me. But, you have to understand, I've met dozens of FBI agents over the years. They live in Oak Ridge; they are my neighbors; they interview me in their office. All it would have taken was for one agent who knows me to see me in the same hotel where they were investigating the IKOR and I would have been in the soup. So I knew I had to get away from the hotel. I told Judith that I'd been informed of an emergency at work, that I had to leave, but that I'd call her soon and explain everything. I packed my things and left the hotel by the stairs. I hailed a taxi, went to the station, and took the first train out of town. I've been laying low until I could meet her at the station. Why did you arrest her?"

"Because she was meeting you."

Koval paused. "But how did you know that?"

"The FBI was listening to her telephone calls. They heard you arrange to meet her at *30th Street*."

"It did not occur to me that her phone would be tapped. I was naïve. Stupid again."

"We would have had you anyway. The FBI had agents waiting for you at the train stations in Washington and Knoxville. Even if you hadn't called her, we would have gotten you."

"But only if I returned to base, which I had decided not to do."

34

The few hours remaining before the Army arrived were likely to be the last ones the civilian authorities had to interrogate a captured master spy. Levitan wondered whether Groves would show up in person when the Army came to claim its property. But he was exhausted. He needed a break, however brief. He stood up from the interrogation table, left the room and went into Brixton's listening post.

"I need a break. He needs a break," said Levitan "Treat him like a human being for a few minutes; give him something to eat, let him wash up. Do you think you could get us a pot of coffee?" He noticed a couple of shopping bags on the floor. "Is that the stuff from his hotel room?"

"Yep. We found an empty gin bottle in his trash. It looks like George Koval has been doing some drinking."

"The notebook?" Levitan asked.

"No notebook. If he kept it, he put it somewhere else."

"What's binary math?"

"Damned if I know," said Brixton. "He's given us a lot. Do you think we can believe him?"

"Possibly," said Levitan. "Let's see how much he gives up about his relationship to the GRU. He seems like too smart a guy to be fooled by Stalin."

Brixton said, "They might be holding something over his head, threatening him somehow. But that doesn't change the fact that he's confessed to murder. And to espionage."

Levitan said. "You're right, but his guilt isn't the question. Now we need to know how far to trust him. Ideally, wouldn't we run him in the field for awhile? Set him some traps, see what he does? But who knows how the Army will handle him."

"Groves is really, really pissed off," said Brixton. "He may not settle for anything less than a firing squad."

"Killing the golden goose?" said Levitan. "Groves wouldn't do that."

"Oh yes he would," said Brixton. "And then he'd gift wrap the body and drop it off in Berlin."

"He wouldn't be that stupid."

"Think about what you're saying," said Brixton. "It's The Army you're talking about."

"So I'd best get back to work," said Levitan.

When he returned to the interrogation room, Koval had a cup of coffee in front of him. Levitan poured a cup for himself. "Listen, George, we don't have a lot of time here. The Army's on their way to come and get you."

Koval digests this. "So the FBI lost," he said.

"Apparently."

"Is there anything you can do?"

"Me? Hardly. This is coming from way high."

"President Truman?"

"Could be," said Levitan. "Keep talking."

"I get it. What can I tell you?"

"Why the hell are you working for the Soviet Union?"

"I've never really had any choice. Do you know what they do to people?"

"That's what I'm saying. How can you work for those bastards?"

"My parents are too old to survive The Gulag."

"What's The Gulag?"

"Prison camps in Siberia. If I don't work for them, that's where they'll send my parents. Or worse, kill them, especially if the GRU think I've betrayed them."

"They're not in Siberia already?"

"Yeah, but in a town called Birobidzhan that's on the edge, way out across Asia near the Pacific. It's an awful place, but it's not a prison camp. They have enough to eat and a warm stove."

"That's where you went in 1932?"

"That was it. The Soviet Jewish Oblast, a pit of misery, the last place on Earth. It takes four days and five nights in a railroad car to get to it from Moscow, but only in the summertime. It's a frontier town surrounded by frozen swamp most of the year. The rest of time, it's infested with mosquitoes. Birobidzhan! By comparison, Sioux City is Paris."

"It was a shock, was it?"

"To say the least. My poor parents. My Dad came from Belarus, in Central Europe, and that was where the Oblast was going to be. That was the deal. That's what they signed up for, to go back to Europe. But there was a lot of resistance from the European Soviets, Belarus and Crimea, so we got the only place where people wouldn't object - Birobidzhan. Screwed again. I could get out. I won a scholarship, but they have been stuck there ever since."

"How do you know that they're still alive?"

"They make sure I know. The waiter with the red pens sometimes puts a recent picture of them under the tab along with my instructions. It's their way of reminding me."

"This scholarship? Is that how they recruited you?"

"Not at first. I was just another student from the hinterlands. I won the scholarship to The Mendeleev Institute of Chemical Technology in Moscow by competitive exam. It's pretty hard to get into. I was in my third year before they started in on me, 1937 that was. They liked the idea that I was American, fluent in baseball and cars and all that. They let me finish college.

"You have to understand how it was. Stalin was cleaning house; there was a purge, everybody knew what was going on: thousands of people were being arrested and sent to Siberia... or worse. You didn't say no to them. Once they told me that they wanted me, I never felt that I had any choice. I just did what I had to do."

"They put you through training?"

"Sure. First there was Red Army basic. Then they sent me to spy schools. Then in 1939, they sent me to The Front."

"What front? Germany didn't attack Russia until 1941."

"They invaded the Baltic countries before that, getting ready, creating buffer states. My job was to find useful equipment, mostly in Finland. I went into factories and university labs and shipped whatever I found back East. But I saw a lot. It was a nasty war. You say you were in Spain? Same thing."

In Spain, Levitan had seen the corpses in the narrow valleys, men and women with bullet holes through their heads. He despised the Stalinists, people who used murder as a political tool. And he despised the Fascists who had beaten them - beaten *him* and his pathetic excuse for a volunteer army of idealists, many of them Jews fighting the anti-Semites on the only battlefield available.

"How bad was it?" asked Levitan, soldier to soldier.

"The GRU and the NKVD killed as many people as possible. It was all very deliberate. Any survivors would be too terrified to resist. They killed hundreds of thousands – cold-blooded murder. That's the kind of people they are. And that is why I work for them."

At length, Koval said. "Then, in 1940, they pulled me back to Moscow and told me that I was going to the States, that I had a job waiting for me in Hoboken. Wonderful news – from hell to heaven, just like that."

"How did they get you back into the States?"

"Through San Francisco on a freighter from Vladivostok. I stopped off in Birobidzhan to say goodbye to my parents and my brother. I told them that they were unlikely to hear from me for awhile. I was in uniform and they understood, like everybody else, that war was coming. It was good to see them. The good news is that my brother Isaiah made it through. They showed me a picture of him standing next to my parents in that pathetic little town hall, so I know they are all still alive."

"Tell me how you managed to get a billet at Oak Ridge."

"It was all legit. I have the qualifications."

"Nobody pulled strings?"

"Not so far as I know. Listen, I enrolled in the Chemical Engineering Department at CCNY as soon as I got settled. I got top marks. Why not? I'd already earned one degree from a damned good school. My professors liked me. By the time I was drafted, I was only a few credits away from the degree. The Army Records Office was looking for anyone with chemistry training to work on the atomic bomb project. I was just one of thousands of soldiers they pulled out of the ranks."

"Whose idea was it for you to go to CCNY in the first place?"

"The Russians'. But I would have done it anyway. I like the work. The GRU didn't want me in the United States Army. In fact they tried to keep me out."

"Really?"

"Yeah. I registered for the draft, like everyone else, in 1940. That was just routine. I am an American citizen. I played on the company softball team and dated American girls. I got called up in 1942, but *Raven* filed for a deferment. They have government contracts for telephone parts, so it was a legitimate exemption."

"Why would they do that? Why would they want to keep you *out* of the Army?"

"Once I was in the Army, who knew what would happen? There are plenty of secret projects that *Raven* bids on, slots where I could be inserted to collect scientific intelligence. When the deferment expired after a year, they actually filed for another year, but Selective Service denied them."

"So you were drafted just like everybody else."

"Yep, just like everybody else. After Basic Training, the Army sent everybody with as little as one or two college science courses for technical training, really just to separate the wheat from the chaffe. Those of us with high marks and a chemistry or physics background were sent to Oak Ridge."

"And your job? Health and Safety Officer?"

Koval said, "I guess they think I do good work. My performance has never been questioned. The opposite, in fact. I'm good at what I do."

George Koval was, in a way, typically American, an ambitious man who'd made the most of his chances, risen high from a humble beginning. Even now, facing the wrath of the American Government, Koval exuded confidence, as if he believed that he could come out a winner. That's *chutzpah*.

"Once you got drafted, how would the GRU know what you were up to? How did they know about your billet at Oak Ridge?"

"I told them. Listen, it isn't just black and white. You don't want me to lie to you, I'm telling you straight out - I like being a spy. I'm good at it."

"So it's not just about your poor old parents in Birobidzhan. You like being a two-faced son of a bitch."

"Two-faced?" Koval said. "I wish it was only two. But yeah. I would be long since dead if I didn't like playing the game."

"So everything just fell your way."

"Yes it did."

Levitan, studied the captured spy. Koval maximized opportunities to suit his purposes. And he was obedient, done what was expected of him all his life: as a dutiful son, diligent student, and loyal soldier. And brutal; he'd strangled a man with his bare hands.

Levitan said, "But, after all of your excuses, you are still responsible for giving away vital secrets to the enemy. You could have turned yourself in at anytime, but you didn't. And you killed a man."

Koval said, "I was at Alamogordo. I have been to Hiroshima. I have seen what America does to its enemies. Without a counter-force, there's no telling what America will do. I cannot put into words how awful these bombs are. I was given a position to do something about it, and I did."

"So, you're an idealist! Bullshit."

"Believe me or not," said the spy, "I am being honest. I think the American Army is trigger happy, too pleased with itself, too righteous, more powerful than any country ever before in history. The Army's running the show in Washington these days, is it not? And I know it is because I work with them. I've met a dozen brass hats who are itching to drop an A-Bomb on Moscow... or on anyone else they decide to teach a lesson. The only way the world is going to be safe from them is if there's a counter force. Call it idealism, call it whatever you want, but the idea that America can use these weapons without facing any consequences is absolutely terrifying. Bob Weber was one man. I didn't want to do it. I didn't plan it. It just had to be done."

"Aren't the men in Moscow just as bad?"

"Worse! Stalin is a monster. But the same thing applies to the Soviet Union as to America; the threat of nuclear retaliation will restrain them."

"That's madness," said Levitan. "What happens if everyone has the A-Bomb? What if it doesn't end with the Russians? What if every two-bit dictator in the world has atomic bombs? You can't just let everybody have one!"

"We don't know the future," said Koval. "But, if the wars we have seen in this century are the examples, then there is an even more horrible war coming. America is getting ready, and they're smart to do so, and the Soviet Union is getting ready too, and both Armies are run by ruthless men who will use any weapon that comes to hand. But not if they get as bad as they give. What if you *knew* that ninety per cent of your urban population would be killed? What if the country you had attacked could make your land poisonous for centuries? The Generals may be ruthless, but they are not suicidal."

Levitan said, "You're wrong. What matters in a war is who wins. I want America to win. Not Russia or Germany or Japan or anybody else. If war is coming, then we sure as hell better win it. You are giving weapons to the enemy, and that is treason."

"So kill me. Hang me. Shoot me," Koval said. "Do whatever you are going to do. I'm ready for it. I've been ready for a long time."

Tick. Tick. It was after seven o'clock, full sunlight bounced off the city brick outside the barred window.

"I am truly sorry that it had to be Weber," said Koval. "I had a lot of respect for him. He was a talented man. Brilliant, I suppose you'd say. He was married, wasn't he?"

"Yeah, to a good woman with two kids."

Koval looked at the tabletop. When he looked up, his face was sad. Levitan reminded himself that he was interrogating a manipulator, an opportunist.

Koval said, "I didn't plan it. It was bad luck, an unfortunate coincidence that I had to deal with. I regret that I had to kill anybody, especially Bob Weber. But that's war, kill or be killed."

Koval thought of himself as a soldier. He had simply been bigger and stronger than Bob Weber, another casualty of war, just one more dead man among millions.

"What's going to happen to Judith?" Koval asked.

"She's in deep trouble," said Levitan. "Because of IKOR."

Koval said, "She took a stenography job – so what?"

Levitan wasn't a hundred per cent sure of that. IKOR had entrusted their legacy to her. Would they have done that with *just* a stenographer?

"She's not one of them," said Koval. "They offered her a week's work and a free room to take shorthand. That's all. She's not a Communist. She's all about going to Israel. She doesn't care about the Soviet Union. You should leave her alone, let her go."

"Time will tell," said Levitan.

"Please," said Koval. "She hasn't done anything wrong. She's a Jew, that's all; the daughter of outcasts. Her politics are about survival, not Communism or Americanism. She's just looking for a safe place."

"It's safe here," said Levitan. "It's our best chance. We can be Americans here, and that's a damned good thing to be."

Koval said, "Until there's a need for a scapegoat. The day always comes when people need Jews to pin their woes upon. We are a wandering people, so it's bound to happen. Even in America, the day will come. Jews are like quanta, one thing until you need them to be something else."

Outside the barred window, the day looked like another scorcher. Soon, the Army would come to collect their Sergeant. Tick. Tick

Levitan said, "I don't follow you." He'd never heard of *quanta*. "And, right now, I don't want to. Judith made some choices. Nobody forced her."

"I feel sorry for her," said Koval. "She would not be in trouble if it wasn't for me. What do you think will happen to her?"

"I can't say," said Levitan. "She is in the hands of the FBI; their prisoner, not mine. I have no say in what they decide to do with her."

"Then I hope that the Justice Department believes in justice," said Koval.

"Let's stick to the facts," said Levitan. "You spent more than a day in Philadelphia before we caught you. What were you doing? Who did you talk to?"

"I didn't talk to anyone. I stayed in my room."

"Well, that just doesn't make sense," said Levitan. "You didn't know that we were on to you. What were you hiding from? You had no reason to think we were after you. You got in touch with Bannerman, didn't you."

"No."

"And why not? This was it! The time had come! Bannerman was your escape hatch. Of course you called him."

"Yes, the time had certainly come to escape, but not to Russia. There was no need to tell Bannerman immediately. At some point, for my parents' sake, I would inform him and convince him that I had acted in the best interests of the Soviet Union. But there were other things to be organized first. I went to the library, did a little research, walked around, thinking it over. But I spoke to no one."

"What kind of research?"

"About San Francisco and California. I think I like it out there. I was looking at maps, checking directories."

"What kind of directories?"

"Phone books. Yellow Pages, looking for electrical supply companies and chemical companies, places I might check for jobs."

"As who? What would you use for identification?"

"I'm not an amateur. That wasn't going to be my problem."

"Not a problem? You can't just create an identity."

"Sure you can, it just takes a little patience. "

"So you left Atlantic City around midday on Wednesday. Walk me through what happened between that time and Friday afternoon."

"Sure. But can I ask you question first? Real quick... How did you knock me out?"

"Doesn't your chin hurt? I hit you with a fistful dimes."

"Huh. I never saw it coming."

"It was a sweet moment, I confess," said Levitan.

Asking subjects about their movements at specific times and places is a good way to check their veracity. The more detail they offer, the easier it is to determine if they are lying. He asked, "Tell me what you did after you left Atlantic City. I want the details."

"When I got to Philly, I took a taxi from the station and had the driver to take me to a big, downtown hotel. He took me to the *Benjamin Franklin*. I checked in, then went outside to get the lay of the land: where to eat, where the cabs and buses are, the kinds of stores, the street names. I stopped in a bar for awhile. I had supper at an automat. I went to a movie – some cowboy thing with Gregory Peck. Then I had a couple of drinks at the hotel bar and went up to my room for the night. I was exhausted. I hadn't been sleeping well.

"Thursday, I slept late. Maybe I had a little too much to drink the night before. But I got up determined. The most important thing would be talking to Judith. I needed to convince her to come with me. I started calling her at *The Breakers* after I woke up, Thursday morning, figuring that she'd be in her room because the conference was cancelled, but she never was. I guessed that she was probably on the beach, she loves it. So, I went to the library. I called her from there, but she was never in her room. I went to another movie; John Garfield and Lana Turner, *The Postman Always Rings Twice*. I finally got her on the phone late last night. But you know that. You were listening to her calls."

"Were you going to tell her everything?"

"Everything… except about Bob Weber. I didn't think it would have accomplished anything. I had no idea that I could be connected to the murder. I thought I was in the clear, that nobody would ever find out. As for the rest of it, I knew she would understand."

Koval's story fit the facts that Levitan knew. He had spent the better part of Thursday afternoon with

Judith on the beach, and on The Boardwalk in the evening. She'd gone to the beach early, enjoying a last day of free time,

"Were you planning to propose to her anyway? Was that part of your plan for the week in Atlantic City?"

"No, sadly. Sentimentality and espionage are a bad combination. It's hard enough to keep secrets at work; I certainly didn't want to have to keep secrets from a wife at home. It was too bad, but that's the way it had to be. If it wasn't for the kind of life I led, she would be a good wife for me. Please, let her go."

"I told you, it's not up to me. Tell me what you did yesterday morning before you went to the station."

"Nothing. I slept hard until late. Again, too much to drink the night before. I didn't even have time for breakfast. I took a taxi, but we hit a lot of traffic as the driver got close to the station. I was a few minutes late."

"Why did you run out of the station?"

"Because I saw the men in suits converging on Judith as soon as I walked in the door. Do you always keep a roll of dimes in your pocket?"

"Yep," said Levitan. "Standard equipment."

"Good idea," said Koval.

35

At precisely eight AM on Saturday the 7th of September, a platoon of Military Police arrived and took George Koval away. In the small listening room in which Brixton had spent the night, Levitan and Brixton went over their notes.

"We could prosecute him. We have enough to get a conviction," said Levitan. "Even Turner and Staup could win it. Even without everything else, it's already a solid case of second degree murder, thirty years to life. But he committed it as an act of espionage, which makes it a Murder One felony."

"But he's not ours to prosecute," said Brixton. "This really aggravates me. We've only scratched the surface of what he knows."

"You know plenty. He's given you his contacts and his methods. Just tread lightly and you'll snag the whole network. You did okay. He's given away the store. Find out who answers that phone in Washington. Watch *Raven* and *Joyners* Restaurant in Knoxville, don't raise any alarms, and you should be able to identify the whole network. Whatever else he knows should be in his reports, and he can write those in a jail cell. That part's all done. But that's not justice. He needs to be punished for what he did."

"This ain't the Nuremberg Trials, Dave. He hasn't committed a war crime."

"How is it different?" said Levitan. "The Nazis got away with blatant criminality because the German courts allowed it. If they had done their job in the 1930s, the Nazis could never have gotten away with all that they eventually did. So now you're saying America should allow murder because it's in the national interest? You're saying our courts should do the same thing as the German courts? That doesn't sound right to me."

"It's not right, but this is not a perfect world. And I think comparing J. Edgar Hoover to Adolph Hitler is a bit extreme. Besides, it's the President's decision, not the FBI's," said Brixton.

Levitan said, "But you do have the authority to let Judith Horowitz go free, don't you? She didn't know about the murder and didn't know Koval as anything but a soldier she saw whenever he had leave."

"And you buy that?"

"I do," said Levitan. "I don't think you have grounds to hold her and I don't think she knows a damned thing about the real George Koval. We don't do things like this in America. Let her go, John."

"I'd have to convince Hoover. He hates people like her. Hates them."

"But she hasn't broken any laws."

"What about fornication?"

"Thank God that's not a crime," said Levitan.

"It is to The Director," said Special Agent John Brixton. "She's a woman, which is two strikes against her to begin with as far as Hoover is concerned, a Communist fornicator who's literally been in bed with a Soviet spy. She's a left-winger who's planning to leave America – so she's disloyal and unpatriotic to boot. She's Hoover's textbook subversive. He'll want his pound of flesh."

"John, for the sake of your conscience, talk him out of it. Our government, an American government, can't be allowed to act that way. You have no legal grounds to keep her in a cell for another second."

Brixton shook his head, "I'll say something to him, but I know him. He's not going to give her any kind of break. He'd love to lock her up in Leavenworth and throw away the key."

"John! No."

"I said I'd talk to him," said Brixton. "You seem to be as nuts about her as Koval is. He took a big risk calling her the other night."

"Not really. He had no idea you'd tapped her phone. Neither did I, for that matter. I think he's genuinely in love with her. But that's neither here nor there. She hasn't committed any crime and she doesn't have any intelligence value at all. She knows nothing. She needs to be freed."

The phone rang and Brixton picked it up. Levitan watched his face.

"Hoover," Brixton mouthed, with a speaking-of-the-devil expression. He nodded. He raised his eyebrows and looked meaningfully at Levitan. After a few minutes, he said, "Yes sir," and hung up.

"That was your boss?"

"J. Edgar Hoover Himself. The Director. He's really pissed off - at Truman, at The Army, at Groves."

"Did he say anything about the woman?"

"No. He was busy venting. I have to go down to Washington and debrief him personally."

Admiral Tom Spiegel, ramrod straight, wearing a crisp white summer uniform and spit-shined black shoes, walked into the listening room. "Ah, the men of the hour! Well done!" he said.

"Thank you, sir," said Brixton. "Dave did most of it."

"Well done, Commodore," said the Admiral. "Atta boy."

"He deserves a promotion," said Brixton.

"I'm afraid not. Commodore's my top Auxiliary rank. But I'll consider a slight raise in his pay."

Levitan dragged a chair next to the desk he and Brixton had been using and the Admiral sat down. "I've been on the phone with Washington," said Spiegel. "The President knows that you guys did a hell of a job catching Koval. Have you spoken to Hoover?" he asked Brixton.

"Yes sir. I just got off the phone with him. He's mad as hell about turning Koval over to the Army."

Spiegel said, "The Army is better equipped to deploy him against the Russians than the FBI, or the State Department, or me for that matter. I sure as hell have no use for him."

"Hoover is angry," said Brixton.

"Given the politics, your Director really doesn't have a choice. And it won't be the last time he loses to The Army. There's a whole new power structure in Washington these days - we're getting ready for a war with the Russians. The Army and The Navy are getting whatever they ask for. The powers they were given during the war are being expanded and made permanent."

Brixton protested, "What about Judge Stacy? This isn't the way he was going to rule. Does Truman know that?"

"Yes. That's why I'm here, to convey the President's decision to Judge Stacy. And it's time for you guys to go home. Get some sleep. You've done a good job."

"Well, if he's told us the truth, we're satisfied ," said Brixton. "We know who he passes his reports to: a restaurant and an electric parts manufacturer. And, goddamit, they are the FBI's jurisdiction."

"If I were Edgar, I would be very careful," Spiegel said. "He shouldn't just send a bunch of agents in and take names. If they even suspect that Koval's cover is blown, they'll go to ground and cover their tracks. If that happens, he loses his value."

Levitan said, "I suppose this means Koval gets away with murder."

"I'm afraid it does, " said the Admiral. "Why did he do it? Did he tell you?"

Levitan explained the accidental encounter between Koval and Weber, that Weber would have informed military intelligence that Koval, a man at the center of the atomic bomb program, was seen talking with avowed Communists. "He felt he had no choice. We were lucky to have found him, he hadn't left many tracks."

"Luck? I doubt it."

Levitan said, "Do you know what bothers me? Weber's wife. She'll never know who killed her husband. That doesn't sit right with me."

"Nor with me," said the Admiral. "But it's a small price to pay for a chance to sabotage the enemy's atomic program. Isn't that right, Mister Brixton?"

"He'll rot in hell eventually," said Brixton.

"One can only hope," said the Admiral.

"I'm concerned about the woman we picked up," said Levitan. "The FBI has to release her; she's had nothing to do with anything subversive."

"I'll discuss it with the judge. Now go home. Get some sleep. You're done."

"No, sir," said Levitan. "I'm not leaving with that woman still in a cell. We have absolutely nothing on her. She's broken no laws and poses no threat. She has to be set free. Letting a murderer go is bad enough; we shouldn't compound the injustice."

"You're convinced she's not a Soviet agent?" challenged the Admiral.

"Not a hundred per cent," said Levitan. "But if she is, we can learn a lot more by watching her than we can by locking her up."

Spiegel said, "The people in Washington want somebody's head on a platter. We have a monumental intelligence failure, a double whammy - the spying and the loss of a top scientist. It's reached the Secretaries of the three most powerful agencies in Washington and landed on the President's desk. Somebody has to pay for this."

"Blame the Army and the FBI," said Levitan. "They gave a Soviet agent access to atomic secrets. These failures are theirs. The FBI failed to notice that George Koval had spent eight years in the Soviet Union before they cleared him. He's been working for the Army for three years and they have had no idea that he was reporting to Moscow the whole time. If you're looking for guilty parties, find them in the Army and the FBI. But Judith Horowitz is responsible for none of that. She had no idea it was going on. She took a job that came with a hotel room at the beach, a place where she could enjoy the company of her boyfriend while he was on leave. She did not know that he was spying, only that he was a soldier working on a secret project. He hadn't even given her his phone number."

Brixton said, "We only have her word for any of that. We have had no chance to verify whether she's telling the truth. She could as plausibly be the mastermind behind the whole Soviet operation in the United States. All we know about her has come from Dave, and he's half in love with her. I'm not letting her go."

Spiegel was taken aback. "What? Dave? What's your relationship to her?"

"I'm a married man, Admiral. I've gotten to know her through the course of this investigation. We became friends. John thinks there's more going on between us, but he's wrong."

Brixton said, "As far as she is concerned, you are too damned close, Dave. Your judgment has been compromised. We are not letting her go until we check every word of her story."

Levitan and Brixton had been good partners, with just enough conflict to keep both men respectful of the other. But this was different. He said, "She hasn't broken the law. You have no legal basis to deny her her freedom. You have to let her go."

"No I don't," said Brixton.

"Yes you do," said Levitan. "Keep a watch on her. Check out the facts she's given you. But let her go."

"Do you have anything on her, John?" asked the Admiral

"Enough," said Brixton.

Levitan said, "You have nothing. How much time do you want? What's your estimate."

"I couldn't say," said Brixton.

"Right," said Levitan. "Since you work for J. Edgar Hoover, it might take years. But, in the meanwhile, she is an innocent woman. There's such a thing as *habeas corpus*, isn't there John? The right thing for the FBI to do is to let her go... today. You have her statement. Check it out. Keep her under surveillance and arrest her on a legitimate charge *if* you find any evidence against her."

"So you're a lawyer now?" said Brixton.

"I'm an American," said Levitan. "And so is she. I'm not leaving this building until I see her walking out the door as a free woman."

"Then you're going to need a tent," says Brixton.

"Admiral," said Levitan. "I want to come with you when you talk to the judge. He can order her release."

"Settle down, Dave. Go home," said Spiegel.

"No, sir. You have to have her released." He stood up, removed his wallet from the inside pocket of his jacket, unpinned the gold badge, slid the ID card out from behind the glassine cover, and held both objects in his outstretched hand, offering them to the Admiral. "Unless I see her walking out the door, I will quit."

Spiegel looked from Levitan's hand, to his face, and then at Brixton, then back at Levitan. "You're sure she's not a threat?"

"Yes," said Levitan.

The Admiral said, "Put those away. I will argue your case before the judge. I think he'll listen to reason."

"Jesus Christ! I can't believe this!" Brixton said. "She is, goddamit, in FBI custody. And that's where she's staying."

"I think that would be wrong," said the Admiral, rising to his feet.

"I'm coming with you," said Brixton, standing.

"Now listen to me, the both of you, settle down. Go home. Get some sleep. Leave this to me."

"I'll be in the lawyer's lounge starting on my report," said Levitan. "Will you find me there after you talk to the judge?"

"Will do," said the Admiral and left for his appointment.

"You're out of line, on this, Dave," said Brixton.

"I'm right. You know it."

"Hoover's not going to let this go," said Brixton. "You've just made yourself a powerful enemy."

"So be it," said Levitan. "He's your problem, not mine. I work for the Admiral, remember?"

36

He stood with Judith Horowitz and her small suitcase on the sidewalk in front of the Federal Court House on Second Street. She seemed fragile, tired, still in the clothes he'd seen her in at breakfast the day before.

He said, "Wait right here. I'll get us a car and be right back."

"Where are we going?"

"I'll take you home."

"To New York. Really?"

"Sure. It's all part of the service."

"Do I have a choice?"

"Of course."

"Then save your service. Just leave me alone. I'll take a taxi to the train station."

"You're tired. This will be a lot easier."

"Don't waste anymore of your charm on me," she said. "Either I'm free to go or I'm not. Which is it?"

"You're free to go."

"Then get lost. Here comes a taxi." She took a step toward the curb and raised her arm. The taxi pulled to a stop. She tossed her suitcase onto the back seat and told the driver, "*30th Street Station.*"

"Let me ride with you to the station."

She paid him no heed and got into the cab. She did not even look at him as the taxi drove away.

§

Home without Helen was depressing. The place was exactly as he'd left it - empty. It was not *his* bed, it was *their* bed. There were no stockings draped over the shower rod.

His car was still parked in the Atlantic City lot near *The Traymore* where it had been sitting since Tuesday night. Tomorrow, Sunday, he would take the train to Atlantic City and retrieve it. Perhaps he'd walk onto a jetty and try his luck catching fish. And he'd take his bathing suit too. He thought about Judith, the way she'd bounced and bobbed through the surf.

He took a shower with his own bar of soap, brushed his teeth with his own brand of toothpaste, and clicked on the radio, already set to the *Phillies'* station. It was the bottom of the seventh in a game with the *Giants* and the score was tied. The *Phils* pulled it out in the top of ninth as he was cleaning cracker crumbs off the kitchen table.

It was early twilight, the sun hadn't even set, but since his midnight meeting with General Groves two nights before, he'd gotten little sleep. He climbed into their bed, put Helen's pillow under the covers so that he had something to sleep next to, and fell asleep.

Hours later, in the dark, Helen slid into bed next to him and pressed her naked body against his skin.

"Hi there," she said.

"You're home."

"I am."

"Good. Very good. I thought you had a gig tonight."

"I decided to come home instead."

"Good. That's very good," he said, and turned into her embrace.

§ *THE END* §

The Historical George Koval

(by Michael Walsh, May, 2009, *Smithsonian Magazine*)

"In 2007 Russian President Vladimir Putin posthumously awarded George Koval the Hero of the Russian Federation decoration for "his courage and heroism while carrying out special missions".

George Abramovich Koval (December 25, 1913 – January 31, 2006) was an American who acted as a Soviet intelligence officer. According to Russian sources, Koval's infiltration of the Manhattan Project as a Glavnoye Razvedyvatel'noye Upravleniye (GRU) agent "drastically reduced the amount of time it took for Russia to develop nuclear weapons."

Koval was born to Jewish immigrants in Sioux City, Iowa, USA. Shortly after reaching adulthood he traveled with his parents to the Soviet Union to settle in the Jewish Autonomous Region near the Chinese border.

Koval was recruited by the Soviet Main Intelligence Directorate, trained, and assigned the code name DELMAR. He returned to the United

States in 1940 and was drafted into the US Army in early 1943. Koval worked at atomic research laboratories and, according to the Russian government, relayed back to the Soviet Union information about the production processes and volumes of the polonium, plutonium, and uranium used in American atomic weaponry, and descriptions of the weapon production sites. In 1948, Koval left on a European vacation but never returned to the United States.

ABOUT THE AUTHOR

Stanley Cutler writes in Philadelphia. He's had careers as a teacher, programmer, and IT consultant to corporations and government agencies. Most of his books are historical mysteries:

- LOW LIGHT
- THE SUBVERSIVE DETECTIVE
- KILLER MATH
- KNOTS
- POLITICAL DYNAMITE

Direct any inquiries to stancutler-at-gmail-dot-com.